DYSFUNCTION

By

GUY ROBIN

Grosvenor House
Publishing Limited

The right of Guy Robin to be identified as the author of this
work has been asserted in accordance with Section 78
of the Copyright, Designs and Patents Act 1988

This book is published by
Grosvenor House Publishing Ltd
Link House
140 The Broadway, Tolworth, Surrey, KT6 7HT.
www.grosvenorhousepublishing.co.uk

This book is a work of fiction. Any resemblance to
people or events, past or present, is purely coincidental.

A CIP record for this book
is available from the British Library

ISBN 978-1-83975-862-1

For my wife Paula
Love you, love xxx

Acknowledgements

Having completed the piece, I felt an enormous sense of achievement to have actually written something, so tangible, so long! I remember writing essays at school and thinking; '*Wow, 12 sides of paper; that's a full piece of work*'. So, you finish the writing and then have so much more to do. I had no idea it was so involved.

There are always people to thank, for those who give the smallest nudge in the right direction, the collection of individuals who make it happen and the organisations and representatives who just help and support.

Angus Darroch-Warren and Sharmaine Matthews (both Reed's school), thank you for suggesting and pointing me in the direction of my publishers.

Grosvenor House Publishers, for guiding me through the process and fielding my sometimes basic and inane questions and getting this thing to print.

I found designer Steve Mead and he immediately got what I had in my head for a cover design. He took that thought and created just what I was looking for. I cannot commend him more highly for his time, effort and artistic professionalism. I will be using him again without hesitation.

Alasdair Day from the Isle of Raasay Distillery, who gave his swift an unconditional support for the project and permission to use of details about the premises on Raasay. Do, if you get the chance, taste their fine range of Malt Whiskies or even visit their site on the island, perhaps even stay at the hotel?

I sought the services of professional photographer John Scofield, to take a few up to date pictures of me. When you embark on a vanity project like this; then you clearly need photos. I can recommend John, who was quick to see what I wanted and provided an excellent portfolio of pictures. If you should ever need his services, then please view www.johnscofieldphotography.co.uk

Finally, my soul mate, sounding board and love of my life; my wife Paula. Without your constant encouragement and unconditional support, this may never have happened!

Love you, love xx

He saw movement by the shoreline. A glint of something reflected across the bay on the bank opposite. He picked up the binoculars from their case and looked out towards the other island. Yes, he saw three people wandering up and down beside the slipway, searching for something. *A boat most likely!* he thought.

He kept a steady watch on them through the binoculars and moved his foot forward to give a reassuring tap to the butt of his rifle. After months of using a long-barrelled shotgun, he now had an Arctic Warfare Magnum sniper rifle (the AWM) fitted with a longer bolt to take the .300 Winchester ammunition and an effective range of 1,100 metres. This was the rifle favoured by the British Army, the rifle that had confirmed kills at ranges in excess of 2,000 metres. This particular version had a folding stock; so much easier to carry with a rucksack.

There seemed no need to move from his concealed position just above the treeline. He reckoned he was about 1 to 1.5km from the three figures. They had glanced in his direction but only for the time it took them to realise that the ferry was berthed on the opposite shore to them; they now seemed more interested in an apparently abandoned car in the car park just to the right of the jetty. He heard the distant smash of a car window shattering, shortly followed by the high revving of a cold internal combustion engine. He watched with little interest as a small red Ford Focus drove out of the car park and away out of his field of vision. The direction of travel would take them back to the bridge that linked the island they were on to the mainland.

He stayed stock still, listening intently as the sound of the car engine became fainter, until it was no more. He maintained his stillness in the undergrowth, his senses attuned to anything unnatural. He saw the heads of a couple of grey seals as they bobbed up on the periphery of his sightline between him and the jetty on the opposite bank. They disappeared as quickly as they had arrived. He stayed put for about another 20 minutes, then, happy with the stillness, he rose from his position, hefted the rucksack onto his back, folded the stock of the sniper rifle and slung that onto his back also. He shook himself to adjust some of the deadness in his legs and began to walk back through the trees away from the coastline.

As he walked, he began to think once again about the strange set of circumstances that had ended with him now based on a small island just off the western coast of Scotland. He had been a resident of the island, not by choice, about four months now. Four months that had changed the world and his own life beyond all recognition. Here he was, a retired police officer who had been trying to enjoy the change of pace that retirement had brought him, suddenly thrust into a world where civilisation had receded to a time before order, civility, the rule of law, common decency and compassion existed. What remained was chaos and brutality. The struggle to survive had dealt him a reasonable hand. To be enjoying a brief touring holiday on a remote Scottish island when the world turned had been a definite head start. Quite what would have become of them in their semi-detached in the South East did not really bear thinking about. He moved out onto a narrow, metalled track and continued up the small rise to a point where he could see the buildings come into view.

This selection of low buildings, now joined together with modern glass and heavy beamed architecture, was originally the stately home of the landowner of this small sparsely populated island, then a hotel. A few years ago, it had been converted into a brand-new malt whisky distillery, so recent in fact that no actual official malt whisky was available yet for general sale. A quirk of the drink is that for Scottish malt whisky to be sold as such, it must have spent at least three years and one day maturing in a cask before bottling. Therefore, the only spirit so far available (prior to the cataclysmic events that had overtaken them) had been a new spirit bottled as a taster for those waiting for the release of the new whisky!

The distillery had been the reason he was originally on the island. He had read of the establishment of a new whisky distillery on Raasay and had seen that it had offered accommodation within the buildings in the form of a rather luxurious hotel. Things had been getting tense in the country; there was the beginning of a shortage of goods in the supermarkets and the level of infection was skyrocketing out of control, especially in the cities and more heavily populated areas. He was a keen watcher of news and current affairs and had always been perceptive of public attitudes and behaviour. In his mind, there was change ahead; the news reports were pointing to the NHS being overwhelmed and death rates were the highest they had been. The public's attitude to remaining at home and abiding by the rules implemented by the government was starting to fracture.

His initial thought was simply to seek a break and a change of scenery for his wife and himself, away from the more densely populated areas. The island, in addition to the attraction of the distillery, had a welcome remoteness, a very small indigenous population and some excellent walking trails to explore and soak up some of the much-needed Highland fresh air. They had booked rooms and packed for a short break. The rugged landscape had ensured they packed large rucksacks and quantities of heavy-duty outdoor clothing, excellent footwear, including crampons, walking poles, all of his accumulated camping equipment, several sleeping bags, stoves, insulated matts, torches, waterproofs, gloves, hats, maps, compass, GPS devices and a range of rations and energy bars. In addition, their 4x4 carried several blankets, a shovel, more torches, rubber boots for each of them and snow chains for the vehicle. Over the years, he had acquired a few 20-litre ex-MOD jerry cans, which were filled with diesel fuel and fastened to the roof rack.

He also went into his first-floor study and opened his gun safe. He had spent a little of his retirement doing some clay pigeon shooting at a local open-air range. As he had started to become more of a regular, he had decided to obtain a shotgun licence and buy a gun of his own. After much deliberation, he had opted for a rather evil-looking 12-gauge that resembled the American M16 rifle. The Akdal MKA 1919 gas-operated semi-automatic was manufactured in Turkey. He had picked this black model up from a local dealer second hand. In addition to the normal five-cartridge box magazine, it had come with a 10-shell magazine too! As he opened his gun safe, he mulled over whether to take it or not. Finally, he pulled out a black leather gun case and placed the shotgun inside. He also picked up two boxes of 12-gauge birdshot shells and put them inside the case with the gun and zipped it closed. When he got to their car, he lifted the false bottom of the boot and placed the gun case under this, packing some other soft items around and over the top to disguise its presence. He knew it was a strange decision to be taking his gun, but he reasoned that the chances were that it would never be removed from the car, let alone from its case.

As they had travelled north up the A1, the radio in the vehicle continued to broadcast disturbing developments about the contagion. Hospitals were declaring states of emergency, people were now dying in ambulances and being abandoned in situ, as there was no one to deal with them. The very people charged with dealing with the sick were themselves too sick to work. There had been isolated reports of looting and disorder at the supermarkets. People had gone into full panic buying mode, leaving very little on the shelves. The elderly and most vulnerable had reportedly been found dead at home by visiting relatives and friends, their pleas for assistance going unanswered in the deluge of new cases.

He decided to push on through the night, sharing the driving duties with his wife rather than stopping at a hotel, fearing any interaction with others could risk exposure. He had read that the infection was most dangerous for the elderly and those with underlying respiratory conditions, but more recently it was becoming clear that the infection, as it spread, was mutating and was now a real threat to everyone, regardless of age or health. As they pushed on into Scotland, it was clear the country was starting to break down. He steered the vehicle off the A1 and took to the back routes to try to bypass any large urban areas.

The stop for fuel had been a test. He found a remote station on a hillside, pulling in and seeing a man inside the shop area. He saw that he was able to pay at the pump and, using disposable gloves, he completed the fuelling, topping off all the jerry cans too. Having disposed of the gloves, he waved at the figure in the shop but received no response. He got back into the vehicle, and they continued.

Once past Fort William, the roads were empty of all but the odd car travelling in the opposite direction.

Eventually, they turned left and headed for the Isle of Skye. At any other time, they would have been marvelling at the wonderful scenery and talking excitedly about a return to Skye, which had been one of their first holidays together. Thinking about the beautiful walks they had done, the wonderful Talisker whisky experience and laughing at the rain that had fallen every day of their stay. The weather today was perversely clear and sunny. It was cold but beautifully crisp and fresh. The distraction of the radio broadcasts kept them focused on getting to Skye, over the bridge at Kyle of Loch Alsh. When he had come to the island as a boy, there had been a ferry to cross on to the island, but since 1995, the bridge had connected the island to the mainland.

As they passed over the bridge onto the island, he felt himself relax just a little. He turned and smiled at his wife as they passed the turning for Ardvasar on the Aird of Sleat. He recalled his time as a boy on the island. He had vague memories of them turning and heading down to Ardvasar and then continuing down the ever-narrowing road to eventually reach their holiday lodge. He remembered it being set halfway up a hillside. It had been a simple building, with a basic kitchen and dining area and a small snug lounge with a beautiful big open fire. The central staircase rose to a first floor of two reasonable bedrooms and a modest bathroom. He remembered the air being so fresh and the night sky being so clear, really seeing stars properly for the first time. He had loved the countryside, climbing the hill behind the lodge to the summit and the spectacular views whichever way he looked. A view across the sound to the port of Mallaig and the mainland of Scotland one way, and out over a bay and towards the forbidding and brooding jagged peaks of the Cuillin mountain range the other.

He broke from this memory and returned to their journey as they came into a small area of habitation. Broadford, the sign on the road indicated as they continued past some more properties and a Co-op supermarket, which seemed to be open for business. He knew from his planning that they were about 10 to 15 miles from the tiny ferry slipway at Sconser. After 20 minutes or so, they arrived at the modest car park, the small roll-on roll-off ferry immediately visible at the slipway. The MV *Hallaig* was probably about 150 feet long and looked relatively new. A man in uniform ushered him forward and indicated that he was clear to drive onto the ferry and that money for the passage would be taken on board. There was one other vehicle in front of him and a large non-articulated HGV bearing the Co-op logo to his right. Once he drove onto the ferry, the same man in uniform who had ushered him forward from the shore appeared at his window with a card reader. He and his wife put on their face masks, and he lowered the window and tapped the card reader with his credit card. He declined the offer of a receipt, and he closed the window.

He remembered his caution had still seemed very uncomfortable and anti-social at the time, almost rude to the uniformed ferry operative. How things had changed. After a short wait of no more than 10 minutes and with no further vehicles or passengers embarking, the ferry ramp behind him lifted and the engine note changed. They moved away from the slipway and out into the sound. The sea was flat calm, the weather still beautifully clear and sunny. The ferry was making good progress around a small headland and out into a channel, from which the island of Raasay could now been seen properly as it came closer.

The crossing had taken about half an hour. The engine note subsided as they slowed, and the front ramp began to descend as the slipway appeared. There was the loud clanging of metal hitting concrete as they docked. The uniformed operative reappeared and waved at the HGV, which was all the prompt the HGV driver needed to start his engine. The vehicle moved forward off the ferry, up the slight incline of the slipway and away up the hill. The brake lights of the car in front came on and it too moved forward and off the ferry. Peter started the engine, put his vehicle in drive and drove slowly forward, waving at the ferry staff. Following the vehicles in front, he drove off and up the slipway, onto the jetty, past a small car park containing two cars and drove off to the right, guided by a sign for Raasay Distillery and Hotel. In no time, they caught up with the HGV from the ferry and followed it down some narrow roads. As the HGV continued, they saw the entrance to the distillery and drove into the grounds of what had formerly been a private home, then a hotel called Borodale House. The new company had converted the buildings into a new malt whisky distillery and fashioned six new deluxe double bedrooms for guests to stay in. They had booked for seven nights, and as they pulled into the drive, it was clear that they were the only car in the car park.

They both made their way to the entrance, impressed with the open plan look of the newly created structure and the views of the large copper whisky stills visible through the vast panoramic windows. The lady at reception was warm and welcoming, quickly finding their reservation and indicating that they were indeed the only guests currently to be staying with them. A proper key was handed over, the type that opens a dead lock as opposed to a plastic card, along with directions to the room and the Wi-Fi code. The room was beautifully clean, with crisp white bed linen, tea and coffee making facilities with lovely fresh milk (not the UHT stuff you get in those little white plastic containers) and the most awe-inspiring view across the bay towards Skye and the Cuillin Hills.

They returned to their vehicle and unloaded all their luggage and walking and camping paraphernalia. Peter also subtly brought in his shotgun. The initially tidy, pristine room was now crammed with all they had brought from home. There was a large flat screen television on the wall that appeared to have a Freeview system. He turned on the set and flicked to a national news channel. Immediately there was a change of tone from the broadcasts they had watched up to this point. They both stopped what they were unpacking and listened intently to the serious tone of the newscaster as he gave the latest information and guidance.

It was now much more deadpan. The guidance was now being given in the form of strictly enforced rules. The basis of the instruction was that all persons, with absolutely no exception, were to stay indoors, wherever that may be. There was an outright ban on travelling. From 1800 hours that evening, every single person in the country was to stay inside. This would be enforced by the police and military. All persons discovered breaching this directive would be immediately detained and moved to newly created holding centres. Any form of resistance to these new measures would be dealt with robustly and with force if necessary. This internal quarantining was to last initially for 48 hours, with further instructions given during that time.

He processed the information he had just heard and stared out of the window at the beautiful scenery and clear blue sky. He turned slowly back to his wife, who was sat on the end of the bed. She looked back at him. He gave a small half-smile... "Fuck!"

"What do we do then, Peter?" his wife Helen said.

"It looks like we are staying here, certainly for the immediate future," he replied.

"Let's go back to reception and have a chat with that lady who checked us in!"

They left their room and went back down to reception, only to find the desk unattended.

Peter rang the bell on the desk to get someone's attention. After a short while, the kindly old lady who they had met when checking in returned. The smile on her face seemed just a little bit more strained.

"Hello, my dears, what a dreadful situation! I am just rushing to get the last ferry back to Skye."

"Where does this change in the rules leave us as guests at the hotel?" Peter asked.

"You are welcome to come with me and get the ferry back over and then try and continue your journey," the lady replied.

"We are too far from home to be able to comply with the new deadline, so we are thinking we would stay here, certainly in the immediate future. Would that be okay?"

"Well, I am only here with two members of the kitchen staff and another person is away on business for the distillery, but we are all heading over to the ferry so we can all get back to Skye, where we live."

Peter was just starting to grow slightly frustrated with the lady's inability to understand that they needed to know what their options were.

"So, what are we supposed to do?" Peter asked in a slightly more direct tone.

"I am just the receptionist here, the owner and manager of the hotel and distillery are away at the moment, so I don't know what I can suggest. All I know is that I want to be back home and am going to have to leave now to get the ferry."

As she finished her declaration, two younger people, a girl in her 20s and a younger male, appeared from the staff entrance, busily putting on jackets and carrying small bags.

The lady took her cue from the two new arrivals and started to put a coat on, which had been hanging from the back of the door.

"That's it, we are going to have to go. As I said, you are welcome to come with us, but we are going now!"

"Is there any food in the kitchen? Where are the keys to the place? When is the next ferry after this evening?"

He might as well have been talking to himself as the three figures disappeared out of the front entrance, past their vehicle and up the road out of sight.

Peter looked long and hard at the entrance, part of him wondering if they would possibly return. But nothing stirred.

"Welcome to Raasay Distillery Hotel, could the last one out please turn off the lights and lock up," Peter quietly said.

"What are we going to do then?" Helen spoke quietly too, but there was a little bit of fear and nervousness in her voice.

"Right, we have a room and a bed for the night. Let's have a bit of an explore of the hotel and the distillery and assess things after that. I am wondering if there are any other people nearby," Peter exclaimed. "Do you want to stay together or split up?" he continued.

"Can we stay together, please? I am feeling a little bit freaked out about this and would rather be with you while we look round," Helen replied.

"Okay then, shall we start down here and see how much access we have to the hotel and see if they have any food in their kitchens."

They walked through the open staff door into an office with two desks. There was the usual assortment of office chairs, computers on each desk, some calendar planners taped to the wall and a white board with what appeared to be the rosters for the next four weeks. Peter stared at the board, and by a simple process of name repetition, it was clear that the three figures scurrying down to the ferry had been the receptionist, Gail, the cook, Ross, and the waitress-cum-chambermaid, Olga. On the far side of the office was another door. Peter opened the door and, with Helen following closely, they entered a dark corridor. There were doors either side indicating male and female toilets; they checked and found the doors unlocked. The next door on the right opened onto a large dining area furnished with half a dozen tables, four chairs at each table. A bar area at the far end had a spectacular display of the New Raasay Distillery (New Spirit) whisky. The opposite end of the room from the bar was a panoramic window wall, with another glorious view of the Cuillins on Skye.

They returned to the corridor and opened another door opposite the dining room. This was a large, well-appointed industrial-sized kitchen, with an eight-ring gas hob, two eye-level grills, a couple of deep fat fryers, some stainless-steel work tops and islands. There were drawers under the work tops, knives affixed to the wall and a variety of other large machines that Peter couldn't immediately identify. There was a corridor off the kitchen leading to another room, which contained a walk-in fridge and another walk-in freezer. Peter tried each of the doors in turn, opening the fridge first, which seemed well stocked with milk, cheese, butter and some meat in packets and other prepared meals. The freezer was also well stocked with boxes of frozen cod and salmon, several boxes of pies and other pastries, a good selection of frozen vegetables and tubs of ice cream and what looked like a range of frozen pre-prepared meals.

"Well, it looks like we won't have to dig into our own rations just yet." Peter smiled.

Just in a large alcove to the side of the freezer was a sizeable dry goods store. Similar to the fridge and freezer, this area was well stocked with lots of packets of rice, pasta, cereals, an array of tinned goods, large bags of flour and other things that would need to be investigated later.

They left the kitchen area and pushed open the final door at the end of the corridor, marked "Fire Exit". Being careful not to lock themselves out, they opened this to find themselves in a large outside yard, with two medium-sized trucks parked next to one another, a large 4x4-type vehicle, a stack of sherry barrels, and they could see three other buildings, which were clearly the buildings of the distillery. He wasn't sure what made him think to do it, but as he stared at the vehicles in the yard, he decided to check them out. To his surprise, he found the vehicles were unlocked and the keys were (as he'd seen so many times in the movies) under the flap of the driver's sun visor. He made a mental note to check the level of fuel of each vehicle, but that could wait.

They both moved back inside through the staff corridor and into the dining area, which in turn opened out into a comfortable modern lounge on the edge of the building. The enormous glass window appeared to be framing the now familiar Cuillins on Skye. A large flat screen television dominated the wall space above the fireplace. Peter could see the remote control on a coffee table in front of the fire. "Let's check out what's happening then," he spoke quietly. Helen looked at him and just nodded. They turned on the television and an information message filled the screen. In bold typed letters, the message was numbingly clear in its starkness!

TO ALL PEOPLE EVERYWHERE
STAY INDOORS
DO NOT GO OUT FOR ANY REASON
FOR YOUR SURVIVAL
STAY INSIDE

Peter flicked across a random number of channels; the same message was being screened everywhere. "Well, this has clearly got serious!" Peter commented.

Helen looked up and said, "More serious than the last 15 months of restrictions?"

"It looks as if we could be here for a while longer than we expected then," Peter said. Helen just nodded her agreement.

"Okay, we need to get ourselves fed, then we need to get organised. We have plenty of supplies here and it looks like we are on our own. We are on a small Scottish island, away from the centres of population, so if, as I suspect, the disease has changed and become deadlier, then we are in as good a place as we can be to ride this out until the government or whoever gets a grip on things."

Helen said, "Okay, food first, then let's make a list of what we need to do here, what options we have and a strategy if where we are now becomes less safe than it appears at present."

Peter smiled. "At least we have each other, love!" He sidled up to her and gave her a hug. Helen turned towards him, and they kissed each other.

"You mentioned food and I'm starving," Helen said.

"Okay, let's see what we can find in the kitchen then because I am pretty peckish myself," laughed Peter as he moved back to the corridor and across into the kitchen...

Peter was jolted out of his reverie and back to his position in front of the distillery building. It looked the same as when they had arrived four months ago. Was it really only four months since they had arrived for their week's break, away from the insidious, silent illness that had been creeping across the country? As he walked into the car park, he saw Helen had reversed their vehicle so that it was facing out the way they had come in. It was an old habit he had always followed, better to be facing in the intended direction of travel if you want to get out of somewhere in a hurry. He moved past their vehicle and around the side of the building, heading to the open yard at the rear.

"Helen, it's Peter. I am just coming around the corner into the yard, alright, love?" The "alright, love" bit was their code to each other that they were moving freely and not under any sort of duress. As he rounded the building line, he could see Helen was busy loading boxes into the rear of a truck. "Hello, how are you doing?" Peter asked.

"Not bad. I have just about loaded all the dry goods and am ready for you to give me a hand with the frozen stuff if that is okay?" she replied.

"Sure, no worries. I spotted something while out on my walking patrol. It was three people moving on Skye; I thought they might be looking at a way to get across to us here, but they took a car and disappeared away toward the bridge at Loch Alsh," Peter commented about the three individuals he had spied earlier.

Helen nodded. "I reckon people will have to be heading for larger towns to try for food and supplies by now."

"Yep, I think you may be right. Did you see anyone while I was down at the jetty?" Peter went on.

"No, there are one or two chimneys with smoke coming from them in the town, but I reckon everyone here is keeping their heads down," Helen responded.

"Did you get everything on the list?" Peter asked.

"No fresh milk and not much cheese left, but I did get a case of long-life stuff on board," Helen answered.

"Let me help you load this frozen stuff into the truck then."

They disappeared back into the hotel part of the distillery and returned with boxes of frozen fish, meat, part-baked bread, ready meals of lasagne, other pasta delights, chilli, casseroles, etc., and best of all, they were all in industrial quantities. After 20 minutes or so, they felt they had loaded as much as they could. Peter had been over to one of the distillery warehouses where they kept the maturing casks of whisky and liberated two firkins of spirit that had been laid there since 2017.

Helen walked back to the front of the hotel where their own vehicle was parked and got in the driver's seat. Peter got into the truck they had just loaded and started it up. He stamped on the clutch and forced the gear shift into first, a few revs and a subtle lift of the clutch pedal and the truck leapt forward as he steered it out of the rear yard and out to the front to join Helen. He had driven this truck a few times now, and in his life, he had driven countless vehicles of all shapes and sizes, but the clutch on this thing was still a bastard!

He drove past Helen in their vehicle, pulled out onto the road and headed back towards the ferry quay. He drove past the turning for the quayside and carried on up the single-track road, heading north. He knew this road avoided many of the buildings and houses on the island. The track hugged the coast, then turned back on itself as it climbed away from the coastline. They eventually came to a junction and took a sharp left turn again heading north, away from the most inhabited part of the island. The countryside was a mixture of low heather and gorse moorland, with a few small areas of forest. The weather was still being kind to them. It was Scotland after all, so rain was always to be expected, but today was dry and quite bright, with the sun occasionally breaking through the clouds, which were travelling slowly across the sky on this almost windless day. The road continued to follow the contours of the ground in front of them and snaked its way around hill and scrub. Eventually, they reached a sign. Callum's Road. Peter knew from the way down to the distillery that the road was now much narrower and less well metalled. There was some fairly large potholes and parts of the surface had clearly been washed away in bad weather.

Peter kept a watchful eye in his mirrors to make sure Helen was still keeping up in their vehicle behind. She was happy to keep a safe distance between them, but not too far. As they rounded a headland, the road looked to come to an end up ahead. There was a signpost indicating this small hamlet of half a dozen houses was known as Arnish. An earlier exploration had found that most of the buildings belonged to a farm that was now deserted and one or two apparently empty holiday cottages, all boarded up. Just before the road ended, there was a track going off sharply to the left and down a small descent to the sea. The track disappeared into the sea at this point, with a usable concrete slipway.

Moored and anchored just to the left of the slipway was a 40-foot catamaran motor cruiser with a large, covered cabin, flybridge above and a spacious open deck area. Peter reversed the truck down the slipway as far as he dared. He jumped down and unhooked the rear drop gate of the truck.

"Okay?" he said as Helen joined him on the slipway.

"Yes, that road doesn't get any better, does it! Did you see anybody?" Helen asked.

"Not a soul, the place is almost too quiet. So, let's get all the stuff on board and get the vehicles secured in case we get a chance of another resupply."

Between the two of them, they unloaded the contents from the back of the truck and managed to get it onto the rear deck area of the catamaran. Once the truck was empty, Peter drove back up the slope and parked the vehicle. He opened the bonnet and unscrewed the distributor cap, removed the rotor arm and put it in his pocket. He then locked the cab and returned to the slipway. Helen had reversed their own vehicle down the slipway, had the hatchback open and was throwing bags of things onto the catamaran.

"Well done, love. Be done in no time," Peter encouraged. "Do you want me to park the car?" he went on.

Helen said, "No, I'll get parked, and you get the boat started and make sure all the stuff is secure on board."

"Okay, reckon we've earned a drink once we get back to base."

"Did you get gin?" Helen smiled.

"What?! From the distillery that we have just left?" Peter laughed.

He got onto the rear of the boat and went into the cabin, pulling a key out from under his coat that was on a light neoprene lanyard. He put the key in the starter slot on the control panel and turned it. Some lights came on and he pressed the green starter button and the engine burst into life. While he was waiting for Helen to return, he sorted out the various containers of supplies and brought the more perishable items into the cabin. The weather was still very clear and calm, but he knew how quickly things could change. Helen untied the front mooring line from a large rock by the side of the slipway. Peter, not as well versed with boats as he was with motor vehicles, had put out a front and a rear anchor. He winched in the rear anchor. Helen clambered on board and walked to the front of the boat. She indicated that she was ready at the front anchor winch and Peter put the boat into reverse. Helen began to winch in the front anchor, holding her left arm in the air so Peter could see she was still winching in anchor chain. After a short while, she lowered her arm and shouted, "Clear!" With the anchors and mooring lines all aboard, Peter reversed the boat slowly out of the small inlet into the channel between Skye and where they were on the north-western shore of Raasay. Once out in the channel, Peter put the boat into drive, and they headed north.

Peter moved the boat out into the middle of the channel, not comfortable with the many rocks sticking above the surface along the shoreline of Raasay. The wind was a little stronger here and there were small waves just lapping against the front of the boat as they headed north, but the catamaran was very stable as they moved along. Helen had stowed the anchor and chain and had joined Peter in the cabin. They were now moving past a small rocky outcrop that Peter knew from his map to be Eilean Fladday, and they would shortly pass another smaller outcrop island called Eilean Tigh. They were heading for the next parcel of land to the north, a small island of about four square miles, with a couple of hills of no more than 350 feet in height, called Rona. Peter had studied the maps carefully and knew that just beyond the island they were approaching was a small inlet, forming the most wonderful natural harbour, sheltered from the elements with a manmade jetty providing safe mooring and large enough for a vehicle to drive right up to the boat. Peter slowed the boat as the channel was quite narrow. He threaded the boat between the small outcrop of rock and the main island of Rona, into the wide sheltered harbour. As the jetty came into view, Helen picked up the binoculars from the cabin table and scanned the land around the jetty. "I can't see anyone!" she exclaimed.

"Okay, let's get going. Is the Ranger thing still there?" Peter asked.

"Yes, right where we left it this morning," Helen replied.

Peter manoeuvred the boat to come alongside the jetty. Without needing to be asked, Helen had placed four large white fenders along the port side of the boat, to protect the boat as they moored alongside the concrete jetty. Helen jumped onto the jetty carrying the front mooring line, which she attached to the purpose-built metal mooring. Peter put the boat into reverse, then neutral, moved out to the rear deck and threw Helen another line so she could secure the rear of the boat. They worked efficiently now; not like the first time, when it had taken several attempts and a good deal of shouting and cursing to get the boat moored here!

Once secure, Peter returned to the cabin and switched the engine off, removing the key from the control panel and once again placing the lanyard around his neck and under his coat. Peter walked up to the small utility 4x4 Polaris Ranger vehicle that they had "borrowed" from the island manager's house. The vehicle was small, maybe a little bigger than a quad bike, but not much. It had a tiny two-person cab and a useful open-backed storage area. There was also a trailer with a flatbed fitted, more than capable of transporting their latest foraged supplies. They both worked hard at unloading the boat onto the jetty and then into the trailer and back of the vehicle. They had the whole amount loaded in about 30 minutes.

"Have we got everything?" Peter asked.

"I think so. I picked up the binoculars, you have your rucksack and the rifle?" Helen asked.

"Yes, it's in the front of the Ranger, between the seats," Peter replied.

"I'll drive if you like," Helen offered.

Peter looked back at her after scanning the sea behind them. "Okay, thank you, love."

They got into the small Ranger, Helen started the diesel engine and put it into drive, released the brake and they slowly drove off the jetty and onto a narrow track into some woodland. As the track turned left, the trees stopped to reveal a small meadow with a couple of outbuildings, from where they had found the Ranger. They turned right onto a better surfaced road and up to a long white building that looked like it had been reasonably recently refurbished, with new UPVC windows and a bright coat of whitewash to the walls. A sign on the front gate simply stated, "Rona Lodge – ISLAND MANAGER". They had knocked here when they had first arrived on the island. No answer. They had both looked around the entire cottage and yard area. Knocking louder on the front door and still getting no answer, they had tried the door and found it unlocked. As they entered, they saw that they were in a lovely old-fashioned kitchen. On the table was a note with a key:

To whom it may concern!
We have gone to see family on Skye
Help yourself to food
This key is for the truck in the barn (may be useful)
Good luck to you!

Dennis Maclaverty

Helen drove past the lodge and continued up the track as it climbed away from the sea and into the interior of the island. After less than 10 minutes, they started to descend towards the sea again and came to a lovely picturesque dry bay with a small rectangular cottage facing out over it. This was a holiday cottage, rented by the manager at Rona Lodge. The keys had been hanging up in the kitchen at the lodge, and after a little exploration, this was where Helen and Peter had chosen to take refuge!

They pulled up at the rear of the cottage, between the main building and the large outbuilding that contained a spare fridge, chest freezer and washing machine. Just to the side of this was a large green plastic fuel oil container. The heating, water and electricity were powered by the fuel oil from here. Peter had found a similar oil container at Rona Lodge and had worked out how to siphon the fuel out of that container into a portable 50-gallon drum he had found in one of the outbuildings.

They started to unpack the supplies from the Ranger and the trailer, putting the frozen stuff into the chest freezer and taking the dry goods into the house, to stock up the pantry just off the kitchen area. This unloading took another 20 minutes or so. By the time they had unloaded everything, brought in Peter's firearm and their rucksacks, they were ready for a sit down.

"Tea?" enquired Helen as they collapsed into the chairs around the table in the kitchen.

"Sounds excellent," Peter replied as he watched Helen fill the kettle and put it on the stove.

Helen brewed the tea and Peter walked through the kitchen into the lounge and opened the French doors to sit out on the small patio with a view of the sea and dry harbour in front of them.

It had been four months since they had driven to Scotland and three since they had left Raasay and found this remote hideaway on this small three- to four-mile-long island. Peter sat down, sipped his tea and watched as Helen sat down, placed her feet on the chair opposite and drifted off to sleep. Peter smiled and stared out to sea, watching a few sea birds routing about in the bay and shoreline where the tide had gone out. Four months; Peter thought back to how they had got organised and survived these last months, from that time when they had sat down to eat that first meal at the Raasay Distillery.

After the initial shock of the stark message across every channel on the TV, they had found some precooked lasagne in the walk-in fridge of the hotel kitchen. Working out how to turn on the oven, they were able to heat the food, cut some slices of bread and throw a few salad leaves and tomatoes into a bowl. They took the food through to the dining area and sat down to eat.

"What do you think we should do now?" Helen asked.

"I think we are stuck here for the moment. The ferry that left a while ago has not returned," Peter replied.

"Should we just stay here?" Helen went on.

"I think in the short term, we are complying with the rules, we have a good supply of food and can use all the facilities of the hotel if no one returns soon," Peter said.

"What about finding out about the latest situation on the mainland and why they have suddenly increased the level of the stay-at-home order?" Helen exclaimed.

"Hmmm!" was Peter's only response (his non-verbal communication had always been a cause of frustration for Helen, but at this moment, with their situation so unknown, it was perhaps the only answer!).

Peter returned to his dinner, thinking as he ate of what might be going on. He had always been a keen observer of the news and had watched the increase in the concern caused by this illness across the country these last 18 months. He had his own take on things. He had always been scathing about the attitudes and values of the general public at large. Perhaps 30 years as a London copper had given him a slightly jaundiced view of the public and he certainly found them, as an entity, utterly contemptable.

When the leaders had begun to realise there was a problem and a danger that the NHS may not be able to cope with an increase in intensive care patients, he had been staggered by their naivety. Expecting the public to do the right thing and follow the ever-increasing level of contradictory guidelines and rules. He knew from experience that the public on the whole would need proper, simple, easy-to-follow guidance; that there would be a significant minority who would ignore the rules and carry on regardless. Then, of course, the conspiracy theorists and other internet warriors, spreading false stories and furthering their own agendas.

He watched the reports as the number of those new cases and new deaths rose each day; the shear lunacy of one expert saying it might be beneficial to wear a face covering and another suggesting that there was no proven clinical benefit to wearing a mask. The mask wearing issue dragged on for months, until someone, clearly using the common-sense brain cell, decided to start making mask wearing mandatory. He had been wearing a mask from the outset, sourcing his masks from an online Chinese supplier. A rumour had built up, mainly by the media, that the leadership were considering a full-scale enforcement of staying at home, closing schools, asking everyone to work from home, restrictions on public transport, etc. This had immediately sparked panic buying at the supermarkets, with toilet paper and soap, of all things, being absent from the shelves for several months. He had watched all this from a distance, with his own time being used to get some more outdoor clothing and camping kit together.

Once they closed the gyms and all the non-essential shops, the amount of traffic started to dramatically reduce. Peter found himself checking in on his elderly neighbours, making sure they had enough food in. He told them not to go out to the shops and volunteered Helen and himself to go and do their shopping for them. He found himself taking advantage of the surrounding countryside, to take himself out for ever longer walks across the South Downs, trusting his planning and map reading skills to walk from home, steering clear of any car parks and roads, where other people might be. He remembered thinking how good he was at avoiding people. If he happened upon someone ahead of him on a footpath, he would challenge himself to watch which way they went at the next junction or obvious route change point and go a different way from the way they had gone. If this meant a deviation for him from his planned route, he would simply recalculate and work out an alternative.

He had always been a keen walker, keeping himself fit as he had gotten older by visits to the gym and by taking long countryside walks. The year before all the upheaval from the onset of the illness, he had challenged himself to take part in an organised 100km walk from Eastbourne to Arundel, along the South Downs path. This was not like him, to take part in an organised event; he usually preferred to do his own thing. But he set himself a challenge and did the whole distance in one go, in a little under 24 hours. Once the restrictions came into force, the walking was one of the few things both he and Helen were able to continue to do. It kept them fit and their minds active.

Peter had begun to see the slight change in atmosphere as the restrictions had dragged on through Christmas. The public love Christmas and it was clear that the leadership were caught in two minds as to what they should do. They had initially made great play of following the scientific advice. Clearly the scientific advice (a bit like the correct advice, but with all emotion and sentiment removed) was that all measures should remain in force throughout Christmas and the New Year holiday. The leadership knew they had to give something of a lift to the flagging spirits of the country, so allowed a slight relaxation of the regulations, for people to meet up with family for an abbreviated period of time. This, of course, was set up to fail, with a vast proportion of the public ignoring pleas to "Stay Local" and instead travelling all over the country, mixing with family and friends and being "festive"!

It was immediately after Christmas that Peter had started to formulate a plan to go away from their semi-detached in Sussex. It was clear that the number of infected people was rising; anyone could see that another regulation to stay at home for all but the most urgent needs was going to be reintroduced. He talked with Helen about maybe a week or 10 days away in a remote countryside location. She seemed keen on the idea; after all, it had been 15 months since they had any holiday at all, and they were owed money from the likes of Easy Jet, Airbnb and other holiday companies. So, he began to do his research and try and find a suitable place for a break, away from where they lived. Looking at the increase in numbers, he knew they would need to get going soon.

Eventually, he happened upon a new whisky distillery on the island of Raasay, which lies just north across a narrow channel from the Isle of Skye. They both knew Skye from an earlier holiday they had had there. He was also a keen collector and lover of Scottish malt whisky. What caught his eye was the fact that this new distillery had a small hotel attached, for guests to actually stay at the distillery. Yep, that was the one for them! This was how they had found themselves all the way up to this remote part of the Western Isles of Scotland.

They finished their dinner and took their plates and cutlery back to the kitchen, did the washing up, keeping the area tidy, and returned to the lounge.

"Let's have another look at the TV, see if there is any update," Peter said. He turned on the set, but still saw the same stark message as before.

"Fancy a drink, Peter?" Helen asked as she moved to the bar at the end of the dining area.

"Go on then, let's try some of this whisky," Peter replied.

Helen poured two generous measures of the light brown liquid into two cut crystal glasses and brought them over to the table where Peter was sat. She then went back to the bar and returned with a small water jug. They sat opposite each other and sipped the whisky.

"Hmm, very good," Peter remarked. "So, let's comply with the rules at the moment and see what happens in the next few days."

"Okay, but how long before we have to make a decision ourselves?" Helen asked.

"I really don't know. Let's get some sleep and see how things are in the morning; there may be more news," Peter replied.

But Peter remembered there had not been more news. The same message continued to be broadcast on all channels. The radio channels had all gone silent. Peter remembered thinking at this point that it had reminded him of the book by John Wyndham, *The Day of the*

Triffids, that he had read as a child. Perhaps part of this story caused him to think about improving their situation at the distillery after they had been hunkered down inside the hotel for five days. The lack of information was worrying, with maybe a slight chance it was due to a poor signal in their remote location, but he didn't really believe that.

There was no internet signal; again, whether this was due to the remoteness of their location or something more serious, he didn't know. He had spent a few days looking at the local maps of the area and felt he was now familiar with the layout of the island of Raasay and the smaller island of Rona to the north. Some guidebooks and other pamphlets in the hotel reception had made him aware of accommodation on Rona that might be more secure for them. He found a pamphlet on boats for hire out of Portree on Skye as a way to get out to Rona. There were still a lot of unknowns; for example, he hadn't known what fuel was available and he had assumed that all supplies would have to be transported out there. He didn't know of the size of the population on the island, but the five days on Raasay had started to become more thought-provoking, as he had seen one or two people wander past on the road. It had spooked both him and Helen, and his willingness and desire to distance themselves from the public had kicked in.

"Let's go down to where we got off the ferry," Peter stated as they sat having some porridge for breakfast.

"Okay, then what?" Helen asked.

"I have an idea. If we can get a boat from the quayside, maybe we can get across the channel to Portree. We can take our time as we approach to have a close look at the situation in the town. They have boats for hire at Portree, maybe we can go ashore there, grab some more supplies and other items that could be useful, then head back here with the boat. We could load up with as much stuff as we can from the distillery hotel kitchen, then take ourselves up to Rona and see what we can find on that island?"

Helen looked hard at Peter. "Why do you want to leave here? We have everything we need. It still feels reasonably safe."

"Helen, it's just an idea. This is fine for now, but I have this feeling we are going to need to be even more isolated than we currently are. I just wish we knew more about what was happening," Peter replied.

"So, can we just stay here for now, please?"

"Okay, but if things change, then we need to think about moving, is that alright?"

Helen nodded and they took their breakfast things back into the kitchen.

That evening, while eating their dinner, there was suddenly a noise from the TV. They had left the set on for the last few days in the hope of getting more information and an update from someone as to what was happening.

An automated voice from the TV stated suddenly, "Stand by for a message in two minutes."

"Helen, did you hear that, a message," Peter said.

They listened to the deafening silence, waiting for the TV to spring into life. After a while,

"Now hear this!" The same robotic voice. No picture, just a voice. "The Illness is now spreading among all ages and causing those with the condition to be unable to breath unaided. There is no more room in hospitals. We are declaring martial law. You must stay indoors to save your lives. We will endeavour to supply food. A state of emergency now exists. More to follow tomorrow at 12 noon. I repeat, stay indoors." The message ended as abruptly as it had started.

"What now then?" Helen asked.

"Let's give it 24 hours, listen to the next message tomorrow at noon, then we can make a plan," Peter replied.

Peter remembered, as he now sat sipping tea on the patio looking out to sea from his secluded spot on Rona, how difficult that next 24 hours had been. They had both spent that day discussing whether to sit tight where they were, complying with the rule to stay inside, cautious of stepping outside. Helen had been keen to stay at the distillery hotel. After their short time there, it had started to become familiar to her and safe. Peter recalled that they had become quite heated with each other. In his opinion, they needed to consider isolating themselves further by moving up to Rona, but that was not what Helen wanted to do. So, they agreed to wait for the message the following day at noon to make a more reasoned decision.

That next morning, the time seemed to drag on after breakfast, waiting for the clock in the lounge to tick round to 12 noon.

"Stand by for a message in two minutes," the TV suddenly announced. Helen and Peter perked up from the dining table to listen to this latest information.

"Full martial law now applies; all persons are ordered to stay indoors for their own safety. Armed security are now patrolling your streets and you run a risk to life if found outside. We will bring food to you all in the next five days."

That was it.

"Well, clearly we have no choice but to stay here," Helen had remarked.

"Somehow I don't think that the provision of food will extend as far as a small island off the coast of Skye, Helen."

"What do we do then?"

"I think we are on our own. We have to take steps to find sufficient supplies to survive this situation on an isolated spot, more isolated than where we currently find ourselves."

"And if we are caught outside?"

"In the same way that I cannot see us being supplied with food here, I don't think that hordes of armed security are going to be patrolling the hills and valleys of the Scottish Highlands," Peter responded. "My proposal is this," Peter went on. "Let's get up early tomorrow and get down to the quay, where we got off the ferry. I think there were one or two small motorboats moored there. If we can get one started, I suggest we go across the channel to Portree, the main town on Skye. We could see if we can get a bigger boat, maybe gather some more supplies and return here?"

"What if we see people?" Helen questioned.

"Yes, the chances are we will run into people, they are going to be panicked by this, and from my experience, I wouldn't be surprised if we start to see the breakdown of social order and law. We will have to be on our guard. Don't forget I do have the shotgun with us."

"Oh Peter, you and that bloody shotgun. I don't know why you brought it," Helen shouted.

"It may be that the 'bloody shotgun', as you call it, is what keeps us safe as we maintain our isolation."

Helen shook her head. "I don't like it. The trip feels unnecessary to me, and I feel if we turn up with you carrying a gun, it will only escalate any confrontations we might have."

"Helen, I hear what you are saying, but we may be embarking on a type of living where the normal rules of decency and lawfulness are disappearing."

As Peter sat sipping the tea, and the sun started to sink and the shadows lengthened, he carried on remembering the events that had led to them being holed up on the small Scottish island of Rona. He thought back to the night before the trip to Portree. Helen was not keen to go outside, let alone take a boat across a stretch of water to the main town of the island of Skye. He had agreed with her that it was a risk, but he pointed out that the amount of food they had in the hotel would only last for a finite amount of time, plus there were quite a few houses in close proximity to them, and the occupants of those houses may well come looking for food when their own stores ran out. He tried to impress on her that they were just looking to improve their own circumstances, plus he reasoned that there may be more information of what was happening in the country.

That next morning, the weather was as beautiful as it had been since their arrival in Scotland. The sky was a clear blue, with bright sunshine and virtually no wind. They were up early and had eaten a quick breakfast of toast and coffee. They agreed to take a few items with them, some prepared food to eat during the day and the usual things they would have taken on a typical day out together. Weatherproof jackets, gloves and hats, as well as a thermos flask of hot coffee. After some hard staring and tutting from Helen, she finally agreed that it might be prudent for Peter to take his shotgun. Peter loaded the ten round magazine, placed this in his rucksack and attached the five-round magazine to the gun, racking it to put a round in the chamber and checking that the safety catch was on.

They left the security of the distillery hotel on foot. Not wishing to draw attention to themselves, they walked down the road to the jetty where a week ago they had got off the small car ferry. As they surveyed the scene in front of them, they could see a couple of boats tied up to the jetty, which was to the right of the ferry slipway. Peter took in the second of the two boats they could see. The small craft was quite an open design, with a small protective half-cabin-like-shelter. On the rear of the hull were the words, "Orkney 14", which he presumed referred to the boat being about 14 feet in length. There was a single outboard motor at the rear, tilted so it wasn't in the water, and a smaller outboard motor out of the water fixed to the rear of the boat.

Peter said to Helen, "Keep an eye out while I see if I can get this engine started."

Helen looked back the way they had come as Peter jumped down into the boat, took off his shotgun and rucksack and placed them at the front of the boat, just under the small, sheltered section. He could see some wires leading from a control panel that led back to the rear of the boat into the engine. He found a catch to lower the engine into its correct vertical position. He saw some instructions printed on the top case of the engine. He returned to the panel and saw a key in a slot. Turning the key, a green light came on. He went back to the engine and, finding a pull toggle, he pulled. Nothing happened. He read the instructions again, returned to the control panel and opened the throttle lever a little bit. Back at the engine, he pulled the toggle again. The engine fired and died immediately. He tried a third time. This time the engine fired and stayed revving. He jumped back to the control panel and opened the throttle to get some more revs from the engine, then, satisfied, he lowered the revs again.

"Helen, we still okay?" he shouted up to his wife.

She looked down at him and nodded. "That engine seems so noisy with nothing else going on," she added.

"Give me your rucksack, then see if you can undo the mooring lines," Peter said.

Helen dropped her rucksack down to Peter in the boat, then untied the front mooring line and threw it into the boat. She untied the rear line but left it looped through the mooring ring. She jumped down into the boat with Peter's help.

"Okay, let's go," Peter said as he put the shift lever into forward on the side of the panel. As the boat moved forward away from the jetty, Helen pulled the rear line through the loop and gathered it into the rear of the boat, being careful not to snag the rope in the revving engine.

"Well done, love," Peter encouraged as he steered the boat away from the jetty and out into the water of the channel between the two islands.

He had studied the maps with Helen the night before. They had agreed to head out into the channel and, once a reasonable way out, they would head north, keeping a fair distance from the shores of both islands. As they headed out into the water, the boat started to bob a little, but there was virtually no swell and the wind was still almost nil. A large headland on Skye was approaching on their left side; Peter knew that past this headland would be an inlet, which was where Portree was situated. Peter throttled the engine back and slowed the boat as they came past the headland, getting their first look at the small town.

Peter turned the boat into the small inlet, and they began to get closer to the town of Portree.

"Keep an eye out, love. See if there is any activity," Peter said to Helen as the town got ever closer.

"Nothing so far. The place looks deserted," Helen answered.

"Okay, you see that straight bit, sticking out on the left of the town bay, I reckon we could try to moor there," Peter offered.

He slowed the boat again as they approached a harbour wall, with what looked like a row of shops along its length. There was a more industrial section at the end with several commercial-sized trawlers moored, a cage of gas cannisters and a reasonably large white building. There were also some olive-green fuel storage containers set back from the jetty area. Peter had spotted a number of boats moored out in the bay on mooring buoys.

"As I pull alongside, can you get a couple of those plastic tubes over the side to cushion us against the wall?" Peter asked.

Helen saw the three objects and tied them to the side of the boat.

"Okay, grab the front line and take it with you while I get us against the harbour wall, then tie it to any mooring you can find," Peter said.

"Okay, Peter, slow down a bit so we don't crash," Helen replied, spotting a ladder built into the side of the harbour wall leading to the top of the wall and the road behind.

Very slowly, Peter edged the boat closer to the harbour wall, watching the slight swell as he approached. Helen was on the side of the boat, ready to jump for the ladder. They were lucky it was calm, Peter thought; trying to do this in a rough swell would have been a challenge! Helen grabbed a rung of the ladder and stepped onto it. As she climbed, she took the mooring line with her. As she did this, Peter put the boat into reverse and then neutral. Helen secured the front mooring.

"Throw me the other line so I can secure the rear," Helen said as she moved alongside the boat on the harbour wall. There was about a three-foot drop to the rear deck of the boat.

Peter threw the rear line and watched as Helen secured the second mooring.

"Okay, let's have a quick look around, maybe pick up anything we can find of use and see if we can find out any more information, shall we?" Peter said as he climbed up the ladder on the harbour wall, placed his rucksack at the top, then returned to the deck of the boat. He reappeared at the top, now carrying the black M16 replica shotgun.

"You going to take that, are you?" Helen scolded as she saw Peter with the gun.

"Better to be safe than sorry," Peter replied.

They both put on their rucksacks, Peter cradled the shotgun with the barrel pointing down and headed along the road, which formed the top of the harbour wall.

"Boat trips around the islands," Peter exclaimed, pointing to a sign on the front of a building as they walked along the road, aptly named Quay Street, Peter noted. There was a guest house, a restaurant and a fish and chip takeaway. As they walked along, Peter was scanning the shop fronts and buildings for any sign of people.

"It's so quiet," Helen remarked as they walked behind a row of buildings and up a slight hill towards what they presumed to be the main part of the town. As they came up the rise, they could see the distinctive green sign of a Co-op mini supermarket.

"Shall we try the Co-op?" Peter suggested.

"Okay, just be careful with that gun," Helen replied.

As they got within 30 metres or so of the supermarket, a male appeared from the entrance brandishing a rifle.

"That's far enough," the male shouted. Peter reckoned him to be in his 40s or 50s, maybe a little younger than himself. He was of medium build, with a beard, about 5ft 6in tall. He was wearing brown trousers and a heavy knit navy sweater, with an open dirty green waterproof jacket on top. Peter also noticed he was wearing a pair of very dirty ancient rubber boots that may at one stage have been yellow in colour. His warning had come with a light Scottish accent.

"Alright, mate," Peter responded straight away, halting their progress up the road and very slowly moving Helen behind him. "We are on holiday, got caught up here and are just trying to find out what's going on."

"Just stay there, the shops are under my control, keeping stuff for local people; you understand? You will have to find stuff elsewhere," the man continued.

Peter was forming the opinion that this was a local fisherman and he had also spotted that the rifle was actually either a .22 or .177 air rifle.

"If you point the rifle down, I'll put mine down and maybe we can talk. You can help fill us in on any information... please?" Peter asked.

The man looked at them, perhaps spotting the M16 replica for the first time, and he slowly lowered his rifle.

"I am Peter, and this is my wife Helen. We are on holiday, as I said, and if you could tell us what's going on, we will keep our distance and go elsewhere, is that okay?"

"My name's Duncan," the man indicated by tapping his chest. "Lived here all my life. The local police put out a message via tannoy last night. This illness is killing folk really quickly and it's spreading fast among everyone. From what they said, mass panic has set in, people are fighting over food; our police have left to control the bigger cities, but it sounds like it's everyone for themselves."

"What about the government, the NHS, the army?" Peter asked.

"The army are on the streets of the mainland, detaining whoever they find outside. No word from any leaders, from either up here or down in England. You are lucky to be up here, I reckon," the man continued. Peter reckoned he was right!

"Is there anyone else about?" Peter asked.

"Most people are indoors and staying indoors. One or two passing through in cars; there has been a bit of looting and other break-ins," the man, Duncan, went on. "I am protecting the food we have here, for the locals, you understand?" he explained.

"Makes sense to us and we understand," Peter replied.

"If you want some medical stuff, there is a chemist around the corner. It's open as the lady who runs it was found dead upstairs two days ago. Just help yourself to what's left. Be careful of the other shops; most of the owners are very protective."

"Thank you, Duncan, we will have a look. Can I ask you; I take it you live in town?"

"Aye, I'm a fisherman, been here all my life."

"Is there anyone running the boat trips at present?" Peter asked. "I am really interested in the boat advertised on the wall of the B&B in Quay Street."

"The people with that boat, MV *Seascape*, are called Owen and Carly. They have young children and are away across the island looking after them. I know they were supposed to be back a few days ago, but no sign of them," Duncan volunteered.

"Do you reckon we could borrow the boat to take us back to where we are based, across the channel?" Peter asked, being vague as to their exact location on Raasay.

"Not for me to say either way, you must do what you think is right at the moment. Seems like people are doing whatever it takes now," Duncan said.

"Well, good luck to you, Duncan. We will check out the chemists, thank you, we'll be off," Peter said.

"You two take care. We're okay here for the moment, but not sure for how long," Duncan replied.

Peter waved his thanks and watched the man, Duncan, disappear back into the Co-op store.

"More serious than we thought," Peter said to Helen.

"What now? I'm not sure I like it here, an air of menace about the place, I think we should go," Helen offered.

"I hear you, but we could do with some more kit if we are going back to the other island and some more food if this thing is getting worse and we have to see it out for longer," Peter said.

"Well, let's get what we can and get going," Helen said.

"Let's try this chemist, get some first aid, painkillers and anything else we can use, then head back down to the quayside," Peter replied.

They walked back down the slight hill the way they had come, then turned right into a street signposted as Wentworth Street, full of touristy shops, a pub, couple of banks and a chemist. Peter went first as they walked down the middle of the street. He could see one or two people inside the shops and buildings staring back at them. He still felt self-conscious about hefting the M16 replica shotgun on a public street, but less so than he had when he first got off the boat, and he stared back at the people he could see. They walked on, Helen clutching his arm as she walked quickly behind him to keep up.

At the door of the chemists, Peter looked in. Not seeing anyone inside, he shouted, "We are two tourists looking for a few first aid bits. We are willing to pay for what we want; is it okay to come inside?" He thought it better to declare themselves and avoid any more confrontation or misunderstandings. Not hearing any reply, Peter went inside, with Helen close behind him. The shop was small with only three aisles and a dispensary at the rear and a couple of tills at the front. The place had clearly been ransacked, with produce littering the floor.

"Helen, get your rucksack off and see if you can get some plasters, bandages, any paracetamol and

52

ibuprofen. Also, anything for burns, bites and some muscle stuff." Peter quickly reeled off a list of things he thought might be useful. "Be as quick as you can," he added.

"Alright, I will. You keep watch and shout if we need to get going," Helen replied.

As she disappeared down one of the aisles, Peter stayed by the tills at the front and kept a watch out of the window, staring both ways up and down the street. Meanwhile, Helen was doing her own version of a pharmaceutical supermarket sweep and emptying boxes of painkillers, muscle rubs, plasters, bandages, zinc cream and complete first aid kits into her rucksack. She quickly filled the bag and returned to Peter at the store entrance.

"Any sign of anyone?" Helen asked.

"I can see movement in the shops, I think they are too nervous to come out, but that may not last if we stay here much longer," Peter said.

"Let's get back down to the quay then," Helen responded.

"Yep, I am with you on that," Peter agreed.

They slowly left the shop, Peter first, eyeing up the street both ways, before they walked back the way they had come. At the junction, they looked back up the hill towards the Co-op store and they saw the man, Duncan, outside, cradling his rifle, smoking a cigarette. He acknowledged them with a brisk wave as he saw them. Peter raised his arm and turned back down the hill into Quay Street, back down to the shore, the way they had come. As they walked, Peter was still very watchful. Helen, too, was scanning the buildings either side of them as they returned to the quayside. They continued to walk past the line of shops and restaurants on their right.

As they walked, Peter suddenly stopped and looked at a large sign outside what appeared to be a small hotel or bed and breakfast. The sign was advertising "Wildlife and scenic boat trips" on board a boat called the MV *Seascape*. There were numerous pictures underneath of this new catamaran motorboat, with other pictures of wild birds, whales and seals, clearly spotted while on one of the advertised trips. Peter turned around and his eyes rested on a blue-hulled catamaran moored out in the bay.

"Hang on, Helen, this is where that couple that Duncan was talking about run their trips from. Maybe they have an office inside?" Peter said.

"Come on, Peter, let's get back to the boat and go," Helen replied.

"Let's just check inside, quickly," Peter said and then opened the door to the left of the sign. Half in and half out of the building, Peter spoke. "Is there anybody here, I just need information about the boat trips, please?" Silence. "I am coming in, anybody there?" Peter tried again.

A faint female voice answered, "I am upstairs, please stay downstairs and can you both put masks on? I could see you from my window."

"Okay, we will," Peter responded, looking at Helen. He got his black cloth face mask out of his jacket pocket and put it on and watched Helen do the same.

"We both have masks on, is there anything we can do for you?"

"No, dear, I have my kitchen up here and go out when I need extra; the man running the Co-op is making sure us that live here are okay," the female voice replied.

"Yes, we met Duncan. Do you know anything about the boat trips?" Peter asked.

"Owen has a little desk area near my reception which he uses to organise the trips for those that want it, but he's away with his family on the other side of the island," the fragile voice offered.

"Okay, we are going to check his desk. I will write my details on a piece of paper and leave it here, as I am going to borrow the boat," Peter said.

"Oh, I am not sure about that. Owen loves that boat," the small voice stated.

"Look, we are staying locally. I am going to use his boat until things return to normal," Peter stated.

There was no reply upstairs.

Peter looked at the desk area; loads of bits of paper covering a desk diary, lots of post-it notes with dates and times. He tried the drawers of the desk, locked! He pulled out a Leatherman utility tool from his pocket, opened the pen knife and, after a brief struggle, prised the drawer open. In among the pens and phone chargers, he saw a black neoprene lanyard with a couple of keys attached. He picked them up and turned to Helen. "MV *Seascape*," he simply said, holding up the lanyard.

There were some other keys inside the desk drawer, which Peter figured may be part of the boat's other lockable areas and storage containers. Bit of a guess, but he put them all in his pocket. He put the lanyard around his neck, under his jacket. Peter wrote down his details on a piece of paper and left it on the top of the desk. As he turned back to the door, he spotted a large pair of bolt cutters, just propped up by the door. He re-slung his rifle on his shoulder and picked up the cutters. You just never know, he figured.

"Hello, upstairs?" Peter called out.

"Yes, dear," the quiet voice answered.

"My name is Peter, and I am here with my wife Helen. We are going to leave now, is there anything we can do for you before we go?"

"No, dear, I am expecting Duncan to pop in later today. Just make sure you close the door properly, please," the voice replied.

"Okay, well, take care of yourself," Peter came back as they both left the building, returning to the street.

Peter looked left and right along the quayside, Helen doing the same.

"Can you carry the bolt cutters while I carry the rifle?" Peter asked.

"Sure," Helen said as she took the cutters. "Wow, these are heavy," Helen added.

"Not sure why I picked them up, but they may come in handy," Peter said.

"I suppose so," Helen said.

They walked back along the quayside away from the town, watching all the shop fronts and buildings carefully. Peter saw there was an open metal cage of large gas cannisters, like the ones he was used to seeing outside of petrol stations at home.

"Hang on, Helen," he called to Helen, who had walked past the cage on her way back to the boat. "Let me just check these gas bottles," Peter said.

Peter put down his shotgun and lifted one of the green gas cannisters, labelled as patio / barbeque gas. "Heavy and they always cut into your fingers when you lift them by the handle at the top, but I think we should take some?"

"Why do we need gas, Peter?" Helen's tone indicated she was not altogether in concert with Peter's idea.

"Well, at the moment we are cooking on the hob and using the ovens at the distillery hotel kitchen. If that supply fails or is cut off for some reason, we might be able to connect these bottles to at least still cook our food," Peter explained.

"Do you think it will come to that?" Helen asked.

"I don't know, but look how spooked that guy at the Co-op was and that lady in the B&B back there," Peter offered.

"Well, how many shall we take?" Helen asked.

"I am going to take three of the medium ones, as they are easier to lift and transport on the boat," Peter replied.

Peter picked up one bottle and walked it carefully to the edge of the quay wall, just above their boat. He repeated this until he had three bottles lined up together. He picked up the shotgun and returned to Helen, who had just lifted one of the bottles.

"They are heavy, but I reckon if you lower them down to me in the boat, I should be able to manage," Helen said.

"Okay, love, take off your rucksack, put it in the boat," Peter said.

Helen climbed down the ladder to the boat and took off her rucksack. Then looking up, she took hold of Peter's rucksack as he offered it to her. Next, he passed down the shotgun, which Helen was careful to stow at the front of the boat.

Peter got onto the ladder, holding the ladder rail with his left hand as he lowered the first gas bottle with his right. Helen cradled the bottle between her arms and was able to squat down and place the bottle in the bottom of the boat. They repeated this twice more.

Peter untied the bow line and threw it onto the boat. He untied the stern line, left it hooked through the mooring ring and handed the end to Helen.

Peter climbed down onto the boat. As before, he started the engine, which fired at the first time of asking.

"Okay, Helen, be ready to pull the line through that ring as I move," Peter said.

Helen nodded and Peter put the engine into forward, and as he moved the boat forward away from the quayside, Helen pulled in the rear line. Peter did a sweeping arc in the bay and started to head out, but over to where other boats were moored on the buoys.

Peter approached the boats slowly. Some looked like they had been there for years without use, with faded canvas covers and discoloured and dirty hulls. A couple looked in good order, with the rails still shiny and the hull and upper parts still reasonably new looking. Peter was heading for the boat furthest out into the bay, slightly away from the others. As he got nearer, it was easy to spot the name on the rear of the hull, "MV *Seascape*".

6

As Peter continued to sit on the porch of the holiday cottage on Rona, his thoughts returned to that first time they had stepped on board the catamaran, MV *Seascape*.

The keys in his pocket had opened the hatch to the cabin and the internal hatches to the flying bridge and lower cabin area. The boat was a good size, he reckoned 35–40 feet long and a good 10–12 feet wide. The rear deck area was spacious. They had tied the smaller Orkney boat they had come to Portree in onto the rear of the *Seascape*, transferring the rucksacks and rifle to the bigger vessel. Peter saw the control panel and pulled the lanyard from around his neck and tried the key in the starter. He turned the key, and a light came on, then he pressed the button next to the keyhole and the engines burst into life with a reassuring roar. He scanned an array of gauges and saw the one for fuel was all the way over to the right for full. Fortuitous, he thought.

"Helen, can you go to the front and see how this is tied onto the buoy and if the anchor is out?" Peter asked. He watched as Helen got up onto the side of the boat and walked along the edge past the cabin, onto the front deck area and up to where a line disappeared out of sight down to the buoy. Helen looked down and could see the boat was simply tied to the buoy. She could see a flap to a locker on the deck. She lifted this to see a large, heavy-looking anchor and long chain neatly stowed in the locker. She closed this hatch and lay on the deck to be able to reach down and untie the line from the ring on the buoy. She looked back into the cabin through the front windows and put her right arm up with her thumb in the air. She felt the boat move as Peter directed it backwards slowly.

"It's got more or less the same controls as the Orkney, just slightly bigger and a bit more refined," Peter offered as Helen came back into the cabin.

"Are we going to head back over to Raasay, where we came from?" Helen asked.

"Why don't we explore the opposite coastline; might be worth seeing what else is further up the coast of Raasay and beyond," Peter replied.

"Well, not too far, Peter. We're not exactly experienced mariners," Helen pointed out. Peter put the engine lever into the forward position and eased open the throttle, and the boat moved off as he took hold of the wheel by the control panel. Peter was aware that there was a similar control system above him on the upper deck; a nice place to control the vessel from on warm sunny days, he thought. He steered the two boats out of the bay area and back out into the channel as before, making his way out into a more mid-channel position.

As they moved north again, Peter kept a close watch on the sea in front of them. As they continued, he saw that there was a large inlet on the Raasay coast shoreline. Peter made a mental note to investigate this on the way back to the distillery later. They continued north and discovered a thin channel between a small rocky outcrop and the bigger land mass. Once through, they had caught their first sight of the sheltered natural harbour and little concrete jetty, with the whitewashed cottage set back from the water, which they now knew to be the Rona island manager's cottage.

"Seems like a nice spot," Helen suggested.

"Well, it's certainly very calm in this inlet and that house is nicely hidden from the sea. Plus, that jetty would make getting things ashore much simpler," Peter surmised.

"Are you thinking we should come here?" Helen asked.

"It would be a good safe place to hole up, but let's head back down to the distillery and check how things are in the immediate area. We would also need to see how much in the way of supplies we could take, as I suspect there will be very little stuff here," Peter said.

Peter turned the boat around, with the Orkney following behind on the short tow line they had fixed. Peter returned to the main channel through the narrow gap again and they headed back south. As they approached the inlet previously noticed by Peter, he steered carefully into it and was rewarded by spotting a recently built slipway with room to moor one boat.

"That's a useful find," Peter went on. "We could use the two boats to transfer as much food and other useful gear up to that white cottage, then once we are happy with what we have, leave one of the boats here. I reckon we could then bring several vehicles up to this point from the distillery; what do you reckon, love?" Peter asked.

"Why bother to leave a boat?" Helen questioned.

"I just think we can use our vehicle and perhaps one of the distillery trucks on our last resupply to carefully check out the rest of Raasay, liberate whatever we find that's useful, and then we have vehicles left up here at the north end of the island, where it's definitely quieter," Peter replied.

"I see," Helen nodded her understanding.

Peter turned back out of the inlet, steered the boat out into the channel and headed back south towards the point where the ferry had dropped them, the point where they had "borrowed" the Orkney boat. After 20 minutes or so, the ferry jetty came into view. With some coaxing and negotiation, Peter managed to convince Helen to get into the Orkney and get the engine started. As per his instructions, he watched as she put the large fenders out again while he then did the same with the larger catamaran. Helen then clambered back into the MV *Seascape*, walked to the front of the boat and took the line. As Peter very slowly manoeuvred the boat, Helen was able to step onto the wall next to the slipway and tie the boat on. Peter put the boat in neutral, found the rear line and threw it to the waiting Helen, who secured it. Helen then secured both front and rear lines of the Orkney to the wall. They gathered up their rucksacks and Peter picked up his shotgun. They left the gas bottles just inside the cabin of the catamaran, along with the bolt cutters. Peter placed the engine key around his neck, locked the cabin and put those keys in his pocket.

"Helen, take the key out of the switch," Peter shouted down to Helen, who was now back in the Orkney.

"Okay, I will," Helen replied and did as he had asked. She joined Peter on the wall and then they walked back to the distillery buildings. Everything looked as it had when they had left earlier that day.

That was where they stayed for the next week. They made little journeys into the village of Inverarish, checking carefully if any people were about. There were one or two buildings with smoke coming from their chimneys and every so often Peter thought he caught a glimpse of a face at a window. The small general shop had clearly been emptied by the locals and there was very little of value left. Peter found some alkaline batteries of various sizes, which he knew would fit the torches he had packed in his camping stuff. The HGV that Peter remembered from their original ferry crossing to the island was parked and unattended on the verge by the green area in front of the small shop. He checked the driver's door and was surprised to find it unlocked. Another mental note for the future.

Back at the distillery, they had loaded as much of the dry goods as possible onto one of the distillery trucks. Peter had ambled over to the distillery warehouses and selected a couple of small firkin-sized barrels and loaded those into the truck too (might as well take some decent whisky with them if they decided to set up elsewhere). All of these preparations were done under the constant blank automated message being repeated on all TV and radio stations, to stay indoors and wait for food supplies to arrive and be distributed.

Peter had suggested that it would be unlikely that food supplies would actually get to as remote a location as Raasay, but he was aware Helen was keen to stay in the relative safety of the distillery hotel, so didn't comment when no food had arrived after the sixth day back from Portree came and went.

"Let's move up to Rona," Peter abruptly stated over breakfast the next morning.

"I knew you were going to want to do this; you are so impatient. Why can't we just wait here?" Helen responded angrily.

"Look, how about this; we move some supplies up to that cottage we saw in that bay on Rona, make ourselves comfortable up there, but return here on a regular basis. Then at least if we need to get away from here quickly, we have somewhere to go with some food and other supplies, how about that?"

"Seems a little unnecessary to me, but I suppose there is no harm in having a look elsewhere," Helen retorted.

So, after clearing away their breakfast, they drove the truck down to the ferry dock and loaded everything onto the deck of the catamaran. Remembering to lock and take the truck keys with him, Peter got the catamaran started as Helen undid the mooring lines. Peter steered the boat out into the channel once again and they headed back up the coast towards Rona. The journey was uneventful. Peter remembered that Portree had looked quiet, no movement on the shoreline, no boats on the move, no people visible, quite eerie.

They got to the little jetty on Rona and moored safely against the side of the concrete dock. Peter secured the boat and, leaving the supplies, they had walked along the jetty towards a track that led into some woods.

It was just a small copse of trees, which quickly opened out onto a meadow with the long whitewashed cottage they had seen from the bay. As they approached the cottage, Peter unslung the rifle from his shoulder and held it ready across his body with the barrel pointing down. A signpost indicated that the cottage was the home of the Rona island manager. Not wishing to spook anyone who may be home, Peter called out,

"My name is Peter, and I am with my wife Helen; we are just looking to find somewhere to stay during the crisis, we don't mean you any harm." Peter remembered they had waited a good five minutes before he opened the unlocked door, and they found the note on the kitchen table from the island manager. They had a quick look around, then they had gone across to one of the outbuildings, unlocking it with one of the keys provided, and found the Ranger utility vehicle. After driving it outside, they had dragged a trailer stored nearby and hitched it to the Ranger. The Ranger had readily fired into life, and they had jumped in and driven back to the dock, unloaded the supplies from the back of the boat into the trailer and then driven back to the cottage.

Peter had checked the cottage and worked out that in addition to a real wood fire in the lounge, there was an oil-fired heating system and an oil-fired Aga in the kitchen, so they would have plenty of heating to keep warm and to cook, as there was a large green oil container outside one of the outbuildings with a gauge indicating that it was nearly full. After a short search, he found that there was an electricity supply, but a quick check of the lights revealed that it wasn't working. Another search revealed a couple of large portable generators that ran on diesel. In another building, there was a stack of over a dozen blue plastic 50-gallon drums with DIESEL written on them in large black felt pen. Peter did some mental calculations as he walked around the cottage and environs. If they retreated here, they would have a good supply of heating oil; they would have electricity from generators when needed. He had his own cans of diesel fuel too. They had brought a good quantity of dry and tinned goods with them today and there were two chest freezers at the back of the kitchen pantry, so they could bring frozen supplies on their next supply run.

Peter had recalled it had all seemed quite calm and rational and Helen, he felt, was sure this was only a precaution that they would probably not need. He had always been the more pragmatic of the pair of them and had always been a researcher and a planner.

As they had finished bringing in all the supplies, Peter came outside to have a bit of a break and had a chance to take in the clearly quite idyllic surroundings. Helen came outside to join him.

"Why don't we stay here for a few days, see how we like it?" Peter asked Helen.

"I knew you would do this," Helen started and was about to continue, then she stopped and looked out to sea, across the channel. "Okay, it is a beautiful spot, let's just stay for a few days, then head back to the hotel, check the car and how things are there," Helen finished.

"It is getting quite late, why don't we get a fire going, get some food inside us and get a decent night's sleep. After all, it is pretty quiet here," Peter went on.

That is what they did. Peter remembered that they had made themselves comfortable in the bigger of the three bedrooms, noting that even the bed sheets were freshly changed. He had investigated the generators and was able to get them going and connect them to the electric of the cottage. Another day they had taken the small Ranger utility vehicle and driven north along the rough track until it came out into another smaller inlet or bay. Here there was the most wonderful cottage with a front garden, which disappeared down to the sea edge. The Rona manager had left keys for this cottage and another hanging up in his kitchen, indicating they were holiday cottages available for rent. Another short drive north had revealed a second more remote smaller cottage.

On the third or fourth day, Peter couldn't quite remember, the weather had cleared from the cloudy miserable way it had been since they had got to Rona. It was a clear sunny day, with not a cloud in the sky. Having driven the Ranger as far north on the track as it could go and continuing over the rocky terrain on foot for a short while the day before, Peter was sure he had seen a building on a hilltop to the north.

"Helen, do you mind if I go for a bit of an explore further up the coast of this place? I am sure I saw a building to the north yesterday," Peter asked Helen as they were sat having breakfast in the kitchen of the Rona estate manager's cottage.

"Well, I don't understand why you want to explore any further," Helen replied.

"We don't know what is beyond here. It will put my mind at rest, so we know that we are safe here if and when we return to ride out the situation", Peter came back.

"What do I do then?" Helen asked.

"Well, you could top up the diesel in the Ranger, check how much fuel oil we have, not only here but if the other cottages we have seen have similar large tanks that serve them. See whether there is any wood or coal for burning in the fire here," Peter suggested.

"Are you going to be gone long?" Helen enquired.

"To be honest, I don't know. I will be as quick as I can be, depends on what I find," Peter answered.

As he had motored out of the sheltered bay in the catamaran, he was aware that Helen was getting quite fed up with the situation and he knew he needed to be a bit more supportive, but he also needed to make sure that they were as safe as they could possibly be. He would sit down and have a chat with her when he got back, he thought.

Peter had motored north, back out into the widening channel. He remembered that the coastline looked to be a continuous line of jagged rocky cliffs and crashing waves, with certainly no visible mooring spots or any signs of life. As the boat neared what Peter assumed to be the end of the island and the start of open water, he came around a headland to find a relatively large inlet. He steered into the bay, and as he came closer to the shore, he could see what looked like some form of tiny harbour to his left, at the northern end of the bay. Peter recalled how difficult this had been to spot when he had first approached it. As he neared the area, he saw there was a well-made, strong-looking concrete jetty, with a wide flat top to it and a dark brick-built building set back from the edge of the jetty wall, up against the rocky outcrop behind. As he got closer still, he saw a tarmacked road, looking reasonably new, disappear from the jetty, round the bay and towards a collection of low, well-built Portacabin-type buildings.

Peter had wondered what he had stumbled across as he came close to the jetty. He was able to steer the catamaran around to the more sheltered side. Having already attached the fenders, he was able, after a while, to get the boat secured to the side of the dock wall. He climbed up a small ladder, similar to the one at the harbour wall in Portree, and was confronted by a large sign next to the building he had spotted by the jetty earlier.

MOD PROPERTY
NO TRESPASSERS
INSTALLATION
MANAGED BY
QINETIQ

Peter, shotgun ever present, moved past the sign and checked the single door at the front of the building; locked. He turned and walked up the road, around the small bay, past a slipway and then past a large metal shed. In front of him and to the right were several other metal buildings, all single storeys; additionally, he took in the three long wheel-based, white Land Rovers all parked neatly next to each other. He remembered thinking on this first visit, *what is this place?*

He had called out when he first walked up the road. This was clearly a military installation; he was carrying a shotgun. *Better call out*, he thought. One of the buildings had a sign on it, designating it as a general office. Peter called out again while he was outside. Nothing, so he tried the door handle. Unlocked! Peter turned the handle and walked inside.

Inside the building, it was a fairly basic office, three desks forming three sides of a square, lots of charts and maps on a wall. Peter saw that a large Ordnance Survey map was pinned on the wall with drawing pins, so he quickly decided that he could make use of that, and after a quick look at the various features, he removed it from the wall and rolled it up tightly. Looking for a rubber band, he found one in a metal pen store on the main desk. He continued his search; a locked filing cabinet, a coffee and tea making area. It was all very tidy. A small under-desk-size fridge contained some out-of-date milk and a tub of margarine. There was a locked metal cabinet on the wall, which from his police days, he recognised as the sort of cabinet used to store spare and master keys. *So, where to find the key to this wall cabinet?* Peter thought.

The drawers of the main desk were locked. But as with the bed and breakfast in Portree, the drawer was easily forced with his Leatherman pocketknife. He could see inside a slim binder that had the logo BUTEC on the cover. As he lifted this binder out, he caught sight of a small bunch of keys! *Bingo!* he thought. Setting the keys down, he sat down behind the main desk and began to read the binder.

MOD BUTEC: The British Underwater Test & Evaluation Centre (MOD BUTEC)

The MOD and QinetiQ working together to provide Defence Test & Evaluation and Training Support Services

The facilities available at MOD BUTEC include:

Tracked Range: The byelaw protected sea area provides:

- The ability to track submarines, dived targets and heavy-weight torpedoes to support platform and weapon acceptance trials activities and submarine crew 'weapon certification'.
- The ability to track surface ship and helicopter firings of light-weight torpedoes.
- Torpedo recovery from the surface or seabed, using specialised recovery platforms or a Remotely Operated Vehicle. There is also the capacity for offsite weapon recovery.
- A tracked deep acoustic range optimised for submarine underway radiated acoustic noise assessment.
- A dummy minefield with three different mine types, accurately mapped and enabling mine-hunters to exercise in a number of scenarios.

Shore Support Facilities: Ashore at Rona, there are services and facilities to support on range operations:

- Range Terminal Building which provides control of the byelaw protected air and water space, including the data capture functions for both underwater tracking and acoustic ranges.
- Specialised facilities for the de-preparation of torpedoes post firing, including the safe handling areas required to support Spearfish.

- The ability to maintain, prepare, deploy and recover autonomous targets that simulate various aspects of submarine operations.
- The ability to conduct production testing of air-dropped sonobuoys with data collection to enable testing and measurement during operations.
- A Trials Safety Manager who is able to offer advice on complex, bespoke and novel trials planning; extensive experience in Hazardous Activity management and access to Subject Matter Experts.
- An Explosive Safety Manager who is able to offer general or weapon-specific advice and extensive knowledge of explosives-related legislation.
- Operation and control of a helipad at the Shore Support Base, capable of accommodating helicopters up to Merlin size; four multi-purpose trials vessels available.

Operational Readiness Testing and Support: Through the LTPA, QinetiQ is able to provide a range of proven services and facilities to support the testing and evaluation of operational platforms, leading to the optimisation of platform time. Services can include:

- Pre-deployment support, including underway acoustic ranging and crew certification.
- Platform calibration, including sonar calibrations, threat assessments, log calibration, underway signature measurement and bearing accuracy checks.
- Operational Training area which can provide a full range of services to support surface, underwater and airborne platforms leading to the best use of valuable operational training time.

What the fuck?! Peter thought as he put the binder down. Who would have thought a place like this would have such a facility on it? But then he considered the location and the remoteness of it, and it made perfect sense. As he thought and reread the opening page of the binder, his eyes were drawn to the words, WEAPONS and EXPLOSIVES.

"They must have explosives and some weapons here then," he said to himself. Standing, he snatched up the keys and began trying them in the wall cabinet. The third key turned in the lock and the cabinet door swung open. An array of keys confronted him, some Yale, some brass Chubb and some of those little locker-style keys, all individually labelled, with a plastic sheet additionally indicating what each key was for. He scanned down the list and saw; barracks A, ratings mess, SBS mess, kitchens, mess hall, acoustic range, small arms range, explosives store, armoury. He stopped reading; *Hello, here we go,* he thought as he read "armoury" and "explosives store". What he now needed was a map of the complex. He went back to the drawer in the desk and found an over-photocopied piece of paper with a plan and description of the layout of the place. He picked up a selection of the keys he thought he would need; each key, in addition to the plastic cover sheet, had a label on them indicating what they were for. He put them in the pocket of this jacket, picked up his shotgun and went back outside, shutting the door behind him.

"Is there anyone here?" Peter shouted as he walked up the slight hill to a much larger-looking collection of buildings. No reply, no sign of life as he approached a concrete path. He noted that as he left the office, there had been two large cylindrical gas cannisters, possibly powering the facility. He got to the path and followed the neat little sign up to a door which indicated it was the mess hall, kitchens, ratings mess, SBS mess and common room. Neat, A-typical MOD signage, he thought. He pulled out the jangle of keys and found the mess hall key (a large brass Chubb). He tried the door; locked! He inserted the key and turned it and opened the door towards him. He then entered a large well-appointed dining hall, with perhaps 10 tables and 30 dining chairs. At the far end was a buffet-style serving area and he could see through a hatch that beyond that were the kitchens.

He walked through a swing door into the kitchens, taking in the large expanse of pristine stainless-steel work tops, grills and ovens. He continued through the kitchen into another room, which looked like a dry food store, he thought. Another door off this room was marked, "Rations". He opened this to be faced with large cardboard boxes, stacked floor to ceiling, with various stamps on the side. He leaned over to read one; "24-hour ration pack".

Well, there is literally enough here for an army, he thought. He opened a box near the door to find 12 smaller boxes inside, each one designated as a one-person 24-hour ration pack. From his experience with cadets and a brother who used to be in the army, he knew each smaller box contained enough food to keep a soldier going for 24 hours. He mentally ticked this off as an excellent find! In other parts of the storage area, he found a large pantry stocked with more conventional dry food supplies. When he came to the double-doored stainless-steel fridges, he was not surprised to find them empty; clean and switched on, but empty! He walked back out into the kitchen, back to the mess hall, noting the ready supplies of cutlery, crockery and salt and pepper pots all neatly stored for future use.

He returned to the door he had come in through and went outside, relocked the door and moved back down the path. Another sign caught his eye, "Armoury". He walked the way that the arrow indicated and left the kitchen/mess hall complex behind as he headed back towards the main office and then turned right before reaching the armoury down a narrow, tarmacked path, descending a slight hill, until he reached the smaller collection of modern prefabricated buildings. They were nestled in the shelter of a natural valley with rocky hills on three sides. Peter approached the main door, a very strong-looking door with steel edges around the frame, and in addition to a Yale lock, there were two dead bolt door locks, one above and one below the Yale. He found the keys from his pocket, and after several attempts to get the right key for the right lock, the door opened. Inside was a clear space with a couple of 50-gallon drums filled with sand.

Peter, while in the police, had spent some years in the Royalty and Diplomatic Protection Group (RDPG). He had passed the police basic firearms course when based at Lippitts Hill. He was familiar with, and had carried for duty a Glock 17, 9mm side arm and also the 9mm

Heckler and Koch MP5. The area in front of him was like any of the armoury front distributing setups he had used on a daily basis when with the RDPG, when officers (in this case, he presumed, soldiers) could receive and return weapons from an armourer, who kept a daily log and inventory of firearms issued and firearms returned. He recalled the oil drums filled with sand being used as somewhere for an officer (or soldier) to make their weapon safe and unloading and doing it with the weapon pointing into the sand in case of a mishap. Peter recalled that during his time as an armed officer, the issue and return of firearms seemed to be the time when the most accidental or negligent discharges occurred.

So here he was, faced with a fairly large conventional-looking armoury. A door to the side of a solid Perspex screen and countertop with three drawers underneath was clearly the door to the armoury store. Peter once again rummaged in his pocket and pulled out a handful of keys. Another Yale and one other dead bolt key labelled "armoury" fitted into the door locks. Peter opened the door and walked through into what he presumed to be the armourer's area. Beyond the countertop area, Peter came to yet another door (unlocked). He opened it; blackness. He felt around to the left of the door at that familiar light switch height and was rewarded by feeling the light switch. He turned the switch, and an ignition of sodium tube lights came to life. Confronting him were row upon row of guns. In the quickness of his scan, he saw 9mm small arms, a familiar array of MP5s, a row of SA-80s and an assortment of other rifles and shotguns. He nervously put his own shotgun down to take in this arsenal of weapons he had discovered. He saw another two large metal cabinets, one marked "ammunition" and the other "grenades, flares, smoke bombs, misc."

Peter was stunned. What was this place? Clearly a military installation, but unguarded, well maintained and completely unmanned. He could only assume that it was the worldwide illness that had caused the facility to be without personnel. Another cabinet, which he opened using one of the locker-style keys, contained belts, holsters, slings and straps and several large black holdalls and kit bags. After a minute or so of thought, Peter grabbed one of the large black canvas kit bags. He walked over to the array of small arms and found what he was looking for; a Glock 17. *Might as well keep to what I know*, he thought. He picked up one of the Glocks and was quickly familiar again, albeit it had been over 20 years since he had last picked one up. He recalled the lightness, due to so much of it being made of a strong plastic-like polymer, the metal top slide and the neat 17-round magazine that slotted into the handle of the weapon. Peter went back to the cabinet and found a plastic box, within which sat the Glock, along with a spare magazine and a cleaning kit. He unlocked the ammunition cabinet and found boxes of 9mm bullets, 100 to a box. Peter took 10 boxes. He took a second Glock, also placing it in another plastic box. He found some belts and holsters on a shelf above the holdalls, and he took two of each. He put all of this into the black holdall.

Peter next went over to a rack of MP5s. These were the versions with the retractable stock, not available when he had carried one in London. He had carried an older version with a fixed polymer stock. This was such a simple weapon but capable of firing up to 800 rounds a minute. Peter picked one up, found four slightly curved 30-round magazines and placed all of this into the holdall. He tested the weight of the bag, shrugged and returned to his search. He walked past some shotguns and then to a thin but tall metal box. Inside he stared at two futuristic rifles. He knew from one of those courses he had done years ago at Ash Ranges in Surrey that these were sniper rifles. In particular, they were possibly the finest sniper rifles in the world. The Accuracy International Arctic Warfare Magnum, a rifle with a proven killing range of anything up to about 2,000 yards. Peter had never seen one up close before. He had watched a collection of snipers using them on the longest ranges at Ash. He knew enough to know that they were a bolt action weapon with a five-round magazine.

Peter leaned in closer to see the telescopic sight fitted to the top of the rifle. A Schmidt and Bender 5x25x56 P11 LP, reading the writing on the top rear of the sight. Peter picked up the weapon and was surprised by the lightness and balance. He also noted the folding stock, which would make it so much easier to transport and to carry. At the bottom of the cabinet was a black canvas rifle bag and a stack of Winchester .300 Magnum boxes containing the cartridges that the rifle fired. Peter picked up the rifle bag and stowed one of the rifles inside, putting little rubber protectors over the telescopic sight lenses. He placed this rifle bag inside the holdall with the other weapons. He then picked up four of the boxes of the .300 Winchester Magnum cartridges and placed them in the holdall. He zipped the bag closed. He lifted it, reckoning he could put it all on his back, as the holdall had the straps with which to do this. As he was just closing the cabinets, he suddenly thought, *what about now?*

He quickly took another Glock from the store, checked it was empty, then loaded four of the 17-round magazines. He picked up a light black canvas belt and threaded a black leather holster onto it so he could carry the side arm on his right-hand side. He also threaded two spare magazine holders, each being able to take two spare magazines, onto the belt. He loaded all the magazines with 9mm ammunition, put one magazine into the recess in the handle of the pistol and clicked it into place. He then drew the top slide back and let it release forward, thereby putting a round into the chamber of the Glock, ready for firing. He gently lowered the Glock into the holster on the freshly assembled utility belt. He put four fully loaded spare magazines into the holders on the belt. *Like old times!* he thought

Peter hefted the black holdall onto his back and then picked up his shotgun. He retreated from the armoury the way he had come, locking each of the doors behind him, until he was once again outside the front of the building. He didn't feel he could travel too far with the large holdall on his back, so slowly walked back up the hill towards the main office. As he looked up towards the area behind the office, he could just make out the top of a whitewashed wall at the top of the hill.

Struggling up the hill with his load, Peter walked up to one of the parked Land Rovers. He tried the door handle and was not really surprised to find it open. Taking the holdall off his back and setting his shotgun down, Peter returned to the main office. After a short search in the office, he found three sets of car keys bearing the Land Rover logo in one of the other desk drawers. Peter took one of the sets and returned to where he had left the holdall and his shotgun. He clicked the fob and was rewarded by the lights of one of the Land Rovers coming on. He clicked the fob again and once again unlocked the doors. He placed the holdall in the rear of the Land Rover he had selected, picked up his shotgun, placed that in the passenger footwell and climbed into the driver's seat, remembering how awkward it was to sit in a vehicle seat with several magazines of 9mm ammunition digging you in the back. He started the engine first time, put the manually geared car into first and drove forward out of the parking space. He drove slowly along the metalled track, now heading back towards the mess hall and what he assumed to be the barrack area. He could check that out another time, he thought. As he got to these buildings, the track turned sharply to the right and then he began climbing a steep hill, up to what looked to be a fuel store of some description. There was a caged stack of oil drums and gas cylinders. The track then turned to the left, still climbing, until it came to a flat area, and he spotted a large concrete helicopter landing area. *What is this place?* he again thought.

Peter continued on, still climbing on the track. The road went off to the right, then left, eventually ending in front of a vehicle-width gap in a whitewashed 8-foot-high stone wall. Beyond the wall, Peter could make out the dark slate roofs of some buildings. But his attention was drawn to the squat whitewashed circular tower within the walled compound, topped by a large rotating light. A lighthouse. *A good spot for it*, Peter remembered thinking. Peter drove through the gate in the whitewashed walls and parked the car in a drive area with a long building on his right-hand side. Peter got out of the Land Rover and walked around the edge of the building line, turning to the right as the buildings ended. He stayed on a path that took him round into a grassed courtyard, where he could see, in all its majesty, the lighthouse tower. He reckoned it was about 40 feet high, with a black-coloured rail guarding a walkway around the top, a single black door at the bottom and one at the top allowing access to the walkway. *Good place for a lookout*, Peter thought.

The top of the structure was a black metal frame, supporting a large glassed-in rotating light. Peter also spotted a tall radio mast just beyond the walled compound. There was a small gate in this side of the wall, presumably to be able to get to the radio mast. Peter turned to look at the long building. There were three red doors and five windows along this side of the structure. Peter walked up to the right-hand door and tried the handle. Locked! He remembered thinking that it was a surprise to be finally faced with a locked door in this place. Peter looked in through the closest window. It was pretty bare inside. No furniture, some large machinery that Peter presumed to be power generators for the clearly automated lighthouse. He could see a fireplace and, through a gap in one of the connecting doors, he thought he saw a sink and some kitchen cupboards. Peter was about to venture further and try to access the building when he suddenly thought that it was something that could wait and that he ought to be getting back to Helen.

Peter made his way back to the Land Rover. There was just sufficient space to turn the Land Rover around within the driveway area and Peter drove back out through the gates and down the track. As he got closer to the helicopter landing areas, he saw a tall pole on his right with a windsock attached. He remembered thinking even this appeared new and not faded or torn. Peter drove on past the helipad, back down the hill and to the mess hall buildings complex, continued past the main office and the other parked Land Rovers and on towards the small harbour, round the bay and up to the building by the brick quayside. Peter had stowed the large holdall of "liberated" weapons on the rear deck of the catamaran, along with his shotgun. He reversed and repositioned the Land Rover so it was facing back up the way he had come. (*Old habits*, he thought.) He locked the vehicle, jumped down into the catamaran and started the engine. He got back onto the quayside to undo the mooring lines, and once clear, he moved the boat back into the bay. Then he headed back out into the inlet the same way he had come. It didn't take him long to travel back down the edge of the island and spot the rocky outcrop that protected the entrance to the small harbour and jetty, where the island manager's cottage was. Peter was about to carry the holdall off the boat, but after thinking carefully, he decided to leave it locked inside the cabin. Some delicate admissions and explanations to Helen about all this, rather than turning up like Rambo, he thought.

That was pretty much how things had stayed. Peter had correctly perceived that Helen was less than impressed with his weapons haul. After some fairly intense discussions, an agreement to put all the weapons somewhere safe and keep them as an insurance policy had been arrived at. They had also agreed to stay at the manager's cottage initially and make this their base until such time as the authorities announced a change in the situation. Even then, after two weeks at the cottage, Helen readily agreed to move to the more remote holiday cottage, mainly as she actually thought it was a more comfortable interior and Peter agreed that the view from the garden patio out into the bay was beautiful.

They had got themselves organised with food and water. They had oil fuel for heating, plus the coal fire in the lounge of the cottage. Peter had got two generators working and now had these stored in an outbuilding nearby. They had moved several drums of the diesel up to this cottage using the Ranger vehicle. Peter had brought all the weapons and ammunition up as well and locked them all in the spare room, save for the

Glock he kept on his belt and his own M16 replica shotgun, which he kept handy in the lounge when they weren't out exploring the island. Peter had found a radio that worked, and they had listened to the automated message every noon, telling everyone to continue to stay indoors, as the illness was now mutating and affecting persons of all ages. It was imperative to stay isolated to try and suppress the spread of the illness. There was also some more rather morbid and emotionless information about removing bodies from the household and remembering to tag them for identification purposes. "That's a line from the old Protect and Serve information films that they produced years ago, in the event of a nuclear war," Peter mentioned to Helen.

After some pleading with Helen, Peter had eventually been allowed to have some practice with the AWM rifle. He had spent a day setting up some empty tins of soup on the other side of the bay, probably about 500–600 metres away, and learning how to load, unload, clean and finally fire the sniper rifle. It took him 10 shots to be able to feel he could confidently hit the soup tins most of the time at the range he had set them. Much to his surprise, he managed to persuade Helen to practise with a Glock and she also fired several rounds from the MP5 in single-shot mode. Peter was at pains to point out that he was just being prudent, he was not turning into a gun nut!

Once the fresh produce had begun to run out, they had started to walk out into the bay when the tide was out and find shellfish to supplement their tinned and processed diet. Peter had never realised how much he missed fresh milk until on the third day of the long-life stuff. Despite their first trip having brought a large amount of food and other supplies, they had ventured back to the distillery twice more; this third and last trip had been more nerve-racking than the previous ones. Peter had worked out the safety phrase with Helen, that they would always finish a sentence with "alright, love" as an indicator that they were moving freely and not under any sort of duress when they came back together, after any period of time apart or out of each other's eyesight.

Peter had discovered a quality pair of binoculars in the island manager's cottage, and he surveyed the sea channel most mornings, when the visibility allowed. They had seen a couple of trawlers heading north up the channel and Peter had been able to pick out a couple of motor vehicles as they drove north up the coast road on the Isle of Skye. Beyond that, they had continued to make themselves comfortable and tried to occupy themselves. They had discovered jigsaw puzzles and some games in a chest in the spare room and would sit down for Scrabble on a regular basis after dinner. They had busied themselves clearing an area of the grass in front of the cottage and planted some potatoes and carrot seeds they had found in the manager's cottage kitchen. Peter found a book all about Rona and read that there were supposed to be deer on the island, but he was yet to spot any.

They had walked as often as the Scottish weather allowed. There had been no further updates on the radio regarding the situation in the country. They had not had any phone signal since moving onto the more remote island. When they walked, Peter wore the Glock on his belt, a rucksack of essential wet weather gear and also shouldered his shotgun. Helen, after some persuasion, also wore a Glock on her belt and carried a rucksack of essentials too. On one of their first walks, they had walked back south down the track towards the manager's cottage. They came to a fork on the track and rather than follow the right-hand main route, they took the less distinct left-hand track which climbed up and over some rocky crags and dipped down into a small dry valley. The route continued south, climbing and turning but essentially continuing south. Abruptly the path had stopped, as they reached a rather pleasant grassy area with some trees off to the right and just beyond some building ruins, which according to Peter's reading, were most likely to be the remains of a crofter's cottage from the 18th and 19th century.

They continued past the ruins and a small meadow area, probably the remnants of an area of cultivation, Peter thought. There was no discernible track as they went on, they simply following some possible animal trails and the contours of the land. As the ground under their feet became rockier, they eventually crested a small rise and were suddenly rewarded with a view south across a narrow strip of water.

"That, I suspect, is Raasay," Peter said. Helen looked out across the channel and right towards the larger island of Skye.

"It really is a beautiful spot, especially when we get the sun and clear skies like today," Helen replied.

Peter lifted the binoculars to his eyes and surveyed the view in front of them. He could make out the small harbour at Portree, where they had obtained the catamaran and run in to the only people they had seen since they had been caught up in the more serious lockdown. Through the binoculars, Peter studied the small town, trying to see any human movement. He scanned the coastline and the sea channel to see if there were any boats out today, or if any vehicles were moving about. But today it was dead, no sign of a soul anywhere. Peter once again studied the channel between the two islands of Rona and Raasay. As best as he could see, the channel may not have been that wide, maybe 150 metres or so, but it looked reasonably deep and both coastlines were jagged and steep, and the current looked to be fairly fast-moving from his right to left. "I doubt anyone will be swimming across to us from Raasay," Peter said.

"It looks bloody cold and far too fast a current for anyone, I reckon," Helen replied.

With that, they had turned and started to walk back north towards the ruins of the crofter's cottage first, then back to the holiday cottage they had purloined, which they now considered to be home. As they walked, Peter began to think about theirs, and the general situation.

"I suppose we should consider ourselves lucky to be here in the bigger scheme of things," Peter stated.

"I agree, but we can't stay here indefinitely," Helen said.

"I know, but without knowing the whole picture, we are at least safe from socially mixing. We have in effect found a pretty secure way to isolate, with the bonus of being able to safely get some fresh air. Imagine if you had been four months living in a flat in Central London?"

"Do you think it's dangerous elsewhere?" Helen asked.

"Well, put it this way; about a week into the loss of conventional media news, we visited a small remote island town and were confronted by an armed fisherman guarding the local Co-op. Yeah, I reckon it's dangerous." Peter was going to say more, but he caught the look on Helen's face and decided to stop talking.

"The radio has not changed the message for over three weeks now; we really need to know the latest information, Peter," Helen stated.

"Yes, you're right, we need to find some other media outlet or at the very least speak to someone," Peter went on. "Perhaps we could go over to Portree, see if that character Duncan is still about and if he knows what's what?" Peter volunteered.

"I'm not sure, love. Do you think it's safe?" Helen asked.

"I really don't know, but we do need to find out what's happening. What about if we go back to the distillery, rather than moor the boat at the top end of Raasay and drive down through the island, we can take the boat and keep going past the jetty where the ferry is and see if we can see the lie of the land, so to speak, from the water. At least that would be safer, what do you think?" Peter said, turning to look at Helen.

"Sounds like a plan; when are you thinking?" Helen asked.

"The next day when we wake up and the weather is half decent," Peter replied.

They continued walking north and got back to the holiday cottage. While Peter opened up the door onto the patio, Helen put the kettle on and made some tea. They had switched to drinking flavoured tea, as that was a pleasant drink that did not require any milk. Peter was currently enjoying a lemon and ginger infusion! He sat down on one of the chairs out on the patio with the sun on his face and looked out over the dry bay and to the sea channel beyond. He once again found himself returning to their situation and more importantly, the situation for the country and, by implication, the entire world!

Peter knew about people; those 30 years as a copper in London gave you a pretty honest appraisal of the human condition. Peter always regarded the general public as an entity, usually to be referred to in deprecating terms. He knew this was very much his opinion, but he felt that in his life, this feeling had served him well. He felt the public, at least the vast majority of them, needed to be led. They needed guidance and direction; in short, they needed to be told what to do, and for the most part, they would do it. They might not readily admit to it, but they acted more positively if they had a set of rules to adhere to. At the outset of the illness, when the leaders had considered it necessary to impose restrictions, Peter had felt that the rules were more of a set of rather woolly guidelines that were clearly open to interpretation and, more worryingly, were to some extent being ignored. He felt there were too many opportunities for the public to meet and mingle while still complying with the guidelines. He had already thought about masks but was reminded of the idiocy of devolved government, when, on a visit to Wales to visit Helen's relatives, they were both shocked to discover that Wales had not, at that time, imposed a mask wearing policy, as had already been implemented in England. He similarly constantly shook his head every time Scotland did something slightly different to England, because that particular leader was seemingly making political capital out of the crisis!

Peter liked to think he was always a step ahead of the game. As he thought back, he remembered that he had a supply of masks straight away. He smiled when he remembered how Helen had thought he was a bit of a "doom merchant" and that he was taking it far too seriously. As things had continued under the somewhat lax restrictions, Peter had ironically shared a clip on social media from the Protect and Serve campaign; the very phrase, in fact, that was now being used in the ever-repeating message when they turned on the radio.

Now that things were clearly much more serious, Peter wondered what the leadership were doing; *probably something different in Scotland*, Peter chuckled to himself. But then he began to think about the public again, that entity that he felt he had a take on. How would they be coping? Peter, as ever, always considered the worst-case scenarios. Those who had failed to conform and comply to the previous restrictions were going to find this hard. The young had pretty much been, health-wise, unaffected by the illness. The elderly and those with respiratory issues had fallen the most seriously ill. So, the young were going to feel the most inhibited by the severe restrictions and were, in Peter's opinion, going to be more likely to literally kick against the traces and run into confrontations now, he thought.

There had been much talk during the initial restrictions about the level of people's mental health and the emotional strain being placed on them. Peter, probably like a good few other emergency service people, was trying to comprehend a modern society, that considered being asked (not told) to stay inside comparable to a different time when an entire generation of young men were asked to climb out of mud-soaked trenches in northern Belgium and walk very slowly towards another line of soldiers firing machine guns at them. *Get a fucking grip!* he thought.

Peter had thought in his life long and hard about where he stood on a range of issues. Politically, he knew he was fairly right wing. He liked conformity, a set of rules which he was either prepared to enforce or, since retirement, happy to follow. The person in charge was voted into power; crack on, he thought. During the first months of the crisis, the political opposition had tried to make points and use the science of hindsight to browbeat the leadership and generally try and discredit them. The media, too, had taken it upon themselves to criticise and find fault with every decision. Peter had heard mention at the outset that this crisis was akin to being at war, and as such, he thought that a coalition leadership should have been formed and the media should have been taken under the control of the leadership to ensure that the message was consistent and not always so negative and harmful to morale. Small mercies showed themselves when it quickly became clear that the United States of America was in a worse state than over here. Mainly because they had a buffoon in charge, he thought.

Because of how Peter thought and what he believed in, he was never going to be what one might call an environmentalist. It was difficult for him to get worked up about a topic that was going to become a crisis after he was long dead. He also felt that it was very nice of the developed world to acknowledge their fault in causing the forests to shrink and the ozone layer to fail and try to switch to less harmful power sources, right at the time when the developing world was going through its own fossil fuel burning industrial revolution. He had marvelled at the hypocrisy of some of the woke celebrities who, having earned millions from their industry, now wanted to jet around the world to encourage us not to jet around the world and to eat a bean burger! *Yes, alright, you can fuck off too!* Peter thought. Peter wondered if wealthy celebrities just woke up one day and were bored. They did all this stuff because they had nothing else to do.

Peter did, however, have one idea about all the environmental issues and climate change. It did, though, require the complete removal of emotion from the argument and utilising the utmost pragmatism. In his opinion, the fault for all the environmental damage and climate change rested squarely at the feet of the human race. The bottom line was that there were just too many of us on the planet. What was required was the controlling of a population that was growing exponentially. How best to achieve this? You could institute a global limit on the number of children couples were allowed to have. A bit draconian, perhaps. Or you could take a global health crisis, like, for instance, the one they were currently experiencing, and let it rip! Let it kill millions upon millions. Environmentally it would be like hitting the reset button for the planet. No emotion, survival of the fittest, just as the scientific luminaries of the past had predicted. *Take that to the World Health Organisation, Greta!* Peter thought.

Still mulling over these ideas in his head, he began to imagine what was actually happening in the more populous parts of the country. If the leaders and organisers were not fulfilling their promise to deliver food to everyone, then Peter's own survival of the fittest would be well underway now. Those with a will and the resources would have had to breach the regulations in order to find food. Peter's thoughts briefly turned to the many thousands who would not be able to rise to that challenge. The elderly, the disabled, those requiring constant care. As a former police officer, he thought about how his former colleagues would be dealing with a perceived lawless society. Would officers now all be routinely armed? Would such a thing as the forces of law and order even exist out there? These questions began to make his head spin. It was clear that Helen had been correct, and they needed to find out for themselves what was actually happening. This was going to be a potentially dangerous undertaking; they would be heading back to a relatively more populous area. A few months ago, they had already encountered an individual armed with a rifle, protecting a supermarket.

Peter knew from their own stores and supplies that they were pretty much out of all their fresh fruit and vegetables. They had no fresh pasteurised milk and all the meat they ate came from the freezer. Peter assumed that compared to most people, he and Helen were doing really well; they had seized upon the resources available to them immediately and had been out for several straightforward foraging missions, without too much danger, to restock their supplies.

So most of Peter's thoughts about the situation for the rest of the country and indeed the world were at best educated guesses and conjecture. From what Peter knew about the reality of the general public, he envisaged lawless anarchy. There was a part of him that hoped he was wrong and that the presence of armed military personnel on the streets would deter people from testing the strict restrictions, as detailed in the briefest of messages from the authorities.

Peter continued to mull over the possible things they might face when they headed out from their safe haven in the days ahead.

"Here's your tea, love. You were miles away," Helen called to him as she came out of the cottage carrying a steaming mug of tea.

"Thanks, love. I was just weighing up the situation and I agree that we need to find out more information, but we need to be extremely careful," Peter replied.

"Well, thanks to you, we are certainly well prepared," Helen offered.

"So, the next morning we wake up to a day as good as today, we will head back down to the distillery part of Raasay on the catamaran, is that okay with you?" Peter asked.

"Let's see what we see," Helen replied.

When they woke the next morning, the weather was damp, cold and grey. *Pretty much your average day in Scotland then!* Peter thought. The visibility looking out towards the channel was poor. Peter sat down at the breakfast table and thought about their options while he sipped his tea.

Helen came into the kitchen and joined him across the table.

"What do you think then?" she asked.

"I reckon without the visibility, there is no point in going down to the Raasay distillery or across to Portree; we wouldn't see anything or anyone until we were too close to avoid any potential drama," Peter replied.

"Okay, but I really fancy a little bit of a change of scenery, albeit a change that is safe," Helen said.

Peter thought for a moment and then said, "I could take you up to the military place where I got the weapons, show you what facilities they have up there.

We could also stock up from the dry stores and rations they have there; what about that?"

"Hmm, do you think it will still be empty?" Helen asked.

"No harm in taking the catamaran at least as far as their dock and see what we see when we get there; it will at least give us some fresh air out in the sea channel," Peter suggested.

"Okay, what do we need?" Helen asked as she stood up from the table.

"I reckon some wet weather gear, a hat and gloves. Take an empty rucksack to put stuff in. Wear your Glock and spare ammo; I'll take a Glock and one of the MP5s. How long do you need?" Peter said.

"Give me 10 to 15 minutes and I will be right with you," Helen replied.

A short while later, maybe slightly longer than 15 minutes if Peter was honest (but what was the rush, he thought), they locked up the cottage and got into the small Ranger utility vehicle and drove back down the track, past the island manager's cottage and onto the concrete jetty, where the catamaran was moored. They slipped the moorings and slowly chugged out of the small harbour inlet and out into the misty channel. Peter steered as close to the island coastline as he dared, going much slower than normal due to the poor visibility. Peter eventually recognised the inlet near the top of the island of Rona. He slowly crossed the inlet until he saw the opening into the small bay area with the concrete jetty visible now on his left-hand side. There was no sign of life at the jetty and visibility was starting to improve as he looked around the arc of the bay and the route of the road he had followed on his first visit here.

"Helen, if you can do the usual with the fenders and be ready with a mooring line, please?" Peter asked as he slowed the boat and approached the quayside. Helen went about her tasks quickly, and as Peter brought the boat alongside the quay, she deftly jumped onto the dock and secured the front mooring line. Peter was ready to throw her the rear line and they had the boat securely moored in short order. Peter threw up Helen's empty rucksack, put his own on his back, checked the Glock was secure on his belt, picked up the MP5 and joined Helen on the top of the jetty.

"Looks quiet enough," Peter suggested as he looked around and towards the MOD complex.

"Where do we go now?" Helen asked.

"If we follow this road around the bay, it leads to the main office and the vehicles I told you about, then the rest of the base is beyond that," Peter said.

"Let's go then," Helen replied and started to walk off down the road.

Peter pulled a set of Land Rover keys out of his pocket and cleared his throat loudly.

"Erhumm! Why don't we take the Land Rover?" He pointed at the Land Rover he had conveniently left parked on the jetty as he had departed from his previous visit.

"Oh, alright then, don't mind if I do," Helen replied and got into the front passenger side.

Peter drove the vehicle slowly around the bay and up the slight rise until they were stationary next to the other two Land Rovers Peter had discovered on his previous visit. He parked next to them and turned off the engine. "Let's walk from here," he said.

Helen climbed out and said, "Where to then?"

"Let's head to the mess hall buildings and I will show you the food stocks here. We can maybe load up on a few things that we have run out of now?"

"Sounds like a plan," Helen replied.

Peter led the way as they walked onwards up the hill until the larger complex of buildings came into view.

"So, this is the main area, I reckon, where the people who use this place sleep, eat and work when they are here," Peter suggested.

"It's so quiet. Does anything look different from your last trip here?" Helen asked.

"Well, from here, it looks the same, but if we just stay on our guard," Peter said, then added, "Let's go in through the mess hall door like I did before."

"Okay, I am staying close. This place is ghostly quiet," Helen said as she gripped Peter's arm.

Peter opened the mess hall door and they walked into the pristine dining area, then both slowly walked through the kitchens and to the stores area. Peter opened the rations door and simply said, "Tadah!" and opened his arms expansively to show Helen the mountain of military ration packs.

"Wow, you weren't kidding," Helen said, looking at the array of cardboard boxes in front of them.

Peter selected one of the bigger boxes, which was marked as a "10-man operational ration pack – Menu A". Peter opened the box to discover a selection of tinned products all simply labelled with a small, printed description on the lid. "Bacon grill; I remember this from my cadet days." Peter smiled. "They pack literally everything into tins. You name it, margarine, sweets, chocolate, cheese. I bet there is some flour for bread making here somewhere," Peter went on.

"It's a bit heavy for a soldier to carry," Helen said.

"These boxes are for a more organised camp, with enough here to keep 10 men going for 24 hours, using more organised but basic cooking conditions. There are other boxes that contain the single-soldier 24-hour ration packs, with the meal pouches and other dehydrated stuff; similar to what I used to carry on those long-distance footpath walks I used to do," Peter said.

"There must be over 200 boxes here," Helen stated.

"Probably more than that," Peter commented.

"Let's take some margarine and cheese. It would be nice to make some bread, so let's see if we can find the flour. Would they have milk?" Helen asked.

"It will be powdered stuff, like Coffee-mate," Peter replied.

They both crouched down and unboxed the tins from the cardboard and selected the produce that Helen had suggested. Peter managed to sneak a couple of bacon grill and baked beans tins into his rucksack (or so he thought).

Helen said, "I saw that! You are such a child, Peter," and laughed.

"What?" was Peter's wide-eyed comeback.

Happy that they had everything from the box that they needed for the moment, Peter closed and relocked the ration pack store. He led Helen through to the other dry store and she looked in at the shelves stacked with more conventionally labelled tinned produce and dried pasta and pulses. Peter then led Helen back through to the kitchen. He checked the water was flowing from one of the taps and tasted it.

"Water seems to be fresh enough," he remarked.

"You are starting to sound like you want us to move here now," Helen said.

"You have to admit, it may not have the scenic beauty of the holiday cottage, but it has more food and is a more defendable location; if it ever comes to that," Peter went on.

"Are you expecting a war, Peter?" Helen asked.

"I don't know what I am expecting. But I am planning for the worst set of circumstances I can imagine," Peter replied.

"Because that is what you always do," Helen replied with a chuckle.

Peter continued, with Helen following, back out through the mess hall and through the door they had entered the buildings from. He relocked and secured the door and they walked back to where he had parked the Land Rover. They stowed both their full rucksacks in the back, and at Peter's invitation, Helen jumped into the passenger side as Peter got in and started the engine.

"Are we heading back to the boat?" Helen asked.

"I just want to check out something at the armoury," Peter replied. He put the Land Rover in gear and drove up the hill the way they had just come, but then turned off left and drove down the slight hill until they reached the small collection of buildings that contained the armoury.

"What's here then?" Helen asked.

"This is the armoury, and I am assuming the explosives and other weaponry store," Peter replied.

They both got out of the vehicle and Peter went up to the steel framed door he knew to be the armoury. He unlocked the door and went inside, Helen following him closely.

Peter found the light switch and the room was suddenly filled with light.

"Where now?" Helen enquired.

"There is another cabinet beyond this issuing counter area that I never got a chance to check," Peter said.

"Okay, I am not sure I like it in here," Helen replied.

"Stay close to me. We won't be here long," Peter said.

They walked through the next door into the weapons store. Helen stood still, her eyes taking in the array of rifles, pistols and other guns. She had never before seen such an arsenal of weapons, apart from on the TV. Peter selected a key from the many bunches in his pocket and went over to a large metal cabinet in the corner. Eventually finding the correct key at the third attempt, he opened the doors to be confronted with a shelf of about 20 to 30 combat helmets and, hanging below them, a similar number of sets of combat body armour.

"I thought there would have to be a selection of body armour here somewhere," Peter said.

"Do you really think we are now going to add body armour to the stuff you have already nicked?"

"The way I see it, if things get a little bit out of shape when we go looking for information at our next opportunity, we would be foolish if we did not at least protect ourselves as best we can," Peter replied.

"Yes, but isn't all this stuff we now have going to be a bit, well, provocative?" Helen came back.

"It's defensive. Everything that I have acquired and made use of is to defend us and our property and stores. If things are as bad as I suspect, and yes, I fully concede that I have painted a pretty grim picture, but if they are as bad as that, then I think we will have been prudent in adding a set of body armour each to our existing equipment," Peter replied.

"Alright, but I hope that you will be putting all this stuff back where you found it when the opportunity arises," Helen said.

"Of course, dear," Peter quickly said and smiled.

"Less of the dear, thank you." Helen smiled back.

"Try this on?" Peter said, handing a body armour vest to Helen.

She took it and put it on, doing it up. "Blimey, it's heavy, isn't it," Helen stated.

"It's got armour plate front and back and the rest is a Kevlar plastic, similar to what I wore in the job," Peter said.

Peter took a set and put it on. He then picked up one of the helmets, the smallest he could find, and plonked it on Helen's head. "Try this for size," he said.

"A bit big, and this is heavy too," a rather annoyed Helen stated.

"We can adjust it when we get back to the cottage. As long as you've got one, I will feel a little happier," Peter replied.

He took a helmet too and a couple pairs of gloves he saw.

Peter then proceeded to lock the cabinet again and ushered Helen out of the armoury, relocking the doors as they went until they were back out in front of the buildings by the Land Rover.

Peter opened the vehicle, and they placed the body armour and helmets in the back, along with the rucksacks and Peter's MP5.

"Anywhere else?" Helen rather pointedly asked.

"I take it that you would like to head back now then?" Peter said.

"I think we have been here long enough. I have this feeling that someone could return to this place at any time and then I do think we could have some problems," Helen said.

"Alright, I understand, and you are probably right, let's get going," Peter said.

He turned the Land Rover around in front of the building and drove slowly back up the hill, turned right at the top and drove back past the main office and the other two vehicles and then down into the bay and around it until he was on the jetty. He then performed a three-point turn so the Land Rover was back facing up the road again. They jumped out, unloaded their newly acquired equipment from the back and stowed it in the cabin of the boat. Peter relocked the Land Rover and jumped down into the boat, started the engine and called to Helen to undo the front mooring line. Helen was ahead of him, and having dealt with the front line, she was now ready with the stern line, which she held while she jumped into the boat and released it as Peter moved the boat away from the jetty. He turned the boat around in the bay and slowly motored out into the inlet and away back towards the small harbour, where they had made their home.

10

For the next few days, the weather stayed as the more traditional thick Scottish misty rain, with virtually nil visibility and fine enough to soak through any sort of protective clothing. It was a time to stay indoors and wait for things to improve. Peter had adjusted the body armour he had given to Helen and suggested that if she were to wear one of their woollen beanie hats under the helmet, it would be both more comfortable and probably a better fit. After some adjustment, Helen found that it was indeed much more comfortable. Peter took his own armour and added some loaded MP5 magazines to the elasticated straps and loops at the front. He also adjusted the shoulders so that he could still wear a rucksack with the body armour. Peter used the inclement weather as an opportunity to clean all their firearms; all the Glocks, MP5s and the sniper rifle. They enjoyed some home-made bread with some margarine and strawberry jam from the recently acquired rations. Albeit they had a plentiful supply of food and other supplies, they were still careful not to overindulge and to be frugal in their consumption. They did more domesticated chores, doing several large clothes washes, drying them with the tumble dryer the cottage was equipped with. Peter brought in two more bags of coal for the fire. Every morning they woke up expecting the power to have failed and it to be necessary to fire up the waiting generators.

After four days of pretty miserable damp weather, the fifth morning started to look a little brighter, and despite clouds in the sky, there were patches of blue and the winds had died down to make it much warmer. It was starting to look like the short summer weather was starting to appear, even in this remote Scottish location. Peter took his morning tea outside to see for himself. After a short walk around the cottage, looking at the sky, he returned to Helen and sat down with her at the kitchen table.

"So, how do you feel about a little fact-finding trip?" Peter suggested.

"Yes I'm up for it", Helen answered.

"How about we take the boat back down to the Raasay ferry and beyond. Check out the distillery from the water and see how much of Inverarish we can see from there. If things look okay, then maybe moor back by the ferry and walk down to the distillery and then down into the village. What do you think?" Peter said.

"Sounds okay, I suppose. What about heading across to Portree?" Helen suggested.

"Let's see how things are on Raasay first. How we get on will dictate whether we venture across to Skye, alright?"

"Yep, sounds good; what are we taking?" Helen asked.

"I reckon wear your body armour. We can put the helmets on the boat just in case. Wear your Glock and spare magazines. Take an MP5 too," Peter said.

"Isn't that a bit overkill? We'll look like an invading force," Helen replied

"If you don't extend the stock, it will be easily hidden under your coat, as subtle as we can manage and hopefully as non-confrontational as we can be," Peter suggested.

They spent a bit of time collecting their gear, checking magazines and attaching them to the body armour. They each wore an empty rucksack on the off chance they had an opportunity to collect anything useful. Peter checked that safety catches were on for both MP5s, then tested putting jackets on over the top of the weapons and body armour. It was a bit snug, but they did manage to conceal the weapons adequately. After locking up the cottage, they drove the small utility Ranger vehicle back down to the manager's cottage, then onward to the jetty. The catamaran was where they had left it. Peter jumped on board, unlocked and entered the cabin and started the engine. Helen, meanwhile, undid the front mooring and threw it on board. She undid the rear, kept it looped around the mooring ring and jumped aboard. As Peter nodded, she let out the line and pulled it in as Peter moved the boat away from the jetty. As she finished with the line, Helen then immediately pulled in the fenders and stowed them in the deck lockers provided. Peter steered the boat gently out of the small bay, past the rock island at the entrance of the bay and out into the sea channel between the smaller islands and Skye.

Peter looked around as they moved south down the channel, staying closer to both Rona and then Raasay as they motored along. He didn't spot any other boats today. Without prompting, Helen had picked up the binoculars from the cabin table and was out on the rear deck, checking the Skye shoreline and the environs of Portree as they moved past it on the water.

"See anything?" Peter called out.

"Nothing at the moment," Helen answered.

"Okay, keep a watch on the Raasay side as we get closer to the ferry dock," Peter said.

"I will," Helen said, and she moved across to the other side of the deck as they started to approach the ferry still docked at the jetty on Raasay.

Peter slowed the boat and moved a little further out into the channel as they approached. He could not see anything different. To his mind, the small collection of cars was still parked as they had been.

"Let's keep going, see if we can see anything of the distillery from here," Peter said.

He motored on beyond the ferry dock, past the protective retaining jetty wall and into a bay, where the buildings of the distillery could be seen. Due to the lay of the land, it was difficult to make out the road, but they continued to move down the shoreline and could now see a collection of houses and rooftops, indicating the village of Inverarish. They were just a little bit too far away to be able to discern any meaningful movement or signs of life.

"We are going to have to go back to the ferry dock and moor up and then walk back into the village," Peter said.

Helen dropped the binoculars back around her neck and nodded. "I agree. At least if we walk, we are less noticeable," she added.

"The first sign of any issues and we head straight back to the boat and bug out into the channel," Peter said.

"I'm following you, but it makes sense," Helen replied.

Peter turned the boat around in the bay and steered it back to the dock while Helen readied the fenders on the left-hand side of the boat and sorted the mooring lines.

They moored quickly and efficiently. Peter once again checked the safety catches on their MP5s, and they both put on their rucksacks over the body armour. Peter secured the boat and they climbed onto the jetty and walked slowly down the road towards the distillery. They may have only been in this part of the world for five months, but the road between the dock and the distillery was very familiar to them. Peter stopped at the car park entrance of the distillery and asked, "Do you want to have a look here or keep going?"

"Let's keep going. If we need to, we can have a look in on our way back," Helen added.

They continued past the distillery, down the pitted and less well-kept metalled track, into a small vale overlooking the sea channel on the right. They passed a community hall on their left, maybe some sort of former church building, with a 1929 stone marker above the door. As they passed this, they got a view of some buildings down closer to the shoreline, which was indicated as a school. As the road forked, they took the left-hand track, Peter deciding that this looked to be a quieter way to approach the collection of buildings spread out in front of them, which had to be Inverarish. They continued on, passing several individual buildings on the right, one with a sign identifying that it was a bed and breakfast premises.

They turned right on the main track and then turned right again at a junction, a small signpost indicating that it was the way into Inverarish. As they continued,

Peter could see a line of terraced houses on the left-hand side of the road.

"Helen, put your mask on. I'm going to call out, see if we get any response. Be ready to move quickly back the way we came," Peter said.

"I'm ready," Helen nervously answered.

"HELLO, IS THERE ANYBODY HERE? WE DON'T MEAN YOU ANY HARM," Peter shouted.

No reply. "Try again, Peter?" Helen asked.

"IS THERE ANYONE HERE?" Peter shouted again.

They waited about 30 seconds, then Peter said, "Come on, let's keep going."

He moved forward, Helen very close behind him.

A figure appeared from a door from the third house in from a line of a dozen or so small terraces. Peter stopped immediately and sunk onto his haunches. Helen followed suit. Peter saw that it was a male in his 40s or 50s, a black woollen hat on his head, dark jacket and trousers. Like Peter, he wore a pair of glasses. He did not appear to have anything in his hands.

"Are you the food?" the man stated in a strong Scottish accent, looking hopefully at Peter and Helen as they stood up.

"I'm sorry, no. We are tourists. We were staying at the distillery hotel when all this started. Sorry, do you mean to say that you are still waiting for the promised food deliveries?" Peter asked.

"Aye, lad. Luckily, us island folk have some pretty deep freezers and grow a fair bit of stuff in our gardens," the man replied.

"Oh, I see! My name is Peter, and this is my wife Helen. We were staying at the distillery back up the hill there when all the extra restrictions were implemented a few months back," Peter said.

"Oh yes, the distillery. I went up there last week and got myself some whisky." The man smiled.

"What's your name?" Peter asked.

"Sorry, rude of me, not used to people anymore. My name's Craig, lived here all my life, worked as a groundskeeper for the Laird's house, just up near the ferry port," the man, Craig, replied.

"Do you know anything about what's happening beyond here?" Peter asked.

"Well, I went across on the ferry about a month ago. Iain, the ferry captain, lives a way down the lane there." Craig pointed the way they had come. "I drove up to Portree, trying to get some food from one of the shops there," Craig said. "I could see there were people in their houses, but I never saw another car. As I got nearer to the town, the road was blocked with some abandoned cars and what looked like an accident," Craig continued.

"Did you turn around?" Peter asked.

"No, I left my car and walked into the town. I got as far as the cemetery by the sign for Portree and I could see that the road was completely blocked with cars and buses and other bits and pieces. There was a group of people behind this barricade. They asked me to stop about 10 yards away from them and this chap with a rifle came to the other side of their wall and spoke to me," Craig stopped.

"Did he have fisherman's waterproofs on? And did it look like an air rifle, Craig?" Peter interrupted.

"Aye! The fella says he's a fisherman from the town and they are not allowing non-residents into the town while food supplies are not being delivered."

"Did you get his name?" Peter asked.

"Aye, he said his name was Duncan. He looked to have the rest of his fishing mates with him," Craig went on.

"I met him a few months back outside the Co-op in Portree. What happened?" Peter said.

"Well, I explained I had got across from the island to try and get some food," Craig continued. "He said there was nothing they could do for me and then he explained that there had been some trouble."

"Oh, what sort of trouble?" Peter asked.

"He said that groups were coming from the mainland in search of food. Clearly there has been a real problem getting these food supplies to us folk that live up here on the islands," Craig explained.

"Did he say what happened?" Peter asked.

"Aye, the group from the mainland said that the food supplies were getting hijacked on the main roads as they drove north from the distribution hubs. People in the cities were on the streets literally fighting for food. They told of people being shot by the military patrols and pitched battles taking place in areas where there are lots of people." Peter remained quiet, listening with a mixture of awe and horror as Craig went on.

"The group started to make demands about wanting food and Duncan said he had to point his rifle at the ringleader at one point to turn them away from the town. After a brief shouting match, Duncan said that the group went back down the road the way they had come. It was at that point that Duncan said that the town had formed a small committee and decided to put a large roadblock in at the edge of town at the southern and northern ends," Craig said.

"Anything else?"

"Well, one of the ladies at the barrier recognised me from the island and gave me some bread and some other bits and pieces; must have taken pity on me, I suppose," Craig said.

"So how are you surviving?" Peter asked.

"Iain got me back here on the ferry and decided against making any more trips, thinking it better to moor the ferry on this side of the channel," Craig said.

"That makes sense," said Peter.

"We know some folk have died, but possibly because they are old anyway. We have been rationing the stores from the local shop, and we have what some of us have grown, which is starting to be used as the weather has got warmer. A lot of locals were away at the time of the curfew, with relatives and the like," Craig offered.

"How long can you survive without any supply?" Peter bluntly asked.

"We have the better weather, and we are getting organised into growing much more of our own vegetables. There are sheep grazing on the island, so we will have meat; if we can catch the buggers!" Craig smiled. "I miss fresh milk and other stuff like cheese and butter, but I reckon we can get through the summer and store enough for the following winter if we go careful," Craig said. "What about you two then?" he asked.

"We moved out of the distillery hotel after a month or so and headed north and ended up in one of the holiday cottages on Rona," Peter offered, worried that he had told someone where they were, but also feeling he could trust this islander, Craig.

"Oh aye, that's a remote spot in the winter; lovely in the fine weather, mind. How are you surviving with food then?" Craig asked.

"We took quite a bit of food from the distillery and, to be fair, some whisky too," Peter answered, deciding not to mention the military establishment at the north end of Rona.

They had also kept their jackets done up, so despite looking quite a stocky pair of tourists, they didn't look overtly paramilitary.

Peter pulled out a pen and paper from one of his pockets and quickly wrote his name and mobile phone number down. He handed the paper to Craig. "We are going to head back up to the distillery and then back to Rona." Again, Peter decided not to mention the catamaran they had been using to get about. "Then we will see what the situation is over at Portree," Peter said.

"I'm not sure you will find much hospitality in Portree," Craig said.

"Well, hopefully if we get to see the fisherman Duncan, he will remember us from our previous visit and at least he can give us some more information," Peter said.

"You take care there. I hope to see you again, on the other side of this," Craig said.

"You too and thank you for all the stuff you told us. I had a feeling that it could be chaos on the mainland. It's a shame, but it makes me realise that we are actually really lucky to have found ourselves marooned here. We'll visit again, cheers, Craig," Peter said as both he and Helen turned and made their way back the way they had come.

"Nice chap. Do you think they can make a go of it here without supplies?" Helen asked as they walked back out of the village and along the road they had walked in on.

"Depends on so much. How many of them there are, the weather being kind to their crops and no disturbances from outside elements."

"So, are we going to drop into the distillery on the way back?" Helen asked.

"We might as well have a look, but as before, stay on your guard. In light of what that chap Craig said, clearly people are starting to take the law into their own hands, and I think the ordered society we have grown up with may well be a thing of the past," Peter replied.

Helen started to speak, then stopped, thinking that perhaps Peter had been right to be so cautious and to have taken the steps to arm and supply themselves.

"Love you, Peter. You keep looking out for us," Helen said as she put one of her arms through the crook of Peter's elbow.

"Love you too, love!" Peter replied.

They retraced their steps back up the track once again passing the bed and breakfast and then the school and finally the old community hall or church or whatever it was, before arriving back at the distillery.

"Let's try round the back first, okay?" Peter suggested.

"Alright then," Helen replied.

They came around to the back of the premises and immediately saw that the rear door into the kitchens had been forced.

"Not entirely unexpected. Okay, let me go first. You keep an eye out behind me as we go in," Peter said to Helen.

"Okay, be careful, Peter," Helen said.

Peter opened the door with his foot and levered it open, clocking that the self-close mechanism had been ripped off. There was debris from the kitchen stores everywhere. They continued into the storerooms and virtually everything not nailed down was gone. There was the odd can of chopped tomatoes and Peter smiled as he spotted a tin of pineapple chunks on the floor. *Even in a crisis, everyone still fucking hates them!* he thought.

Peter flicked a light switch, and the kitchen lights came on. He switched them off again.

"They still have power here then," Peter commented.

Helen just kept looking around.

"I don't think there is anything left here for us, love," Peter exclaimed.

"No, it's sad to see it like this; it was so lovely when we first came here," Helen responded.

"People have got increasingly desperate and eventually plucked up the courage to take whatever they could from here when their own stuff ran out; no different from what we did, I suppose," Peter stated.

"You were just so quick to realise what could happen and got us organised and away from here before any of this happened. Hate to say it, but you were right, love," Helen replied.

They continued through the kitchen and into the dining area and saw that the TV set was still switched on, still broadcasting the message they had been hearing on the radio whenever they had tuned in.

Peter went over to the small bar area and began to open some cupboards behind the bar.

"What are you looking for?" Helen asked.

"Man cannot live on whisky alone," Peter replied, rising to his feet with a bottle of Raasay distillery gin in each hand and a broad grin on his face.

"Can you pop these into my rucksack, please?" he asked.

Helen opened the rucksack on Peter's back and placed the two bottles inside.

"Very thoughtful," she said as she secured the rucksack again.

They had a rummage around the rest of the ground floor of the hotel, and not finding anything of use, they walked back through the kitchens and out into the rear yard.

"Okay, back to the boat then?" Peter said.

"Suits me. What do you want to do when we get back to the boat?" Helen asked.

"Let's get back there and then we can weigh up our options, is that okay?" Peter suggested.

They walked around to the front of the distillery and back up to the road, then did the short walk down to the small island ferry port. They were much more cautious since the conversation with Craig in Inverarish and kept a watch both in front and behind them as they closed in on the dock. The boat was as they had left it and they jumped down onto the rear deck and removed their rucksacks.

"We could go across towards Portree as we head back up to our cottage?" Peter offered.

"Do we have time?" Helen asked.

"I think so. It's kind of on the way back up to Rona, a slight detour maybe," Peter replied.

Helen climbed back onto the jetty, untied the rear mooring line and threw it into the boat as Peter took the rucksacks into the cabin and started the engine. Helen untied the front line and got back on board. Peter took his leave and they moved forward away from the dock, Helen busying herself with bringing in the fenders. She then joined Peter in the cabin and picked up the binoculars from the table.

"Okay, keep an eye out as we get closer to the town. Look out for any movement, people, vehicles, anything," Peter said.

"Right, love, I'm on it," Helen replied.

Peter steered the boat back out into the channel until he was more or less in the middle. From their position, the large headland on the Isle of Skye to their front left was blocking their view of Portree.

"See anything yet?" Peter asked.

"Nothing, no movement on the road, but until we round the headland, I cannot really get any view of the town," Helen said.

"Do you see those clouds just beyond the headland, quite dark," Peter commented.

Helen looked through the binoculars and remained quiet. Then she looked again.

"Peter, I'm not sure they are clouds, you know. It looks a little bit like smoke, the way it's swirling and billowing up; looks to be coming from the town," Helen quietly said.

"Take the wheel, love, just keep us straight on this heading. Let me take a look?" Peter asked.

They swapped positions and Peter took the binoculars from Helen and had a look. It took him a while to focus on the mass of cloud just above the area where he knew the town to be. He slowly put the binoculars down and stared at the headland as it approached.

"Helen, you are right. Something in or near the town is on fire."

The smoke became darker as they rounded the headland. The origin appeared to be a little way out of town; it was the way the smoke was drifting that had fooled them. Peter slowed the boat as they took in the smoke rising from the south of the main settlement.

"Can you see anyone?" Peter asked Helen as she looked through the binoculars.

"I can't see anyone down by the dock and sea wall," Helen replied.

"Okay, let's go in. I think all ideas of hiding our weapons have now gone; we must be ready for the worst," Peter commented.

They worked quickly and efficiently to secure the boat at the far end of the harbour wall, up near where the small fleet of trawlers were moored. As they clambered onto the harbour road, Peter pulled open the sliding stock of the MP5 and put the safety switch on to single-shot mode. "Helen, get your MP5 ready, put the safety switch to single shot, like I showed you," Peter said. Helen did as she was asked and they slowly walked down Quay Street, and as they were about to climb the hill to the road by the Co-op, Peter spotted a flight of steps to the left. They climbed, Peter leading, until they reached the main street, opposite the Royal Hotel.

"Let's keep going. We have to find out what is going on," Peter said as they continued to walk down the road towards the billowing smoke.

"Go careful, do you think we should go too far from the safety of the boat?" Helen asked.

"It's a tricky one. We need to find out what's happening, but I agree, we have to be ready to get back to the boat quickly," Peter conceded.

They continued to walk away from the harbour down the main street, on past the Portree Independent Hostel, heading out of town. After about half a mile, as they approached a building indicated as the Portree Resource Centre, they saw some people on the road in front of them.

"Hey, we mean you no harm, can you tell us what is happening?" Peter called out to the two people he could see.

One of the people turned and screamed loudly at the sight of a heavily armed pair walking towards her.

Peter put both his hands in the air. "It's okay. We are just tourists, trapped up here in this situation; we mean you no harm. Can we help at all?"

The other lady, who looked a bit older than the first, came a little closer until they were about five metres apart.

"Are you the couple that took the catamaran from the harbour a few months ago? You left a note in my B&B; it's Peter, isn't it?"

"That's right, and my wife Helen. We saw the smoke from the water and stopped to investigate. What's going on?"

"Marauders from the mainland, I reckon from as far as Inverness, have rallied together and are trying to gather all the supplies from everywhere they go. I reckon they thought they would try here again; they've been before. Duncan, you remember him from the Co-op, built a barricade up by the Portree road sign. He's up there now with a few of the others trying to keep them out," the lady said.

"How far up the road is that?" Peter asked.

"It's about a mile, past the high school and keep going past the petrol station and you will see the barrier. Duncan said he was going to set fire to it," the lady added.

"Does he have any way of stopping the group that's coming?" Peter asked.

"He's got that pop gun of his and they have a stack of petrol bombs which they are going to use, but if there's loads of them, what can we do," the lady said.

Suddenly, there was an almighty explosion and a great ball of flame and smoke rose ominously into the air about half a mile up the road.

"What the fuck was that?" Peter shouted.

"It looked like where the filling station is, at least that's what's in that area," the lady said.

"What are your names, ladies?" Peter asked.

The lady from the B&B said, "I'm Margaret, this is my sister Minnie; she works in the kitchen at my little place."

"Well, ladies, you stay here with Helen while I find out how Duncan is," Peter added. "Will you be okay to stay here, love, while I see if everyone is alright?" Peter asked Helen.

"Don't go far and get back here at the first sign of anything untoward," Helen said.

Peter kissed Helen and carried on up the road. He came to a junction with a road off to the right that he assumed must lead inland and across Skye. As he passed the junction, he could see the modern-looking high school on his right. He stopped and listened and thought he heard a high-revving engine. He could see the thick black smoke curling into the sky, just a little further ahead. Around a corner came a black vehicle, driving fast and weaving as it came around the bend.

Peter stepped to the side of the road and put both his arms in the air. The dark 4x4 continued at pace towards him; Peter shuffled a little further off the road, arms still raised. A gamble, he decided, but he hoped he was right.

The vehicle screeched to a halt right next to him, and from the open driver's window, he saw the fisherman, Duncan.

"Peter, isn't it? Good time for a visit," Duncan suggested.

"What's going on?" Peter asked.

"Well, we stopped them at the barricade and then blew up the petrol station as they started to get around the barriers. There are 20 to 30 of them, some are armed with shotguns; not much I can do with my air rifle. I see you have more stuff than fuckin' Action Man on!"

"I'll tell you all about it another time. Is there anything we can do? Helen is with Margaret and Minnie at the resource centre," Peter said.

"Jump in the back and we will get back to the town and see who is about. This is David in the front and Scotty next to you."

Peter jumped in the back of the 4x4. "Hi, how are you guys?"

"Aye, busy day," Scotty said.

David in the front turned and nodded at Peter.

Duncan gunned the engine and they drove back past the school and the junction and up to where Helen and the two ladies were stood.

Once again, Duncan screeched the 4x4 to a halt. Everyone got out.

"Helen, you remember Duncan?" Peter said, "This is Scotty and David," pointing to the two other men who got out and stood next to Duncan. "Duncan, how long have we got before they get past the petrol station and into the town?" Peter asked.

David answered, "We put the tanker across the road by the filling station and then just set the place on fire and got away before the whole lot exploded."

"The tanker formed a pretty big barrier across the road at that point; it should keep people from getting any further for maybe 20 minutes to an hour or so," Duncan added. "So, what happened to you? Looking to invade somewhere?" Duncan continued, pointing at Peter's armour and firearms.

"It's a fairly long story. What are you going to do if they get into the town? Do you have any chance of staying here and surviving if they catch you?" Peter asked.

"Honestly don't really know. A couple of them were firing their shotguns. They didn't seem to want to discuss anything; they just pulled our first barricade apart, so we retreated to the filling station and set it alight."

"Can I make a suggestion?" Peter asked.

"Go on," Duncan replied.

"Helen and I have set ourselves up on the holiday cottages on Rona. It's pretty basic and the food supplies will need some thought, but there is enough space to get you all somewhere to stay and try and ride this out until things improve. What do you think?" Peter offered.

"Aye, I know those cottages. There's not much on Rona; we'd be pretty cut off," Duncan replied. His two buddies nodded.

"But we can plant crops. You can fish; I take it your trawler is still operational?" Peter asked.

"Judging by the level of desperation on the faces of the marauders at the barriers, we may not have a choice. Let's get everyone back to the town." Duncan helped Margaret, Minnie and Helen into the back of the 4x4. "Peter, you're with me; Scotty and David have a car in the resource centre," Duncan said.

"Everyone get some clothing and as much useful stuff as you can carry and meet us at the end of the dock wall on Quay Street in 15 minutes," Peter called.

With that, he jumped into the front of the 4x4, and Duncan got them going and headed back into town. He stopped by the steps that led down to the quay to let Peter, Helen, Margaret and Minnie out.

"Be as quick as you can, Duncan. Bring as much as possible and anyone else you can find who wants to get out of here. Have you got any diesel?" Peter asked.

"In the flatbed, under the tarpaulin," Duncan smiled. Peter lifted the canvas cover and took in the 15–20 jerry cans neatly filling the flatbed of the 4x4.

"Okay, we will be with you in 10," Duncan shouted and roared off in the direction of the Co-op and around the corner out of sight, closely followed by the saloon car containing David and Scotty.

"Right, ladies, let's get you back to the B&B and help you get some stuff together, okay?" Peter suggested.

They got down the steps to Quay Street and entered the small hotel run by Margaret and Minnie. Peter and Helen stayed downstairs as the ladies rushed upstairs.

"Helen, see what you can grab and help them. I'll keep watch outside," Peter said.

"Be careful," Helen said as Peter stepped out of the hotel.

Back inside, Helen took off her rucksack and found some navigation charts and a compass, some flashlights, a flare gun, a first aid box, some weatherproof matches and a flint striker and box of batteries. She put it all into her rucksack.

"How are you doing, ladies?" she called out.

"Aye, we are nearly done. Could you come up and help us with our bags and a box of food," Margaret called back down.

Helen climbed the stairs and saw that the ladies had filled two large soft-shell bags (easier to store, she thought). She was also heartened to see two boxes of dry food supplies and tins of this and that. Helen carried the two bags downstairs one at a time and returned and repeated the feat with the two grocery boxes. She went to the front door and looked out. Peter was standing with his back to the door, looking towards the town, an old sack barrow next to him.

Helen came outside. "Where did you find that then?" she asked, pointing at the sack barrow.

"It was up by the fish stall at the end of the quay. Did you notice the large oil containers hidden by the last of the buildings? If we had more time, I'd love to see if we could drain them in some way," Peter said.

"We don't have time. Let's get the ladies on the boat and be ready to help the others when they get here," Helen said.

They both went back inside and brought the bags and boxes outside and loaded it all onto the barrow.

At that moment, the ladies joined them. Margaret locked the front door. "Right, young lady, thank you so much. I think we are both as ready as we will ever be," Margaret said.

With that, they all walked up to the end of the quay to where the catamaran was moored, just by the trawlers. Peter and Helen helped both ladies down onto the rear deck of the boat, helped them into the cabin and brought their bags and the boxes inside and stored them in the forward cabin.

"Will you ladies be alright to stay here while we help the others as they arrive?" Peter asked.

"Yes, dear, this is so exciting. We thought our adventures were over, but thank you," Minnie offered with a twinkle in her eye.

Peter and Helen returned to the jetty wall at the end of the quay to await the arrival of the others. They both kept a watch at the other end of the street.

They didn't have long to wait. They heard rather than saw the vehicles as they tore down from the high street and roared into view at the other end of Quay Street. Suddenly, the 4x4, now towing a fairly large, caged trailer, and the saloon, also towing a large trailer, were coming to an abrupt halt right by the two of them.

Duncan got out of the 4x4 and joined Peter while other occupants got out of the two vehicles.

"We don't really have time for introductions; how about we just get all this stuff on board and then get going," Peter suggested.

"Aye, Peter, pretty sure the group at the barrier will be heading this way any minute. We had these two trailers loaded, ready to go, all food and other items from the Co-op. It's mainly tinned and dried stuff," Duncan replied.

"Okay, let's form a chain and get this on board," Peter said.

So, between them, with a couple of new arrivals to the group that Peter could ask about later, they formed a human chain from the trailers and transferred the mainly cardboard boxes down onto the rear deck of the catamaran. They then moved the second vehicle and trailer up to the trawlers and started to load the trawler closest to the dock.

"This is my trawler, *The Hebridean Queen*," Duncan said. "I crew this with Dave and Scotty; it's full of diesel and fresh water, so I thought we would take this too," he added.

"Great idea. I suspect the addition of fish to our diet will become more important the longer we are surviving on Rona," Peter replied.

They got the second trailer unloaded onto the trawler, and then returning to the catamaran, they got about 20 of the jerry cans onto the rear deck.

"Can you take our wives and kids, Peter?" Duncan asked as he got the group together. "This is my wife Mary and our boy Callum, Scotty's wife Sonia and David's partner Rebecca, and their dog, of course."

"We can meet properly as we get going, but it's a real pleasure to say hello. Jump on board and we'll go. What's the dog's name, Rebecca?" Peter asked.

"Call me Becky, and this little chap is Talisker," Rebecca replied as she picked up a very excited small Border Terrier.

Just then, there was a large crash and the sound of breaking glass, followed by shouts and cursing, and then more ominously, a couple of shots were heard.

"Everyone on board then. Helen, get the lines. Duncan, let's regroup out in the channel," Peter said.

Duncan, Scotty and David ran up to the trawler and disappeared on board. Peter got the engine of the catamaran going and Helen ushered everyone into the cabin, where they nervously watched from the windows, all looking in the direction of the far end of Quay Street.

Peter put the boat into a tight circle as he steered away from the dock and out facing away from the town and began to move forward, towards the channel between the islands. He watched as Duncan, on board his trawler, got his boat away from the dock too.

Just as it was turning out into the bay, there were some clear shouts from the town and more shots were heard. Everyone now looked back through the rear window of the catamaran cabin to see a group of 8–10 people appear at the very far end of Quay Street and begin running up towards the now abandoned 4x4 and another vehicle. Peter estimated they were about 400 or so metres out into the channel; it was difficult to see what was happening on the quayside, but he saw smoke, then heard the report of guns firing, presumably at them.

"Everyone okay?" Peter asked of all the passengers he now had on the catamaran.

"Thank you, young man, for your timely intervention. I'm not sure we would have enjoyed the kind of visit those men were intending," Margaret said.

"No problem, we just happened to be passing and saw the smoke from Duncan's barricade. So, hello to you all, my name is Peter, and this is my wife Helen," Peter said.

"Thanks, Peter," a dark-haired woman in her late 30s said. "I'm Duncan's wife Mary and this young man is our son Callum, who is 12," Mary said.

"Hello, Callum, nice to meet you both," Peter said.

Callum just looked up from his mop of sandy-coloured hair and smiled nervously.

"Hello, I'm Sonia, Scotty's wife," a tall thin lady, probably in her early 30s, said.

"That just leaves me then. I'm Becky, David's better half, and this wee chap is our dog, Talisker," a slight blonde girl in her late 20s said.

"Do you all know Margaret and Minnie?" Peter asked.

"Oh, we all know them, young man. We make it our business to know everybody," Margaret laughed.

"So, do you all know of the holiday cottages on Rona?" Peter asked.

"We know of them but have never been over to see them. They always get booked up by tourists every summer," Mary said.

"We sometimes see them arrive with their stuff for a week's stay and looking at finding a boat from our town to take them over to the island," Becky added.

Peter watched the trawler on his right-hand side as they headed out into the channel. Either Scotty or David waved from the front deck of the trawler; it was difficult at this range to work out which one it was.

"So, there is a large island manager's cottage that has four bedrooms, perhaps that would be good for Mary and Callum? Becky and Sonia, there is also another detached cottage closer to the sea, with a lovely meadow between it and the manager's cottage. There also another holiday cottage just beyond where Helen and I have set ourselves up, which has two bedrooms. That might be good for you and Minnie, Margaret. How does that sound, everyone?" Peter asked.

"We know the island manager; he's a lovely man. I know he left just before Christmas to go and see his grown-up kids down in northern England somewhere," Sonia said.

"Thanks, Peter. Is there much on the island?" Mary asked.

"Apart from what Helen and I brought with us, we did find a large supply of diesel oil and coal to burn in the fires. There is diesel oil in large tanks to utilise the central heating systems, but how much of that we have will need checking," Peter said. "Are there any others in Portree who we could have helped?" he asked.

"A lot of folk had already moved out and gone north towards Uig. Duncan had loaded the trailers with food and stuff, and we were just about to head up that way too. If you hadn't come along and suggested Rona, I think that's where we would be heading," Mary said.

"I think that quite a few of the elderly have died in the last few months and are just laying where they fell," Margaret spoke softly.

Helen came up next to Peter. "What now then?" she asked.

"Well, we have a group to help, and they can help us. If Duncan can get out and fish in the sea, then we can extend our food supplies and maybe given time and some decent weather, we can grow some fresh stuff of our own," Peter replied.

Helen turned and looked behind them at the smoke rising from the outskirts of the town of Portree.

"Will we be safe on the island? I mean, is the channel between the town and us a good enough barrier to keep us safe?" Helen asked.

"I really don't know; there are so many questions. Do they have ready access to some of the other boats in the harbour, like we did? Is there enough food in the town to keep them satisfied for the moment? If they are not local, do they know what is on the island we have chosen to seek refuge on?" Peter stopped as he could see the faces of the new guests on the boat all listening to what he had to say.

"Duncan knows these waters; his dad fished them before him, and he knows how quiet it is up here. We have always regarded Rona as a forgotten part of the islands. There used to be farmers and crofters on the island many years ago, but they all moved back to Raasay or to us on Skye, or just simply moved away from the islands," Mary said.

"I'm sorry, I didn't mean to alarm you all, but I suppose we have to consider how safe we are going to be across the channel on Rona and how long we can make a go of it on the island. It may be that we will have to go out on our own trips to try and resupply ourselves when things run short," Peter said.

"Let's get settled on the island with a nice cup of tea and then we can see what's what!" Margaret offered.

"Sounds good to me, Margaret." Peter smiled and concentrated on steering the catamaran towards the gap between the rock and the shoreline as they approached the island harbour, with the trawler about 200 metres behind them.

Taking them all off the boats and then unloading the supplies had been backbreaking work, even with all of the extra people lending a hand. They had taken Margaret and Mary up to the second of the holiday cottages, beyond the cottage that Peter and Helen were using. Peter ensured that both the ladies had the makings for a cup of tea, gave them a brief tour of the cottage, then said he would return when everyone was settled to bring them back to the manager's cottage, where they had chosen to meet for a discussion of their situation. Peter then returned and helped with unloading the boats, using the Ranger and trailer to transport the supplies to the large storage barn near to the manager's cottage, where the supply of diesel fuel and coal was. David, Becky and Talisker decided to make themselves comfortable in the cottage right down by the sea front, nearest to the jetty. Duncan, Mary and Callum agreed to share the manager's cottage with Scotty and Sonia.

After having got all the supplies off the boats, they secured them as best as they could and all met at the manager's cottage kitchen at 6pm that evening. Peter had gone and fetched Margaret and Minnie in the Ranger. Mary had got the kitchen organised with a few extra chairs, allowing everyone to have a seat around the table. Everyone welcomed a hot cup of tea, albeit made with long-life milk.

Peter looked up and waited for everyone to have a seat. "I am so glad we came along when we did," he began.

"Aye! Not half as much as we are," Duncan replied. "I reckon our plan to get up to Uig was okay, but getting across here might just be a better option," he added.

"What have you got here, Peter?" David asked.

"Okay, well, we have fresh water; I think it must be fed from a well or other underground reservoir from back up the hill. There is fuel oil for each property in the large green containers. There is a fairly good supply of coal in the shed to feed the open fires in each of the cottages. We can distribute that to you all as you need it. There is a good supply of diesel fuel in the oil drums you saw in the barn, where we put all the other stuff today. We brought quite a bit of stuff from the distillery on Raasay, where we had been staying before we moved up here." Peter was going to continue, but he could see there were questions that needed answering.

"That's fine for the two of you, but now there are 11 of us, is that going to make things more difficult?" Duncan asked.

"I have to agree, but I still think we are better off over here, rather than taking our chances with the mob that invaded your town," Peter replied. A few nods around the table seemed to concur.

"May I ask you about the weapons we saw you with in town?" Becky leaned forward and asked.

"Of course. Look, you may as well know. I am a retired London policeman; we live down on the south coast of England. We had driven up here to have a bit of a mini break, then all this happened, and we were kind of stuck here," Peter said.

"Our police disappeared, probably to help on the mainland," Margaret said.

"I came to this island with Helen, and on one of our walks to the north of the cottage you and Minnie are staying in, Margaret, I caught sight of a building," Peter said.

"I reckon that was the lighthouse," Duncan interrupted.

"Yes, Duncan, it was. I went up to the north of this island on the catamaran and found a little harbour and jetty in a small bay."

"Aye, that place is guarded by men with guns; we always steer well clear as we head out into the sea," Scotty offered.

"When I got there, it was deserted, not a soul about. I walked around the bay, found three almost brand-new Land Rovers all parked. The main office was open but empty. I found keys and basically discovered this military base, set up for maybe 100–150 people, with barracks, mess halls, kitchens, and of course, an armoury," Peter said.

"Bloody hell," Mary said.

"Go on, Peter," Duncan requested.

"I got into the armoury to find a fully kitted setup, with side arms, MP5s, a couple of sniper rifles, ammunition. To be honest, I didn't really scratch the surface of what is in there. I think they also have an explosive store and other equipment, which I didn't stay to look for. I took three Glock pistols with ammunition, a couple of the MP5 9mm small arms and one of the sniper rifles," Peter added.

"So, you know about guns then, Peter?" Duncan asked.

"For several of my years in the police, I was part of the Royalty and Diplomatic Protection Group, so I know how to handle and fire lots of different guns. It's been 20-odd years, but it came back to me quite quickly," Peter said.

"And this place was just abandoned, you say?" Scotty asked.

"Well, it was all locked up and secure; I just happened to find all the keys," Peter smiled.

"I bet the guys we used to see on the jetty with the guns went home to be with their families," Becky suggested.

"Oh, and one other thing. There are pretty large supplies of army rations up there, boxes and boxes of the stuff; all appear to be in date and usable."

"What about power?" Duncan asked.

"Seems to be a gas cannister system in two large tanks by the main office and a couple of other tanks near to the barrack blocks," Peter replied.

"How many times have you been up there then?" David asked.

"Twice. Once on my own and the last time I took Helen; that's when we acquired the body armour and Kevlar helmets that you saw on the boat," Peter replied.

"So, do you have a plan then?" Duncan asked Peter.

"Not really, we have been kind of making it up as we go along. Now that you have joined us here, and you are all locals, I would welcome some advice and ideas. Let's not forget, Helen and I are just tourists really," Peter said.

"Well, for a couple of tourists, you seem to have done alright for yourselves and certainly saved our bacon when you got us out of the town earlier," Margaret piped up.

"Thank you, but like I said, we were just there at that time, just in a position to help."

"Well, cheers, Peter and Helen," Sonia said, and they all raised their cups of tea in salutation.

"So, I maybe have some questions for you, if that's okay?" Peter said.

"Aye, go on then," Duncan said.

"Well, I take it you can catch some fish for us, Duncan?" Peter asked.

"We can certainly rig some smaller nets and get plenty of fish for us," Duncan smiled.

"What about growing stuff on this island?" Peter asked.

"It's a short growing season, but I noticed the meadow by the cottage we moved into looked flat and would be easy to grow some stuff on," Scotty answered.

"Well, there are some potatoes left in our supplies; maybe we should plant those?" Peter said.

"What do we do about the risk from the town?" Mary asked.

"What can any of you tell me of the situation with food and supplies in your town?" Peter asked.

"We had pretty much emptied the Co-op by the time we loaded both of those trailers onto the boat. The other shops in town were empty of all but the last of the tinned and dry foodstuffs," Duncan said.

"I suppose what we need to know is how many of those people have invaded your town and where would they go next, on realising that there is no food there for them," Peter asked.

"Like Duncan said, we had thought we would head across Skye to Uig or Dunvegan next, but to be honest, they are smaller than Portree and there is less in the way of shops than we have here," Mary replied.

"Didn't you say you thought that the men at the barricades may have been from Inverness?" Peter asked.

"Aye, maybe as far as Inverness or Dingwall. That is really the closest area where there are a lot of people," Duncan suggested

"Let's take some positives then," Peter started. "We have boats and fuel to keep them running for now. We have heating, power and light. We have enough food and fresh drinking water for the moment. The weather is in our favour, so we need to think that if this crisis drags on, we need to prepare for the winter and have sufficient supplies for that," Peter said.

"I think we can grow stuff here over the next few months," Becky said.

"We have the beauty of this place to explore, eh, Callum?" Duncan said to his son, who looked up and smiled at his dad.

"I suppose we have to consider what might happen if the group, who are now in your town, decide to head over here somehow and try to take what we have from us," Peter commented.

"Well, we fight them," David shouted back quickly.

"I hear you, David, but clearly those men were armed, and any fight would be serious and may lead to casualties; you appreciate that?" Peter explained.

"Yeah, I hear you, but you are armed and presumably we could all get guns from the base on the north of this island?"

"Agreed, but as long as you understand that it's one thing to carry a gun and quite another to actually aim and fire it at another human being. I am just being honest when I say to you that it's not always the easiest thing to do, even if you are in the right and you are defending yourselves and your property," Peter went on.

"Have you ever shot anyone, Peter?" Sonia quietly asked.

"I carried a gun for about five years in London, and in all that time, I only drew my firearm in anger once and never actually fired it apart from on a range at my regular reclassifications," Peter said.

"Who did you aim your gun at?" Scotty asked, receiving a sharp elbow in the ribs from Sonia.

Peter looked at Helen and took a deep breath and spoke to them all. "When I was on a routine patrol in a vehicle, we were just driving back to the base, which at that time was in a place called Walton Street, almost around the back of where Harrods in London is, for those interested. I was driving with two passengers; we were all armed. It was dark, probably about 9pm at night. If memory serves, I believe it was a Sunday evening. As we drove along Lupus Street in Chelsea, past a parade of shops on our left-hand side, I saw a glint of something in the hand of a man walking past the shops. It was the faintest of glimpses but enough for me to think I had seen a knife in his hand. I told the boys on board, and we carried on for about 50 yards, then I did a quick U-turn and we drove back. The man I had seen was still walking along, now on our right. I pulled up and got out of the car. Immediately I looked at his right hand and saw the end of a blade. I remember I drew my Glock and shouted, 'ARMED POLICE, STAND STILL.' The man turned, and in an instant, the blade became a three-foot samurai sword he had concealed down the inside of his coat. I distinctly remember taking up the pressure on the safety on the trigger of the Glock, like a little pre-firing pressure. I was a millisecond away from firing my gun when he dropped the sword on the floor and put his hands in the air."

The room was silent, all eyes on Peter. "Would you have shot him?" Duncan asked.

"Without a doubt, if he had held on to that sword for a split second longer, I would have put a round in his chest, and from the distance between us, chances are I would have killed him," Peter said.

David whistled. "You remember that in such detail?"

"I remember everything about that incident. It's not a question of whether I could shoot someone, because clearly, I could and would have. It's about dealing with it. If those men come across the channel, with intent to take from us, using force, then what are we, as a group, prepared to do to defend ourselves with what we have?" Peter said. "We can plan what we do, I suppose, and we can post lookouts to keep an eye out while we go about our daily chores, but can we do that 24 hours a day?" Peter asked. He continued, "We can all arm ourselves and learn to use the firearms that are readily available to us, but it will change us. I suppose what I am trying to say is that whatever course of action we choose, we must all be mindful that it will change us all and we will have to live and deal with that going forward. I hope you all understand that?" Peter said.

"Thank you, Peter. I think we all need to decide if we want to be armed and defend our new land and property," Duncan said.

"Let's vote on it then," Scotty said.

"Aye then. All those in favour of arming ourselves and defending this place using our guns, raise your hands," Duncan ordered.

There was a pause, then everyone slowly raised their hands.

"Okay then, let's get ourselves organised. More tea in the pot, Helen?" Peter said.

During the course of the next couple of weeks, the group of locals, with Peter and Helen, began to work out how to survive on the remote island of Rona. Helen, Mary, Sonia and Callum organised the food stores into manageable items and created a shop-like premises in the barn, where the goods had first been taken. The idea was that this "shop" would be open for business to all between set hours and would be run by the girls on a rotational basis for everyone to come and get what they needed, in a similar fashion to how they would do their normal food shopping prior to the crisis. They had agreed to try and be as sparing with the supplies as possible while not knowing how long they were going to be isolated on the island for. After a few days, it was clear that everyone had settled down after the initial burst of activity to stock up their respective cottages.

Becky was most keen to get the field between the cottage she and David had taken and the manager's cottage ploughed and some crops grown as soon as possible. They found an old rusty plough at the back of one of the outbuildings and somehow rigged it up to the back of the Ranger utility vehicle, and after about a week of constant stopping and starting, they had the field ploughed and ready to plant. Both Becky and Sonia had brought a small quantity of potatoes with them. They looked pretty old and tired and had certainly been chitting for a while in their brown bags. To eke out the crop, Becky cut the potatoes in half and planted about 60 pieces.

Peter had remarked about her agricultural skills and smiled at Becky's response: "To be honest, all I've got is the bit of stuff I learned from watching Matt Damon growing potatoes on Mars in the film, *The Martian*," she laughed.

Sonia also dug out a small packet of carrot seeds and similar packets of leeks, spinach, kale, chard and French beans, which had clearly been swept up in the emptying of the Co-op by Duncan and the others.

Either way, before long, Becky, with help from Sonia and David, had the whole field planted and they were busy watering and tending the soil in anticipation of the first shoots to appear.

Peter was delighted to see Helen take charge of the stores and create the faux shop in the barn area. She seemed happy and focused on their new colleagues on the island and was clearly very fond of Callum, who was keen to get involved with organising and itemising the food supplies. Peter met with Duncan, Scotty and David and brought his arsenal of weapons together. He explained the simplicity of the Glock pistols, showing them how to disassemble, clean and reassemble the guns. He went back up to the makeshift range he had created with Helen and showed them how to aim and fire them. Once Becky had got the crops growing, he made time to take her, with Sonia and Mary, out to the range area to become familiar with the Glocks and also MP5s, which he had already done with the men.

Duncan had remarked on his fearsome-looking M16 replica shotgun. Peter had explained that with the after-market magazine, he was able to load the shotgun with 10 shells and was confident that they would find more ammunition for a shotgun when he revisited the military facility with them. He brought out the AWM sniper rifle and let them feel the lightness and balance of the weapon. He explained the accuracy and distance that the weapon was effective to and let them all have a practice with it.

Although they heard and saw nothing from the mainland or out in the channel, it was a short time after their arrival as a group on the island that Peter had suggested they perhaps conduct a daily patrol. He instigated a watch on the main headland of their harbour, just opposite the large rock that was at the entrance to the channel that allowed access into the harbour. Peter knew it was going to be a pretty onerous chore, but he felt it necessary; he remained ever watchful and suspicious of events on the mainland. As a consequence, he took the lion's share of the duties himself, quite often joined by Duncan, who he was getting to know as a really reliable and thoughtful person. When not on these extended walks with Peter,

Duncan had been out in the trawler with either Scotty or David (on one occasion, Mary and Callum too). He had not gone out far, just beyond the end of the island into more open water and simply caught some mackerel with several lines of feathers over the side of the boat. They had then spent a few hours with more lines baited with mackerel and caught a selection of herring, haddock, cod and monkfish. Their return to harbour soon became the source of a welcome break in the chores of the day for everyone, as the catch of the day would certainly feature in most people's dinners that evening.

Peter made several trips on foot up to the most remote cottage where Margaret and Minnie had been making themselves comfortable. Keen as they both were to do their fair share of chores, Peter suggested that they organise weekly meals for the whole group at their cottage and, while the weather allowed, hold these events outside like an alfresco barbeque, where everyone could catch up with how their own existence was going. Becky could impart her progress with the planted field. Duncan was always able to bring the fattest salmon or brownest trout to these gatherings, having hooked up one of the outside chest freezers to a generator to preserve his catch as long as possible.

They began to gel as a small community, each with their own tasks and each able to report on how their own parts of the whole were progressing. Duncan had been responsible for the diesel fuel levels and was able to reassure everyone that they were using very little of their diesel supply. Power had gone off after about

10 days of them all being on the island, so they were now reliant on generators for powering fridges, freezers and light. The cottages were all equipped with oil powered Agas, so with a little instruction from Minnie (who knew about such things), they all started to use the Agas rather than the electric cookers. They also had three gas barbeques, the largest of which was the one that ended up at Margaret and Minnie's cottage, to cook their weekly group meals.

Peter had kept a radio tuned to BBC Radio 4 so that in the event of any updates on the country or world situation, they would become aware of it. The robotic voice message had stopped, and most days that Peter turned the radio on, all he got was static. Always leaving one of the men at the jetty, the others, not necessarily Margaret and Minnie, would take walks across the island as a way to keep fit and for them to appreciate the limits of the area they now called home. They had ventured back south, encountering the deserted crofter's cottage that Peter and Helen had mentioned to them over supper. Becky had wondered if it might be another area that they could plant with crops and they decided that a small area should be prepared and seeded at the earliest opportunity, heartened as they had all been at the sight of the first green shoots appearing in the field they had sown down near the harbour.

The daily patrols did not reveal anything untoward. There was nothing to be seen from Portree, not even any smoke. A discussion had wondered if the men who had been intent on forcing their way into the town had moved on when the limit of the supplies available to them there became apparent. Discussion also turned to whether they should take a closer look and possibly venture back to the town to see if anybody was still there and if there was anything left that might be useful to them on Rona. Clearly it was something the locals were keen to undertake, and Peter could see that it was an obvious desire by them, to check up on their homes.

They had decided that they would undertake a trip. But before venturing back to Portree, Peter would take Duncan and Scotty up to the military facility to secure enough firearms and ammunition for them all, some additional protective vests and helmets and any other items that they might find useful. The trip was planned for the next day.

They had taken the catamaran. Peter reckoned it was slightly more economical on fuel than the trawler, and when it came to loading the boat with fresh supplies, it would be easier to fill the open rear deck. The weather had been a little cloudy at first but now seemed to be brightening up and there was only a light breeze. They left David and the girls down at the jetty, David taking charge of one of the MP5s to protect those left behind. Peter had skippered the catamaran out into the channel. They had slowed as they entered the channel and Duncan, using the binoculars, had taken a long careful look in the direction of the town of Portree. After about 10 minutes, on not seeing anything, they decide to head up to the military facility and perhaps have a closer look on the way back.

Peter moored the boat at the jetty up at the base. They climbed up onto the quayside and he produced a set of keys from the large white canvas bag he carried, which contained keys to everything that he had so far explored on the base.

Peter unlocked the vehicle. "Jump in, boys. We'll use this to show you around and then we can fill it with gear to bring back here." Duncan and Scotty jumped in, and Peter climbed in behind the steering wheel, started the engine and drove the vehicle around the small bay and up to the main office area, showing the other two the additional Land Rovers parked outside.

"And you just found this whole place unmanned and unlocked?" Duncan asked as they drove on past the office and up to the main living accommodation, barracks and mess halls.

"It was deserted! The only thing open was the main office door, and from inside there, I was able to acquire the keys to everything else," Peter replied.

"Why would they leave the office unlocked?" Scotty asked.

"Maybe they left in such a hurry that the last person out simply forgot," Duncan said.

"It would make sense to me. They knew of the crisis and decided to head for home, and someone simply forgot to lock the door," Peter argued.

The vehicle stopped outside the accommodation block and the three of them climbed out of the vehicle. "Let's start with the accommodation; I didn't have a look inside on my previous visits," Peter said. They walked past the path that Peter knew led to the mess hall and kitchens and onto another single-storey structure. They got to a door marked "Barracks A and Barracks B". Peter once again pulled out the bag of keys from his jacket, and after a brief search, he found a Chubb key with "Barracks A and B" written on the label. Peter inserted the key and unlocked the door. He pulled the door towards them, and they all went inside.

"Is there any power?" Duncan asked. He flicked the switch and light flooded the corridor in answer to his question.

"I think there must be some sort of generator block further down the hill, beyond here; probably soundproofed, like so many generators are these days, which is why we can't hear it," Peter said.

At the end of the short corridor, there was a door to the left marked A and a door to the right marked B.

"Shall we try A?" Peter suggested. He opened the door, and they entered another unlit corridor. Duncan once again did the honours and the corridor lit up.

The corridor was a long carpeted walkway, with numbered doors both left and right. Peter tried the handle of the first door on the left and he walked into a very spartan but nevertheless clean bedsit, with a single bed, desk and chair and a built-in double wardrobe. It was all utility MOD-looking furniture, functional rather than luxurious. There was no sign that it was occupied, but the bed was made up with what appeared to be clean sheets and a duvet.

"Everyone gets their own room in the modern military," Peter said.

"Where are the washing facilities then?" Scotty piped up.

They exited the bedsit and walked down the long corridor. Duncan tried the odd door as they went. "Same basic accommodation rooms all the way along here. I reckon there must be well over 100 rooms in this block," he said.

"And probably the same in the other block, not counting the fact that I saw signs for an SBS mess, so I reckon there must be some sort of separate officers' accommodation too; that's what the military would do," Peter surmised.

At the end of the corridor, two doors swung open to reveal a shower block with free-standing urinals and cubicle toilets on one side and a bank of 10 individual shower cubicles. "Try the water, Duncan," Peter said.

Duncan went to the first cubicle in the line and swivelled the water faucet, and water started to cascade from the shower nozzle. After about a minute, Duncan said, "Well, that's scolding hot now! How is it working?"

"Did you see those large cannisters as we drove past the main office? That must be the gas supply for the heating and for the water. I am pretty sure there are another couple down by the armoury block and another one up by the helipad, near to the lighthouse," Peter replied.

They returned to the corridor and walked back to the connecting corridor where they had come in and opened B. After a brief search, they found it to be an identical block of similar size, in the same condition, just waiting to be occupied.

"So, this place looks like it could cope with in excess of 200 people living, sleeping and eating here for quite an extended period of time," Peter said.

"The thing is, we never see any large groups of military personnel here when we pass by on our way out to fish," Duncan said.

"Do you see any large navy ships ever moored near here?" Peter asked.

"We see plenty of ships out there between us and the Hebrides, but I never see them come into this area," Scotty added.

"Who is this place for?" Peter asked to no one in particular.

They returned to the path outside the block and decided to continue over the rise to see how much more of the facility there was.

As they walked, Peter pointed out another couple of the large gas cylinders he had mentioned. "These must keep the heating on and the water hot!"

At their vantage point, they could see a tarmacked path go down towards the other side of the island. The path took a sharp turn to the left about five metres short of the 40-foot-high cliffs, which formed the coastline on this side of the island. "Cliffs get higher a bit further along," Peter said as he pointed to a steep rise in the land right on the edge of the island. The path they were on skirted this high promontory and kept looping around behind the blocks they had just been in. Another similar block was behind the one they had explored, marked "Officers' Mess and Accommodation".

"There we are, chaps! I told you, the armed forces never disappoint with their predictability," Peter said.

"There's some other buildings a bit further down the path, right by the foot of that rocky crag," Scotty said.

"Aye! And then the path turns left again and disappears down the hill," Duncan added.

"If I have worked this out, if we were to keep walking down the hill, we would eventually come to the armoury and other buildings that I didn't look at last time I was here," Peter said.

They came to a square detached brick-built building, which looked older than the rest of the prefabricated base. On the door was marked, "PENS ONE AND TWO".

"Stationery cupboard?" Peter offered, smiling.

The others laughed as Peter turned the handle and the door opened outwards.

They went inside and immediately it was obvious that this was just a disguising shell because there was nothing inside the room. It was completely bare. Peter then saw that at the far side from the door were two large warehouse-style lift doors. He walked across the room to the lift on the left-hand side. "It reads here that these lifts can cope with up to 33 people or 2,500kg; that's a pretty large amount of equipment or people to move, bearing in mind there are two of them," Peter said.

"Do they work?" Scotty asked.

Peter pressed the button between the two lifts and the left-hand doors slid open, revealing a cavernous lit cabin with handrails at either side and closed door on the opposite side from them.

"What do you reckon? Suppose we've come this far?" Duncan observed.

"Yeah, we may as well keep going," Peter said.

The three of them stepped into the lift, Peter pressed the button indicating downward travel and the doors slowly slid shut.

"No music then," Peter nervously laughed and looked at the pensive faces of his two colleagues. After about 10 to 15 seconds of movement, they felt the lift stop and what had been the rear doors now opened behind them. The three of them turned together and looked out in awe at what they saw.

"Bloody hell," Peter started as they walked out of the lift into a well-lit cavern about 100 feet in height. Directly in front of them, beyond the two forklift trucks, was a water-filled subterranean dock. Peter reckoned it to be about 300–400 feet long, and the width must have been maybe 100–150 feet. Running along the edge of each side of the dock was a 20-foot-wide concrete corridor.

"Aye! Bloody hell indeed," Duncan answered. "What is this place?" he continued.

"Nobody mentioned James Bond yet?" Peter said. "You know, I reckon this is a submarine base, and judging by the size of this place, it could probably cope with two submarines at the same time. If you add that to the amount of accommodation we saw earlier, then this has got to be a secret submarine base," he added.

"Where's the entrance then?" Scotty asked. "I cannae see the sea."

"They must have to enter the base while submerged, which means there must be a really deep trench under the rock and a trench along the sea floor so they can enter here without being detected. We were in that lift for a good 15 seconds or so and it felt like we were descending fairly quickly, so we must be a fair way down," Peter said.

"They must have built all this right under our bloody noses," Duncan said. "I remember they said they were building a testing range and an underwater detection facility in the sea area to the east of Rona, and all the time they had been building this underground base."

"If you think about it, it makes sense to tell the public one thing while creating a more secret defensive facility," Peter said.

"So, once again, I have to ask; where is everyone?" Scotty challenged, sweeping his arms around the cavernous empty underground dock.

"Submarines are out at sea for months, sometimes years on end. From what I have always understood, they seldom surface and are seldom at liberty to give away their positions. They became our first-strike nuclear defensive strike weapons in the late 1960s," Peter stated. "Do you see all the railing systems and hoists, ready to equip them with probably replacement torpedoes and possibly the transfer of the nuclear cruise missiles they also carry," Peter added.

"Okay, well, I've seen enough for today. Can we head back to daylight, please?" a definitely nervous Duncan asked.

"Aye! I'm with the skipper," Scotty quickly added.

"Sounds fine with me," Peter answered and ushered them all back into the lift and pressed the ascend button.

They got out of the lift at the top and quickly made their way outside the building.

"Fresh air; that's definitely better," Scotty smiled.

The other two laughed as they carried on past the sign for the officers' mess, and as the path descended, they now came upon another larger, low prefabricated structure, marked "Gymnasium"!

"Well, they have to keep fit and occupied while they are here, I suppose!" Peter suggested.

The next brick-built structure was close to where Peter had discovered the armoury on his previous visits. "It looks to me like we have basically walked in a large circle; if we continue past here, we will come back to the armoury, and from there, a short walk back up the rise will return us to the main office and then we could walk back up to where I parked the Land Rover," Peter said.

"What are these unmarked buildings then?" Duncan asked, pointing at the two sturdy-looking brick-built structures with pretty substantial heavy metal doors securing them.

Peter scratched his head then remembered his large canvas bag of keys and squatted down on his haunches and started to rummage through the bag until he pulled out a large brass key with a label attached.

"Let's try this one, see if it fits?" Peter suggested.

"What does the label say?" Duncan asked.

"Explosives and Ordinance," Peter replied as he walked up to the metal door, which was, in effect, a set of double doors that could both be swung open if necessary.

Scotty whistled. "Fuckin' brand new! Explosives, is it now?" He laughed, as did the other two in response to his outburst.

Peter tried the key in the upper of the two locks and it turned. He then repeated this with the lower lock, which also turned. He grabbed the handle and pulled. Nothing happened.

"Duncan, Scotty, pretty heavy door, bit of a hand, please?" Peter asked.

The two fishermen immediately grabbed the handle and frame, and between the three of them, the door eventually gave, and they pulled it slowly open.

They all took a step back, then Peter walked through the door and found a switch to his left, which he clicked, and the large warehouse-sized room was flooded with light.

Immediately in front of them was a row of large obvious torpedoes, though to Peter they were so much larger than he had ever imagined. "They must be 25 feet long," he blurted out to the others, who also stood in open-mouthed awe at the size of the weapons.

Each torpedo was sat on a wheeled carriage. Peter pointed this out. "They must wheel them to the lifts and then down to where the submarines are moored to re-arm them," he deduced.

"Aye! There are about 30 of them in here," Duncan observed.

"Shall we keep going?" Peter asked.

"Yep, let's see what else is in here," Duncan said.

Beyond the torpedoes was another single door; Peter tried the handle and pulled it open. He entered and again found a light switch to bathe the area in light and reveal a smaller room, but this was a room with boxes and tables and racks of all sorts of different weaponry and accessories.

Peter picked up a block of something on the desk and held it out to the others. "C-4. This is plastic explosive," he said.

He then picked up a box marked "detonators" to show the others.

There was another cabinet filled with 9mm ammunition, shotgun cartridges and .300 sniper cartridges. Duncan and Scotty just stared as Peter picked up a small object and stated, "Fragmentation grenade; there is another box of smoke grenades, white phosphorus grenades and stun grenades."

Peter picked up another standard-issue black canvas bag from a small stack.

"May I suggest we perhaps avail ourselves of some more ammunition and a selection of grenades?" he asked.

"Are you sure we need all this stuff, Peter?" Scotty asked.

"Aye! We do," Duncan quickly came back, interrupting Scotty. "You saw the intent on those men at the barricade in Portree; they were armed and fired on us. I reckon Peter is right, we need to be prepared to defend ourselves and this stuff will do very nicely," he added.

So, they each filled a canvas holdall with a selection of ammunition and safely boxed grenades. As they were busy filling the holdalls, Peter spotted yet another door. He was in the process of thinking he might take a look when Duncan picked up a block of the C-4 explosive. "What about some of this then, Peter?" he asked.

"Erh! Yeah, take some of the blocks in one bag and put a container of the detonators in another," Peter replied.

"Guys, let's just have a peak in this other door before we go?" Peter suggested.

He opened the door to reveal yet another storeroom, filled with racks of what looked like machine guns, more pump-action shotguns, a store of what looked to Peter like a selection of anti-personnel mines, mortars and some other fearsome-looking bits of kit that he had never seen before.

"Well, you two, if we ever do need to defend our position on this island, might I suggest that with this and all the other equipment, stores, supplies and places to hide, this is our ideal fall-back location," Peter said.

"You're not kidding," Duncan answered, staring again at the array of weaponry neatly stored in front of them.

"Okay, let's leave with what we've got and head to the armoury and then probably back to the Land Rover; what do you reckon?"

"Sounds good, Pete. We've been gone a while and all this talk of fall-backs and defensive positions has got me spooked. I want to get back to Mary and the boy," Duncan said.

"Yeah, I'm with the skipper," Scotty added as they all left the main metal doors. Between them, they pushed it closed and Peter relocked it.

"Okay, the armoury is just this way, chaps," Peter said as he led them across the circle of tarmac, around which this selection of arms stores were arranged.

Once again, Peter unlocked the door and entered, followed by the other two. He opened the door leading to the storage room. "Okay, boys, let's get a Glock for you two, David, Mary, Becky and Sonia; so, six Glocks and an MP5 for you two, one for David, and three more, in fact, fuck it! Get six more MP5s too and then as much ammunition as the three of us can carry," Peter suggested. "Grab some more sets of body armour, enough for everyone, including Callum," Peter added as he picked up six belts and holsters for the Glocks.

"How we going to carry all this from here, Peter?" Duncan asked.

"Put it all into another couple of the canvas bags; they are just over by the ammunition cabinet there," Peter said, pointing to where the pile of canvas bags was stacked. "If we load up and carry it all outside, I'll walk up to the Land Rover just at the top of the hill and drive it back to you two, then we can load up and drive back to the boat," Peter said.

"Aye! Good plan," Duncan replied.

They quickly loaded all the guns and another stack of the boxes of 9mm ammunition and between them carried it all outside to the tarmacked roundabout.

"Give me five," Peter said as he jogged up the hill and back up to the front of the accommodation block and got behind the wheel of the Land Rover. He drove back down to the turnaround in front of the armoury and re-joined the others, and they piled the selection of black canvas holdalls into the back of the vehicle and all climbed in.

"I didn't show you the kitchens, mess halls and the rations store, but presumably we can return and do that another time?" Peter asked.

"Aye, for now let's get back to the boat and then back to our harbour, make sure everyone is okay," Duncan said, with Scotty nodding in agreement from the rear seat of the Land Rover.

There were some raised eyebrows when they spread out the additional arsenal of weapons on the kitchen table in the island manager's cottage. Everyone was present, except Margaret and Minnie.

"We took the liberty of getting a Glock and an MP5 for everyone," Peter said.

"And loads of ammo," Scotty added.

"I appreciate this is not to everyone's taste, but I am just thinking we need to be prepared for any intruders, and above all, I see this as stuff to defend ourselves with; I am not proposing that we undertake raiding parties," Peter said.

"Are you suggesting we wear one of these gun belts the whole time?" Becky asked.

"I am certainly suggesting it might be prudent, but it is just that, a suggestion," Peter said.

"I'm not sure I want to carry a gun the whole time or Callum to be exposed to an environment of everyone being armed," Mary added.

Helen had been listening and suddenly stood up. "Peter upset me at the start of our trip with his decision to bring a shotgun with us, but from what I have seen in these last five months, it would be naive to think we can stay here and not expect someone, at some stage, to become inquisitive and come and investigate us here on Rona. I expect if more people are scouring the country for food and other essentials, it's only a matter of time before someone decides, rather like us, to borrow a boat and come looking at what's over here. So, I respect your view and actually share your concern about firearms, but we have to be practical and ready to defend ourselves," she said.

The debate continued for some time around the kitchen table, with an agreement that everyone would take the weapons that had been brought for them, but it was up to each individual to decide whether to carry them or not. All Peter asked was that each weapon be kept cleaned and loaded and be in a position where it could be grabbed quickly if the need arose. Everyone agreed to this, and Peter and Duncan distributed the weapons and ammunition, and the meeting broke up.

Life on Rona began to take on a normality and routine. As the weeks passed, Becky was able to report progress on the field of crops that had been sown and it was clear for all to see the green shoots of new plants thrive in the warm late spring sunshine. Duncan and his colleagues took the trawler and sometimes the catamaran out into the channel and beyond to catch plentiful supplies of fish. Every so often, Margaret and Minnie would venture down from their more remote location to enjoy the company of the others, and as the weather became warmer, it became a pleasant walk for the pair of them. Peter would offer them a lift back up to their cottage in the Ranger, as the route back was mostly uphill. Callum had grown fond of Talisker the dog and was put in charge of taking him for walks, mainly down to the old crofter's cottage ruins and north as far as the cottage where Margaret and Minnie lived.

Peter asked Mary if he could take Callum with Helen and himself on a walk north up the spine of the island, beyond the limits of the footpath. Mary was unsure, but on seeing the pleading look on Callum's face, she eventually agreed. Peter also asked Becky and David if they could take Talisker too. It was a lovely day and Peter was reminded of why he had always loved this part of the world so much, the freshness of the air, the smell of the heather and the saltiness of the sea. They had spotted the odd seal and possibly a whale as they looked out over the sea on the eastern side of Rona.

"Stay close, Callum. The cliffs on the eastern side of the island are very steep and very high," Peter said, trying to be safety conscious but not overbearing.

"Aye! Alright, I'll not go near the edge," was the surly reply.

"I always knew you'd have been an overprotective dad," Helen laughed.

Peter shrugged and they walked up past the cottage occupied by Margaret and Minnie.

"Where do we go now?" said Callum at the end of the track.

"Well, let's climb up that hill to the north and see what we can see from the top. The ground looks fairly rocky, but if we watch our footing, we should be okay," Peter replied.

So, they all zigzagged their way to the top around some of the larger boulders, and after about 20 minutes, they reached the top. From the vantage point, they could see clearly across to Skye, away to their left, across to the deserted-looking mainland between a deep channel of water to their right. But ahead they could see a dip, filled with what appeared to be a small lake and then another slightly lower hill than the one they were on, and just visible on this hill was the whitewashed building that Peter knew to be the lighthouse at the edge of the military base.

"You see the lighthouse?" he said to Helen and Callum.

"Can we go, please, please," Callum excitedly asked.

"I don't see why not. It's not that far and we can check out the lake as we pass," Peter said.

They walked down the hill and along a shallow valley with a tiny little stream bubbling along it. Sure enough, there was a small lake of water surrounded by some trees. As they approached the trees, Peter spotted a path that skirted to the right-hand edge of the lake.

"Well, look at that, another path. I reckon this must lead to the lighthouse," he remarked.

They walked, now on the path, past some heather and bracken and other ferns and foliage that smelt very sweet in the sunshine. The undergrowth gave way to bare rock as they continued north, and suddenly, they were walking towards a small gate in the whitewashed walls of the lighthouse compound Peter had previously investigated.

"Can we go inside?" Callum asked, and with the exuberance of youth, he was through the gate and into the compound before Peter had chance to comment.

Peter and Helen followed, just in time to see Callum disappear through the door of the circular lighthouse, only to reappear on the guard railed platform around the light itself.

"Mind yourself up there, Callum; it's probably not been used for many years," Peter warned.

"It seems okay. It's a great view up here," Callum replied.

"You're in charge!" Helen said and smiled as Peter watched his authority disappear, undermined by the youngster's excitement.

Helen and Peter climbed up the spiral staircase inside the lighthouse tower and ducked their heads to climb through the iron and glass door onto the platform outside.

"Looks quite recently painted," Peter remarked, seeing the pristine black metal railings, devoid of rust and wear.

"You can pretty much make out the whole island from here," Helen said, pointing in the direction of where they had come. "It's only that first hill we climbed that obscures the view of the cottages," she added.

By now, Callum was staring at the complex of buildings on the northern side of the tower spread out before them.

"Is this the military base, Peter?" he asked.

"It is," Peter replied.

"Can we go and have a look, go on, please?" Callum pleaded.

"Not today, young man! I think I ought to ask your mother before we explore any further," Peter said.

"Arh! You know she'll say no," Callum moaned.

"Well, she's not here to say yes or no, and because of that, we will end our exploration here; perhaps to return when your mum has given her permission, okay?" Peter offered.

"I suppose so," Callum said as he sulked down the staircase and out into the compound, where Talisker was busy marking the territory as his own.

They went back out through the gate the way they had come in and walked slowly back to the lake and then up and over the hill to the first of the cottages and then on down the track to the manager's cottage.

They found Mary busy in the shop unpacking a box of tinned tomatoes and reunited Callum with his mother.

"We went all the way to the lighthouse, Mum! It was brilliant; the view and everything. I saw the base up there too. Can we go and explore up there, please, Mum, please?" Callum gabbled his questions quickly before Mary could get a word in.

"We'll see. We can talk to your father," Mary offered.

Callum slunk away, shoulders down. Talisker, tail wagging, followed him in the direction of the crop field.

"He knows his father will say no," Mary said. "Thanks for taking him and thanks for stopping him from exploring that base," she added.

"No problem, he's a good lad," Peter said.

"He has his moments, growing up too fast for my liking," Mary said.

"Well, he's a credit to you, Mary," Helen replied.

They bid Mary farewell and walked down to the crop field, to find Becky, Sonia and David busy watering the field as best they could with a selection of buckets and rusty watering cans.

"You want a hand?" Peter asked.

"No, we're fine, thank you. Duncan looks like he's back; he might need some help?" Sonia suggested as they watched the catamaran returning.

Helen and Peter waved and headed down to the jetty and waited for the boat to come alongside. Scotty threw a line, which Peter caught and secured to the mooring. Scotty quickly threw a second line, which Helen caught and secured too.

"Thanks. How are you doing?" Scotty asked after the engines stopped.

"We're good. How was your trip? Catch much today?" Peter asked.

"We got some lobsters, crabs, along with a selection of other fish and a couple of excellent salmon," Scotty said as Duncan came out of the cabin and greeted them.

"Do you want a hand with the catch?" Helen asked.

"Aye, that would be great," Duncan said.

Between the four of them, they hauled the plastic boxes of fish off the boat and onto the dock and loaded them onto the trailer at the back of the Ranger.

They all jumped in, and Duncan drove back up to the rear of the manager's cottage.

Inside one of the outhouses, Duncan had set up a generator to power a large chest freezer, which is where he stored his catches. He had also found an old dirty aquarium, which he had cleaned and filled with salt water; this is where he put the lobsters and other shell fish, keeping them alive so they stayed fresher for longer.

Mary walked in as they were just cleaning the now empty plastic trays and boxes.

"Would everyone like tea and a slice of freshly made fruit cake?" she asked.

"Oh, that's the ticket, Mary. That would be lovely," Peter replied.

"Helen, would you mind nipping down to the field and asking the others to join us, please," Mary asked.

"Not at all. I don't think they will need much persuading," Helen replied, and she walked back down the track to the crop field and invited the others to come up to the manager's cottage and join everyone.

"Good day?" Peter asked Duncan.

"Aye! Bloody good day, what about you?" Duncan asked.

"We walked all the way up to the lighthouse with Callum," Helen said.

"Oh, I bet he loved that," Duncan replied.

"More interestingly, it was only about a mile and a half to get up there and the going was fairly easy underfoot," Peter said. "If we ever need to get out of here in a hurry, we could make it on foot up to the base quite easily," he quietly whispered to Duncan.

Duncan looked seriously at Peter and nodded.

Then returning to the mood of the table; "Now, where's this cake you've been talking about, my love," he said.

As they all sat down to eat the cake and enjoy the tea, Peter stood up.

"I've been thinking that we need to consider our position here. We are still vulnerable to attack from the sea and possibly from the land too. There are not enough of us to always be patrolling the areas that need defending," he said.

"What do you think we can do then?" Becky asked.

"It's a question of knowing what to do if we do get attacked or we have uninvited guests. So far, between us, there have not been any instances of illness or disease; a lot of that has got to do with the remoteness of the area and the fact we have not been in contact with anyone new for some time. We have, in effect, formed what the government used to call a 'bubble'."

"Aye, makes sense, and any new people may not only pose a threat of violence, but if they came in a more peaceful fashion, then they would still pose a health threat to us," Duncan stated.

"Basically, yes. I suppose if we were to gather any additional people to our group, we would have to quarantine them somewhere for a couple of weeks. Do people think that's fair?" Peter asked.

"It's the most sensible and obvious thing to do. Do we all agree with Peter's suggestion then?" Duncan asked as he looked around the table, getting nods of approval from all those there.

"The other thing that's been on my mind..." Peter went on.

"Sometimes you think too much, dear," Helen interrupted.

"No, it's just a safety thing, as we are often out and about in different areas and on different parts of the island while we go about our daily chores and work,"

Peter defended his thought processes. "As some of you know, Helen and I took Callum on a walk north, beyond the end of the track where Margaret and Minnie's cottage is," Peter went on. "The walk was not too hard, and it was only about a mile and a half to reach the lighthouse, which is at the very southern edge of the military facility. If, God forbid, we do get intruders or other people come, who are clearly hostile to our situation, we need to have an emergency-type protocol in place," Peter said.

"A what?" Scotty replied.

"What we should do in the event of an attack; maybe a signal of some kind, of something dangerous or hostile that makes us follow a course of action, which I am going to discuss now," Peter explained.

"What did you have in mind?" Helen asked.

"Okay, well, correct me if I am wrong, but you probably have a flare gun on your trawler, Duncan?"

"Erh! Yeah, we have flares for emergencies!" Duncan answered.

"Well, there are flares on the catamaran too. What I am suggesting is that at any sign of any issues that any one of us sees, you get to either of the boats and fire the flares, which would warn the rest of us, and from there, we take a course of action that we can plan out now."

"And if we are not anywhere near the boats, and no one else is, what then?" Sonia spoke.

"Yeah, appreciate that. You all now have a set of body armour. When I first joined the police, we used to carry a whistle on a chain in our tunics; it was part of your appointments. Sorry! The things you had to carry and show to the duty officer at the start of your shift. Anyway, the armour has a whistle attached to it. What if everyone takes the whistle off their armour and keeps it on themselves at all times, perhaps on a rope or cord around their necks. At the first sign of trouble, blow three short bursts on the whistle as loud as you can to alert the rest of us and then we implement our protocol," Peter said.

"I am with you; this all sounds okay. So, what is our protocol then, Peter?" Duncan asked. "And sit down, man. You're making us all nervous," Duncan went on, to the amusement of the table.

"Sorry, he gets carried away. Sit down, love!" Helen said.

"Sorry, everyone," Peter smiled as he sat down. "Okay, I have an idea about the base at the north end of the island," he said.

"Aye! Go on, lad," Duncan encouraged.

"Well, firstly everyone needs to have what the military and emergency services would call a grab bag.

You put a selection of essential clothing, equipment, including our weapons and ammunition, in an easily carried rucksack or holdall; and all the holdalls we have been using have straps and harnesses, so they can be carried on your backs like rucksacks. We put all our essential emergency gear in a bag each and we keep that bag somewhere safe, and then at the first sign of trouble, or a signal flare, or on hearing the three blasts on a whistle, we can, as the name suggests, grab our bag and head to our fall-back position," Peter said.

"With you so far. So, what is our fall-back position, as you put it?" Scotty spoke for the first time.

"If we can make it to the catamaran, then we all get on the boat and head north and use the base up there, which is probably more defendable, and we certainly have supplies there," Peter replied.

"And if we can't get to the boats?" David asked.

"Which is actually pretty likely, as I would expect something to come from the sea!" Duncan added.

"Agreed. If we can get to the boats, then we use them to escape, even if only a few of us can get to them. If we can't get to the boats or see that they have already gone, then head up the track to Margaret and Minnie's cottage, and from there, we help them walk over land, the mile and a half to the base."

"How would we know when to move the boats?" Scotty asked.

"If you and Sonia were to get to them and no one else was with you, then I would suggest that you go and the rest of us will regroup at Margaret and Minnie's cottage and start our trek up to the base, which is where you would head for in the boat."

"Depending on where we are and at what time this happens, I reckon the most likely people to be able to get to the boats would be Becky and me," David said.

"Agreed, David. I can only suggest that if Becky, Talisker and yourself get to the boat, then get going and the rest of us will make our way over land. We can try and use the Ranger if we are able to, but it's most likely to be on foot," Peter answered.

"Thank you, Peter. I think that all makes sense. Now, is everyone happy with what we should do?" Duncan said.

"Do you really think this could happen? Do you really think people will come across here and attack us, Peter?" Becky quietly asked.

"Most likely not. We will be able to continue our existence here for the months ahead, possibly head back to Portree to see what's happening there and maybe get an idea of what's happening in the rest of the country and the world. It just seemed to me that we needed to have a contingency plan in place for the worst set of circumstances I could think of... sorry!" Peter replied.

"Ever the optimist, my husband," Helen broke in, trying to lift the mood around the table.

"We have not seen any boats from anywhere in the channel for the past few months. It appears that the town invaders may have moved on, but we now have some sort of idea what to do if the worst should happen," Peter came back.

"So, let's move on and thank Mary for this wonderful cake," Duncan said, and he stood, saluting his wife with his teacup.

The summer was upon them, and the days were long and, on the whole, dry. The crop field looked abundant with varieties of growing vegetables. Duncan now took Callum fishing with Scotty or David and himself, teaching him where the best areas were for the best returns of fish and shellfish. Peter had made another trip with Scotty to the military base, and they had raided the rations store and brought back supplies to augment their dwindling stocks in the "shop". Mary and Sonia were both baking fresh bread and rolls, now using the flour to be found in the rations that Peter and Scotty had returned with.

Peter was quietly heartened to see everyone was wearing a whistle around their necks and were all more often than not wearing a Glock attached to a belt around their waists.

He didn't press anyone on the issue of having assembled grab bags, trusting that such things had been done. He didn't feel it right to labour the point.

He found himself walking down to the entrance to the harbour on the southern headland, right down to the narrow entrance channel. This gave him the best view across the stretch of water between the islands. He would spend half an hour or so staring at the opposite coastline through the powerful binoculars. Sometimes he would look through the telescopic sight of the sniper rifle and scan the channel, up and down.

There had been no sign of life, no movement of vehicles, no instances of smoke for over two months. They had brought the others to Rona just over three months ago and the group had gelled and were working as a well-drilled team, for the benefit of all.

They would gather as the entire group once a week up at Margaret and Minnie's cottage, to enjoy a meal and some beer, wine and a little of the new spirit from the casks Peter had liberated from the Raasay distillery. Peter and Helen would also visit them a couple of times a week from their closer cottage. Duncan enjoyed having his fishing buddies and their wives come and eat with them regularly. They had even all been invited down to the cottage that Becky and David lived in and ate a couple of lovely meals, which Mary enjoyed as a night off from her own cooking. They had all become good friends. Peter and Helen knew they were always going to be outsiders, but they had enjoyed plenty of evenings with the others at the various cottages they had all now inhabited.

The one thing that they couldn't do was know what was going on elsewhere. It didn't seem to matter initially, but as time passed, it was clear that the questions about the country's situation and the world as a whole would not go away. At the latest gathering at Margaret and Minnie's cottage, while they were all sat in a large circle around a large warm fire, Duncan had pulled out a bottle of Talisker whisky and charged everyone's glass, then he sat down and raised a toast to them all, for their friendship and hard work together. Then he turned to Peter.

"You know, we need to find out what's going on. We are doing fine here; Becky and David have got us a fantastic field of crops, almost ready to be harvested, and that should see us well on the way to getting through the autumn and winter ahead. We can fish these waters, as long as I have fuel for the boats, and even when that runs out, we can still catch fish. You said you thought there were deer on the island, and we have the means to kill them for additional food, but we need to know if this is to go on beyond the next few seasons and if this is now life for the foreseeable future," Duncan stated.

"I agree with everything you say, yes, we need to know what's going on. That is going to mean a journey across to Skye and possibly further afield if we can't get enough information there," Peter replied.

"Can we take a boat back to Portree, just take a look from out on the water, and if all looks quiet, then actually go ashore there?" Mary asked.

Duncan leaned forward. "Mary is right, Portree is our home; it's where we live and have lived all of our lives. We need to see what's happening there."

"I completely understand and agree with you. Who should go then?" Peter asked.

"How about I take the trawler with Mary, David and Sonia. We can ask Margaret and Minnie to give us a list of anything they want from their B&B, which we can pick up. The four of us can check each of our houses and also see if there is anything worth collecting or, for that matter, anyone in town we can help," Duncan suggested.

"Good plan, you should take some guns to defend yourselves, and you are leaving enough of us here to watch this place. Yeah, I think that's a sensible suggestion. Obviously, any radio or TV signal over there will give us a steer on what's happening elsewhere," Peter replied.

So that next morning, with the exception of Margaret and Minnie, who had produced a detailed list of clothing and other goodies that had been in their B&B for the others to collect, they all walked down to the jetty. Duncan got on board and started the engines while Mary and David took care of the mooring lines. They then jumped on board with Sonia, and they all waved back at the figures on the jetty as they headed out into the sea channel. Peter turned to Scotty, "Would you be okay to keep watch here on the jetty? I'll walk round to the headland with the sniper rifle and Callum and the girls can go back up to the manager's cottage."

"Aye! Sounds good," Scotty replied.

"I have my whistle and I've taken a flare from the catamaran," Peter said as he walked away from Scotty, catching up with Helen, Becky and Callum.

"You look nervous, love," Helen said.

"I suppose it's a mixture of nerves and the anticipation of knowing whether or not we can possibly return to normal or whether we have to stay here for longer than we first thought," Peter replied.

As they got back to the manager's cottage, Peter took his leave and continued up the track and then skirted around to the headland and walked along the ridge line to the place that had become his observation spot. From here, he could see the trawler as it grew smaller in the sea channel. He could also make out the figure of Scotty, who had found a deck chair and was sat facing the harbour on the concrete jetty. Peter waved, but clearly Scotty did not notice. *Let's hope he sees a flare or hears a whistle!* Peter thought.

"Peter looked a bit spooked this morning," Mary said to Duncan as they cruised down the channel, heading towards Portree in the trawler.

"Aye! Well, he'll be nervous alright. I was surprised he didn't come with us," Duncan replied.

"I reckon he wanted to come but could see it made sense for a group to stay and look after the place on Rona," David replied as he popped his head into the small cabin.

"I really hope he's wrong about the situation and that we can move back home now," Sonia said.

"Remember what he said, put your body armour on and have those guns ready if we need them," Duncan said.

He slowed the engine as they came into the inlet, at the end of which lay the town of Portree.

"David, do you see anyone?" Duncan asked.

"Not a soul," David replied as he walked out beyond the small cabin to the front of the boat, along with Sonia.

"Okay, let's get to the dock and then see what's what," Duncan said.

He very slowly eased the trawler alongside the quayside wall and David, Mary and Sonia got the boat moored and they all gathered on the quayside.

"Is everyone's gun loaded and cocked, as Peter showed us?" Duncan asked, getting three positive nods in reply. "Okay, let's go. Let's just take it slowly, and if we see anyone, we better think about face masks."

"Okay, we're right behind you," David said as they all walked in a line across the road down Quay Street towards the town of Portree.

Mary tried the door of Margaret's B&B and found it unlocked.

"We'll check it out on our way back, okay," Duncan said.

The others nodded as they continued past the line of buildings and up the slight hill to come onto the main through road and up to the shell of what had been their local Co-op, now burned to the ground.

"There's a lot of smashed windows. Virtually every shop and building are completely ransacked," Sonia said as they took in the wreckage of their hometown. They all kept together as they walked past the Co-op, turned left at the burned shell of the Bosville Hotel and walked up Stormy Hill and into their street, York Drive.

"Okay, at least these look to be in one piece," Duncan said as he surveyed the line of terraced houses, where the three of them all lived. "Get what you need and what you can carry on your backs, but be quick; 10 minutes tops, okay?" he said.

David and Sonia ran off down the street towards their houses while Duncan and Mary went inside their home, which looked to have been left as they had last seen it.

"Well, that's something, I suppose," Mary said.

Mary raced upstairs, grabbed a large holdall and began stuffing clothes into it while Duncan went into his lounge and to a bureau behind the table and opened the top draw. He found a selection of sea charts and rolled them up, found a plastic band to secure them and stuffed them into his jacket. He picked up a couple of torches and spare batteries and put them in the rucksack he had brought. Mary came downstairs and was in the process of opening the front door when there was an almighty blast very close. Mary instinctively ducked as Duncan came through to the hall, grabbed her and pulled her back through to the kitchen.

"Okay, check your body armour and take the safety off the gun to single shot, like Peter showed us," Duncan instructed.

They were crouching on the floor in their kitchen as their front window shattered with another blast from what must have been a shotgun.

"Right, out through the back garden, see if we can link up with David and Sonia. Get to the end of the garden and hide behind the shed. Ready? GO!"

Duncan pushed Mary out into their garden, and they ran down to the small wooden shed and crouched behind it, catching their breath.

Sonia took the full force of the shotgun blast in the chest. The force of the impact literally blew her back through the front door and into the hall. She knew nothing about it; she was dead before she hit the hall carpet at the foot of the stairs. She had been waiting for David to gather his stuff from upstairs before they did the same at her house, which was only next door but one. David heard the blast and instinctively ducked, then he peered down the stairs, to be confronted with the sight of

Sonia lying at the bottom of the stairs in a pool of her own blood. He sat there stunned for a few seconds, then he focused himself, picked up his MP5 and clicked the safety to single shot. He was just at the top of the stairs when he heard another blast and a window breaking further up at Duncan's end of the street.

He climbed out of the back-bedroom window onto a small uPVC conservatory roof. As he carefully crouched down, he heard "Dave!" from another garden.

"There he is on the roof of his conservatory." Duncan had spotted David climbing out of the window at the rear of his house. "Dave!" he called and saw David look up. Duncan waved at him from his position. "He's seen us," Duncan said as he watched David climb off the conservatory roof and then over the four gardens between them until he joined them at the shed.

"Where's Sonia?" Mary asked.

"She's dead. She took a shotgun blast waiting for me at the door of my house," David shakily answered.

"Oh my God," Mary exclaimed. "Are you sure?" she added.

"Mary, I'm sorry, she was gone. I've never seen so much blood. She was in bits, she…"

'Alright mate!' Duncan interrupted sympathetically, 'Let's get out of here'

They managed to get over the back fence as yet another shotgun blast echoed around them.

"When we get back on the road, run across to Martin Crescent and wait there, but keep hidden," Duncan ordered. "Are you all ready?"

David and Mary nodded, and following Duncan, the three of them ran about 10 metres across to Martin Crescent. Duncan peered back down the hill just as four darkly clad figures appeared at the end of York Drive. They were all males and Duncan could see that two of them had shotguns. Duncan aimed his MP5 and fired four or five shots towards the group. He then stood and shouted "Run!" to the others.

They ran down Martin Crescent and, at the corner, disappeared through some trees, just beyond the fire station and down a hidden track onto the main A855, where the Scorrybreac Road led down to the Cuillin Hotel. As they looked down the road towards the town, another group of maybe four to five people were walking up the road by a line of buildings.

"Right, we're ahead of them, but they have closed us out of the town. We can't get back to the quayside," Duncan said.

"Aren't there some boats on the beach near to the hotel, maybe we get on one of them?" David suggested.

"Worth a go! You two get going and find a boat. I'm going to slow them down a bit," Duncan said.

"Duncan, come on, let's all go," Mary pleaded.

"No, Mary, we need a bit more time to get out into a boat. Just go, please," Duncan replied.

"Okay, come on, Mary." David picked her up and they ran down Scorrybreac Road.

Duncan took up a defensive position by some buildings behind a low brick wall and began firing.

The group scattered, three of them running back around the corner towards the Bosville Hotel. Two shotgun blasts were returned, but clearly Duncan was out of their range. He was just changing magazines on his MP5 when he heard a quiet voice.

"Is that you, Duncan?" a familiar voice said from inside the building he was sheltering by.

"Aye! Who's that?" Duncan replied.

"Glen Ritchie, you daft twat," came the reply.

"Sergeant Ritchie, well, you pick your moments," Duncan stated.

"I'm coming out," came the reply.

A well-built male in his early 50s appeared carrying a large shotgun.

"Down to my last 10 shells. Do you have a way out of here? I've been one step ahead of these muppets for about a week now, since I got back from the mainland," Glen Ritchie said.

"Come on, let's get down to the beach by the hotel." Duncan stood, and they walked quickly down the hill towards the beach.

"Here's one that will do; engine looks okay," David said as they got to a small fishing boat on a trailer.

"Where is he?" Mary fretted as she scanned the way they had come, looking for Duncan to appear.

Suddenly, Duncan appeared, along with a larger male, who Mary recognised as their local police officer, Sergeant Ritchie.

"Looks like he's found a friend," Mary commented as the two of them walked out onto the beach.

"Hello, Glen, how very nice to see you." Mary hugged the portly officer and he smiled.

"Mary, good to see you," he replied.

"Duncan, this one's okay. Let's get it in the water," David said.

Between them, they manoeuvred the boat into the water, then floated it off the trailer and turned it so it was facing out to sea in the shallow water. They all jumped on board.

The engine coughed into life on the third pull of the cord. Just as they began to move, a large group of maybe 10–15 people burst onto the beach, running towards them.

"David, you steer. Mary, give your MP5 to Glen. Glen, let's keep this lot back," Duncan instructed.

"Keep your heads down," Mary shouted above the noise of the engine.

Duncan and Glen began to fire at the crowd as they moved into deeper water. Duncan noticed that they had hit at least three people before they stopped firing and considered themselves to be out of range. As they pulled further out into the bay and the danger receded, Duncan and Glen sat back down in the back of the boat, oblivious to the four to six inches of water sloshing about them at the bottom of the boat.

"David, slow the engine. At this speed, you will swamp us, and judging by the water in the bottom, I'm not sure of the soundness of this hull anyway," Duncan said.

"Is anyone hurt?" Mary asked as David slowed the boat to a slow cruise further into the bay.

No one spoke; they all looked at the water slewing about in the bottom of the boat and then back to the shore, where the small group on the beach looked to be tending those injured by the shooting from Duncan and Glen.

"Glen, how long have you been hiding in town?" David asked as Glen put the MP5 on the seat beside him.

"I only got back from the mainland five days ago. They had seconded us to deal with serious disorder in the towns, where people had been literally fighting each other over the scraps of food they could find in the shops," Glen said.

"Is it bad then?" Duncan asked.

"Aye, lad, we had no chance to stop the masses. Several groups formed and got organised and had armed themselves with baseball bats, golf clubs and one or two shotguns; that's apart from the usual collection of knives, screwdrivers and anything else that they could lay their hands on," Glen added.

"I thought the army was on the streets to keep control of things?" Duncan asked.

"We thought so too, and at the start, it was clear that they were deployed to some of the bigger towns and cities to the south, but like us, there are simply not enough of them to keep order everywhere. From reports we received, the military have fortified the towns and called for the public to shelter within the now barricaded city boundaries, leaving the more rural areas to be fought over by gangs of people who are desperately seeking food for themselves. There are thousands of dead up and down the country. We are pretty much cut off up here; the closest city barricaded is Glasgow," Glen continued.

"Without support, we began to be openly attacked around Inverness and I made the decision for the three lads and me that come from the Western Isles that we should return to our islands to look after our own people. We all split up and I made it back here, only to find a group from the mainland had already seized control of our town. It took me two days to get through the town, going from house to house, mostly at night, until I got down to the apartment where I saw you fine people upsetting the visitors," Glen said.

"How many of them are there?" Duncan asked.

"I don't really know. From what I observed, they have taken over the Royal Hotel. I moved inland to avoid them, and like you, I got down to the shore by way of the path behind the fire station. I saw probably 40 to 50 people; some of those may have been locals."

"Locals?" Mary exclaimed.

"Aye! There are people that are still alive in the town who didn't leave or seek shelter in the hills or other towns and villages. I think some are working with the invaders. Whether by choice or not, I don't know," Glen said.

Suddenly, the talk was interrupted as a large, blue-hulled catamaran swung around the headland and into the entrance of the bay. Glen instinctively reached for the MP5 on the seat next to him. Duncan gently grabbed his arm and lowered the gun.

"Easy, Glen. I reckon Peter must have heard all the shooting and come for a bit of a look!" Duncan said.

16

Peter had found a rock at just the right height for him to be able to sit comfortably, place the sniper rifle next to him and survey the channel in front and mainly to the south of his position. His attention had been drawn to some small puffs of smoke, very quickly followed by the unmistakable report from a gun. Peter was up on his feet, running back along the headland ridge, towards the harbour. When he got down to the harbour jetty, he could see that Scotty, Becky, Callum and Helen were all busy with the mooring lines of the catamaran.

"You heard the shots too?" Peter asked.

"Yeah, we were just going to go and investigate. Who should go, do you think?" Helen asked Peter.

"I'm not sure we should all go. Scotty, would you mind keeping things secure here while I take Becky with me to go and look?" Peter suggested.

"Why Becky?" Scotty asked.

"I need you here, Scotty. Helen, you can look after Callum and help Scotty. Becky has the local knowledge I need if we have to go into Portree," Peter explained.

"Makes sense, Peter. Right, you better get going." Helen could see the logic and was keen that someone should go and see what was happening. She literally pushed Peter and Becky onto the boat and started to undo the mooring lines. Scotty jumped in to help.

"We will be as quick as we can. Just stay here and be alert," Peter shouted as the catamaran pulled away from the jetty.

Peter gunned the engine once they cleared the narrow entrance of the harbour, and they began to bounce along the surface of the water as they headed south across the channel.

Becky stood next to Peter in the cabin, nervously biting her fingernails.

"Becky, would you mind just checking in the forward cabin to see if the first aid kit is in there and just see what we have," Peter asked as he steered the boat closer to the headland, around which sat the Portree town harbour.

"Okay," Becky replied and lowered herself into the smaller cabin and found an orange plastic box with a green first aid sticker on it affixed to the cabin wall. She pulled it from its bracket and returned to Peter in the main cabin.

"Open it up. Let's see what we have," Peter said.

Becky opened the box to reveal the usual collection of bandages, calico slings, plasters, safety pins and eye wash. There were a couple of burn cloths and some antiseptic cream and micropore tape, Peter noticed.

"Well, it will have to do," Peter stated.

As they pulled around the headland, Peter had been careful to take the turn wide to keep well clear of the headland itself.

"Peter, there!" Becky pointed at a small boat low in the water that appeared to be coming slowly out of the bay.

Peter spotted the boat, slowed the catamaran to idle and picked up the binoculars from the control panel, where he had put them when he had got on board.

After a quick check, he put the binoculars down. "I can see David at the controls and Mary just behind him, and there are a couple of others in the back, but they must be sat on the floor, because I can only just see them," Peter advised. "Okay, Becky, you go outside and be ready to grab a line from them if they have one as I pull alongside them," Peter ordered.

Peter slowly manoeuvred the catamaran alongside the smaller boat, and he watched as Becky caught a line thrown by Mary. She then tied the line off before first assisting Mary, then Duncan, a quite fat older man and finally David onto the back deck of the catamaran.

Duncan untied the line and was about to throw it when Peter shouted, "Tie it to the back just in case."

"Aye! Okay, Peter. Have to say, we are pretty pleased to see you, thanks," Duncan replied, tying the small boat to the rear of the catamaran.

"Everyone get inside the cabin and get warm," Peter suggested as he returned to the controls, opened the engine up and turned and steered the boat out of the bay and back into the channel.

Becky and David were busy reuniting with a fairly lengthy hug and a kiss as the group came into the cabin and sat on the cushion-covered seats.

"Peter, this is Sergeant Glen Ritchie, our local town police," Duncan explained, introducing Glen to Peter.

"Nice to meet you, Glen," Peter replied, taking a step back and offering his hand to the new addition to their group.

"Aye! You too, Peter. Thanks for the rescue," Glen replied, gripping Peter's hand firmly.

"Where's Sonia?" Peter asked innocently.

There was a moment's silence, then David removed Becky's arm from around him and spoke.

"She was shot and killed in our house. I'd gone upstairs to get some stuff for us, and she was waiting at mine before we did the same at hers. She must have taken the full force of a shotgun round to her chest," David quietly spoke.

"Oh my God!" Becky burst into tears and Mary went over to comfort her.

"Jesus, how did the rest of you make it out?" Peter asked as he cleared the headland and moved the boat out into the middle of the channel.

"We got out through the back of our houses after we heard the shot, then we were chased down to the shoreline. I met Sergeant Ritchie as we stopped to work out how to escape. Lucky for us, David found that boat and we got into deeper water just as the group running the town appeared and started firing at us too," Duncan said.

"God, you were lucky; you could have all been killed. How many of them were there?" Peter asked.

"I was telling Duncan that I reckon there are maybe over 50 people in our town now, mostly from the mainland, but I am sure that one or two locals are with them; it's whether they are with them willingly or by force," Glen answered.

"Scotty will be devastated. Him and Sonia have been together since school. Who's going to tell him?" Mary asked.

"I'll tell him," Duncan said.

They had given Scotty a couple of sleeping tablets, found in the large bag of supplies that Peter and Helen had taken from the pharmacy in Portree all those months ago. Mary gently put him into bed, closed the door and came back downstairs.

"Well, he's certainly calmer; that will hopefully be the effects of the sleeping pills. We just need to keep a very close eye on him over the next few hours and days," Mary said as she sat down at the kitchen table next to everyone else.

"So, is this everyone?" Glen asked as he sipped a fresh cup of coffee.

"All except our two ladies, Margaret and Minnie, who stay up at the second guest cottage at the furthest extent of the road," Peter said.

"You know them, Glen; the sisters who have run the B&B on Quay Street for as long as I can remember," Duncan added.

"Aye! I know them. How are they coping?" Glen asked.

"They keep themselves to themselves up at their cottage. We use the large garden up in front of the cottage to have our weekly group meals and meetings," Duncan said.

"I felt it was a safer place for them and they have got probably the best view from their cottage of any of us," Peter went on. "So, is someone going to tell me what happened?" he quietly asked.

"Who do you want to hear from first?" Duncan asked. "Obviously, Glen has more of an idea of the bigger picture around the country, then I can explain what happened when we got to town earlier today."

"Glen, what can you tell us about where things are at? Did you get an idea of what is happening beyond us here in the Highlands?" Peter asked, turning to Glen.

"Well, I can tell you what I know and what I heard from colleagues from different parts of Scotland and then about how I got back here and came to be sheltering in that apartment block, when I saw Duncan and the others come running down the hill behind the fire station," Glen said.

"That sounds like a good idea," Peter replied.

Glen proceeded to tell his story. He explained how he had been called away from Skye to support officers in Inverness in controlling the mass distribution of the food boxes to households and trying to enforce the 24-hour curfew when it had been implemented. Initially it sounded like everything had been conducted as they would have expected. It then became clear from local police channel radio reports that armed groups were hijacking the food distribution lorries and the military were engaged in armed battles with some of these groups, who had formed near the bigger cities, where it was becoming impossible to adequately supply the sheer numbers of people needing food. It became clear that central government had ceased to issue instructions and the decision making was being taken at a more local level. Most of the cities had created safe zones within their boundaries and many people were flocking to them to escape the lawlessness in the other parts of the country.

Glen went on to describe how the illness had mutated and it was clear that it was pretty much killing everyone over a certain age with the so-called underlying health conditions. Because of the breakdown of the normal social structure, bodies were being left where they died. The ambulances and hospitals had been overrun and appropriated by the lawless groups who had formed their own armies, intent on their own survival. Glen detailed the experiences of wanton destruction of property and people he had witnessed as he had made the decision to try and return to his own home on Skye. Most communications were gone; there were no mobile phone signals available, the majority of the electricity generating stations had ceased to operate. Most people were without power, heat, light and essentially food and were starving to death. Those with a will had taken the initiative and were just taking supplies from wherever they could.

It was clear that Glen's journey back to Skye from across the mainland of Scotland had been extremely hazardous, involving changing out of his uniform, switching to an unmarked vehicle when he was able to and then pretty much walking off-road from when he got to the island of Skye.

Peter had listened with awe and admiration for the large police sergeant as he told his story of the breakdown of the society they all knew, and the lengths people were now clearly going to in an effort to survive. "So how did you get past the group who have taken over the town?" Peter interrupted.

"Well, I had all my camping gear, which I had kept with me as I changed cars and was returning from the mainland. I hid the car near to the Sligachan Hotel and took what I thought I would need, including a shotgun that I knew the hotel owner kept hidden in the office," Glen explained.

"How long did it take you to get to town?" Duncan asked.

"Aye! Well, all the while, I was sticking to the forests and was keeping an ear out for any sounds of activity. I know the paths and where the bothies are, so I kept hidden in the forests all the way up to the Glen Varragill Forest, where I camped for a few nights, as I could hear voices and the odd gunshot coming from Portree. I eventually, under cover of darkness, walked along the power lines up behind the town. Finding the college building deserted, I stayed there for a couple of nights, then moved on to the industrial estate, finding the odd bar of chocolate and packet of biscuits. I suppose I just skirted the town; I was making for the fire station, to see if I could find anyone local or anything useful. If you lot hadn't come along, I was essentially going to make for the retirement cottage I have been building on the slopes of Ben Volovaig, right up at the northernmost extent of Skye," Glen finished.

"Did you see any of our friends in town?" Duncan asked.

"The place looks pretty much empty. I thought I might have seen Tom, who works in the bakery, talking with some of the group," Glen replied.

"What about their guns; did you see anything other than shotguns?" Peter asked.

"Maybe one or two hunting rifles and some older rifles and pistols; the sort of thing that used to circulate among criminals on the mainland," Glen answered. "A lot of stuff probably dates back to World War Two," he added.

"Duncan, David and Mary, maybe you can tell us what happened, if that's okay?" Peter gently asked the others.

"Well, it all looked pretty abandoned when we moored and walked up Quay Street, but they must have seen us and been hiding," Duncan started.

"Aye, waiting for us to split up. They must have seen us go into our houses before attacking," David interrupted.

"Poor Sonia; she had been waiting for me to gather some things before we did the same at hers. She had taken off her body armour by the front door when we got into my house; she said it was uncomfortable and dug into her," David said.

Mary was weeping as she heard what had happened. Duncan put his arm around her and hugged her as they sat around the kitchen table.

Duncan looked up from his wife and spoke. "The rest of us heard the shot and Mary and I got out through the back of our house. We saw David at the rear of his and he joined us. It was then a case of climbing over the back fence and running across to the fire station. We saw the armed men walk out of our street; they must have had another group moving up the coast road, but obviously not enough to trap us. I suppose because we knew of the small path through the woods behind the fire station, we kept ahead of them. We could then escape down towards the hotel, where David managed to get that small boat going. It was really close."

"I heard more firing; did you shoot any of them?" Peter asked.

"I fired at them as we ran down Martin Crescent, which maybe slowed them down. Then Glen and I fired at them as we moved off down Scorrybreac Road. Finally, we returned fire again, as they appeared on the beach while we moved out into the bay," Duncan said.

"Did you see if you hit or injured any of them?" Peter asked.

"I reckon we hit three of them on the beach," Glen said.

"What do we do now, love?" Helen asked quietly.

"Yes, what do we do now? Are we safe here? Do you think they will come looking for us?" Mary fired off a succession of questions at Peter and anyone around the table.

"I really don't know is the honest answer. If they have food and shelter and can survive where they are, then what reason would they have to bother us, but they may not know what is over here, think that we have some massive store of food and come looking to take it from us. Plus, we did either injure or kill three of their own people," Peter replied. "Glen, what do you think? Can we expect any help from elsewhere? Is this situation going to at some stage return us to the type of society we had prior to the outbreak of this illness?" Peter said.

Glen looked up from the table and at the small group gathered around him.

"It gives me no pleasure to say this, but as far as our government and society as we used to know goes, it's gone, probably with no chance of returning any time soon. I think that even if those in charge are able to get back in control, it's going to take an awfully long time to get back to the sort of law and order that we all used to know and especially in remote parts of the country like us up here in the Highlands and islands," Glen answered.

"So, it looks like we are on our own here and we may very well have to fight for our very survival against the people that have taken over our town," Duncan summarised.

"I think you are right, Duncan. We need to be able to defend ourselves here, or do we take the fight to them?" Peter argued.

"I don't like the idea of going back over there to take them on. We don't know exactly how many there are; 50, might be several hundred! And what weapons do they have?" Mary interrupted.

"I have to agree with Mary. I have seen these people and they clearly will not tolerate anyone who does not agree with their philosophy," Glen added.

"That's fine; it was just a suggestion. Perhaps one of a number of options we have," Peter came back.

"Do you think this part of the island is defendable, Peter?" David asked.

"I don't know. We know that the other side of the island is made up of sheer cliffs and jagged rocky coastline, with virtually no way to get on shore from a boat. There is a small inlet that could be used to drop off men, just to the south of where the old crofters' cottages are," Peter explained. "They could try a full-frontal, head-on attack from the water, coming through the narrow harbour entrance, and land on the island that way. I reckon they could try to outflank us and land to the north, by the cottage that Helen and I use, and of course, near to Margaret and Minnie's cottage. If there were enough of them, they may try to split their forces, land to the north and south and trap us."

"Bloody hell. So, we are not safe here then," Becky spoke for the first time.

Duncan turned to Peter. "Do you have any ideas then, Peter? How can we not only survive an attack from the people in our town, but also survive for the foreseeable future on this island?"

"Well, subject to all your approval, as a matter of fact, I do," Peter answered.

"Can you manage that?" Peter asked Duncan and David as they half-lifted and half-rolled the 50-gallon drum full of diesel out of the store shed and into the sunlight.

"Yeah, we've got it. This is the last one in there," Duncan replied as he hefted the plastic container up a ramp and into the trailer attached to the Ranger utility vehicle. "Okay, Peter, we'll just do a last sweep through all the storage areas and check that we haven't left anything of value behind," Duncan said.

"Thanks, you two," Peter replied. Peter and Glen waited in the vehicle, and after five minutes, Duncan and David jumped into the back of the Ranger and they all headed down the track to the jetty, to the waiting catamaran.

The four of them immediately began loading the diesel drums on board. This was the last seven of them, after having moved in excess of 20 drums already over the preceding two days.

The job was quickly finished, and Peter turned to Duncan.

"Thanks again, guys. So, we will head up to the base in this; if you let us know when you get up to Margaret and Minnie, pick up the rest and then make as much progress over land in the Ranger as you can to the lighthouse and then down to the officers' mess block I told you about," Peter asked.

"Understood, Pete! We will radio you once we are on the move from the cottages," Duncan replied as he and David jumped back into the Ranger and roared off up the track and out of sight.

"Good men, the pair of them! I've known them all my life, knew their fathers. They'd be proud to see how their boys have turned out, a real credit to them," Glen offered.

"I know I was lucky to happen upon them when I did," Peter answered as they both put on rucksacks and walked back up the track to the wooded area, just before the track came out by the crop field.

Glen and Peter had struck up a close understanding and the beginning of a close friendship in the short time they had known each other. Glen had asked a number of probing questions about Peter's past life as a policeman in London. Peter had explained his situation to Glen; the unique set of circumstances that had placed Helen and himself on the Isle of Raasay right at the moment that the world had turned on its head.

Glen had marvelled at the extent of the military facility when Peter had taken him up there that second morning after Glen's rescue from Portree. Peter had kitted him out with some body armour and a helmet, an MP5 and a Glock and sufficient ammunition. Glen was not a firearms officer, but he had, during his service, been on several familiarisation courses about firearms and was constantly checking the shotgun and firearms licences of the community he used to serve. It was while Peter had been obtaining kit for Glen that he had happened upon a room full of personal radios and two banks of batteries fully charged in their wall-mounted charging pods. He and Glen quickly took another holdall and took 10 radios and spare batteries to distribute among the group. They also took some of the more sinister-looking explosive devices, which included the old-fashioned crescent-shaped Claymore anti-personnel mines, with both trip wires and control wire activations.

Peter had showed Glen the large accommodation blocks, kitchen and mess halls, the large gym and exercise area. Then the main admin office and the spare Land Rovers, waiting to be used, parked outside. Peter and Glen had explored the officers' mess and discovered that the rooms, albeit the same as the other accommodation they had already looked at, were slightly larger, and the general finish was of a higher quality and some of the rooms even had double beds. The officers' mess also linked to an officers' dining room, that in turn linked to the general kitchens.

Peter had decided that when they implemented his plan, this would be where the group would house themselves. If things became more desperate, then he had a last-ditch redoubt location in his mind. *Must have watched* Zulu *too many times!* he thought. After three days of ceaseless working, moving their supplies and all their meagre collection of belongings up to the military base, Peter felt they were actually in a position to move up there. Helen, Mary and Callum had been left at the base jetty with the mountain of boxes and equipment, with the instructions to move all of it into the officers' mess block and into the kitchens. Becky had taken Scotty up to Margaret and Minnie's cottage; he was still numb with shock and Peter thought it best to let the two older ladies look after him while they cleared all the gear out of the other cottages.

All the time they had been doing this, one of them, be it Peter, Duncan, Glen or David, had been stationed at the headland, to keep a close eye on any movement from anywhere on Skye. This task had been made so much easier with the addition of personal radios to each of them. A quick rudimentary knowledge of how they worked, and they were able to keep tabs on each other as they moved about the island and de-camped themselves to the more, in Peter's opinion, defendable position at the north end of the island. Glen and Peter had placed several Claymore mines either side of the track, secured the trip wires between the trees by the old crofters' cottages and concealed them as best they could.

Glen and Peter again took off their rucksacks in the wood, down near the jetty of the island manager's cottage area, brought out a number of the Claymore mines and began setting them at various points within the wooded area around the track, arming them with trip wires and covered those wires with leaves and lichen to disguise their presence. They worked backwards through the woods and ended up back on the jetty, by the side of the catamaran.

"Good work, Glen. Let's get going and join up with the others," Peter shouted as he jumped on board, watching as Glen undid the mooring lines and made himself ready to jump on board at an indication from Peter.

"Okay, let's go," Peter shouted from the cabin. Glen jumped on board as Peter slowly moved the boat forward out into the harbour and then through the gap between the rock and the main island, before turning right and heading north up the main channel.

As Peter and Glen motored north up the channel, Duncan and David were driving the Ranger up to Margaret and Minnie's cottage, talking about the conversation they had had with Becky and her anger at having to abandon the crop field. Becky had taken the news of their movement north quite badly. She was in the process of harvesting some of the crops and had fresh seeds to plant and wanted to experiment with some mixed salad seeds that she had found in the bottom of one of their food supply boxes.

"All that work to cultivate the field and actually grow crops and prepare the soil for the next season and

Peter decided he wants to move us all to this military base. I'm not happy!" Becky stated to the two men in the front of the Ranger as she got in.

"He did explain how much more secure the base is and how it is a much easier location to defend," Duncan tried to placate her.

"We can always try and find another field within the confines of the base and get stuff planted again. You've been brilliant with all those potatoes and carrots we now have. We have a really good quantity of them," David offered.

"Yeah, and you pulled up leeks, onions, garlic, spinach and various other things," Duncan interrupted.

"And we have runner beans, some green beans and shed loads of beetroot," David continued, tag teaming with Duncan in an effort to reassure Becky.

"Well, I hope all this moving is going to be worth it," Becky said.

"Peter asked us what we thought of his idea to move up to the base and we all agreed it made sense to be settled into a more secure area," Duncan said, defending Peter's plan to move the group up to the base.

"There were always going to be a few negative sides to moving there, but the balance of safety over the homes we had created had to come first, Becky," David answered, supporting Duncan's view that it was the right thing to do.

"Just between us, here, now, do you think those people will attack us here on Rona?" Becky asked.

"It's the not knowing their situation. Clearly they are armed; they shot at us and killed Sonia without any attempt to talk to us. You have to believe that if their store of food and other equipment runs out, then they are naturally going to come looking for food elsewhere and that is going to almost certainly end up with them making a trip over to us on this island," Duncan surmised.

"So, what's this place like then?" Becky asked.

"It's probably more functional than beautiful, but it's built into the landscape more, a lot of it so well hidden that David and I had no idea of its existence until we had a look round with Peter," Duncan said.

"It has a power supply and therefore heating, power and light. We can feel secure with high sheer cliffs on two sides of us, a relatively narrow piece of land to defend from the south and a little harbour and bay, which a small group like us can probably defend if the need arises," David added, in answer to Becky's question.

They put Scotty in the back of the Ranger with Margaret and Minnie. Becky and David got in the front,

Talisker jumped in for the ride too. Duncan secured the trailer, full of the last of their gear. He then did a physical check to make sure all the cottages up at the more northerly point were locked and the windows were all as secure as they could be. Scotty was still very quiet. Everyone was sensitive around him; Mary had been at pains to make sure Callum was respectful and quiet in his company. Margaret and Minnie had clearly sensed it was their duty to take him under their wings and look after him.

"Okay, David, you start up the hill and I will walk behind you," Duncan said, then added, "You may have to get out at points, once the track stops and you are trying to negotiate the bare rock and hidden dips between them, but we will keep an eye and assist as we walk along at the back."

"Understood, Duncan," David shouted above the noise of the utility vehicle's engine.

So, they moved off north of the last of the cottages that had been their homes for the past few months and headed up the slight hill. Duncan turned and looked out to the water, where he could make out the catamaran cruising along the middle of the channel on its way north to join up with them. Duncan walked slowly up the hill, taking his time to keep an eye out behind them. David was steering the Ranger carefully along the last of the track and then around the edge of the small lake. He waited for Duncan to join them, then he continued on up the next slight rise to the crest of this second hill.

The lighthouse was now clearly visible about another half a mile over the uneven terrain.

The Ranger was up to the challenge and made it all the way to the whitewashed brick wall and then skirted around the edge of the compound to re-join the metalled road that existed, and David drove down the hill, past the helipad and stopped in front of the mess hall and accommodation block.

Peter picked up the radio from the control panel of the catamaran and called to his wife. "Helen, receiving? Over."

"Is that you, Peter? Over," came the unmistakable voice of his wife, who he could just make out as she slid a large cardboard box into the back of one of the two Land Rovers parked by the jetty.

"Just heading towards you through the inlet. Can you be ready to help us moor the boat? Then we can work together to load as much as we can," Peter replied as he steered the boat across the inlet at the top of the island and towards the small partially hidden concrete jetty.

A short while later, with the boat now moored, both Glen and Peter helped Helen and Mary load the two Land Rovers with as much stuff as they could carry.

"When you get back to the mess hall, if the others have arrived from over land, can you ask if Duncan and David can join us down here with the Ranger once they have unloaded it so we can get all this diesel fuel loaded onto the trailer, please," Peter asked.

"Yes, I will also return with one of the Land Rovers to use the winch to help lift the drums out of the boat up onto the jetty," Helen replied.

With that, Helen and Mary jumped in a Land Rover each and drove slowly around the bay side road and up out of sight towards the mess hall block.

"Glen, how are you doing?" Peter asked as the two of them sat on the jetty wall and waited for the others to return.

"Aye, not too bad. I'll have earned a kip tonight for sure," he replied, smiling.

"Try this while we wait." Peter offered a small silver hip flask to Glen, who took it and helped himself to a generous glug from the container and then passed it back.

"Cheers, Peter! What is that?" Glen nodded approvingly at the flask.

"It's some of the new spirit I liberated from the distillery on Raasay; not bad, is it? And it can only get better in the cask!" Peter replied.

The noise of a vehicle engine stopped their continued appreciation of the contents of the flask, and they watched as first a Land Rover, followed by the Ranger utility came down the hill from the main part of the base and into view as they both drove around the crescent of the bay and onto the jetty in front of them.

Duncan jumped out of the Land Rover. "Caught you two slackers supping whisky, is it?" he laughed as David climbed out of the Ranger. "These two just sitting here having a whisky while we do all the work, eh, David!" Duncan continued.

David laughed as he walked up to the others.

"Care for a blast," Peter said as he again offered his flask to the new arrivals.

"Go on then." Duncan took the flask, had a swig and passed it to David, who did the same.

"Well, if any of us has this illness, then we all have it now, I reckon," Glen observed.

"I think it's safe to say that we have formed a fairly limited bubble among the group and the enforced isolation on the island has kept us clear of the highly contagious infection," Peter replied.

"So, we left the girls and Scotty getting all the rest of the gear into the accommodation complex. They were happily choosing the rooms for each of us, all within the officers' mess building," Duncan said.

"It may not be as scenic as where we were, but I think we can make ourselves pretty comfortable here," Peter observed as he put the hip flask away and walked up to the winch on the front of the Land Rover.

Between the four of them, they quickly winched the diesel drums up onto the jetty and into the trailer of the Ranger. Peter secured the boat and then jumped into the Land Rover with Duncan, while David and Glen got into the Ranger. They drove around the bay and up the rise to the main office and past it, then left down the hill to the armoury and other weapons stores. They had decided to store the diesel in a metal hangar just at the end of the road, where the circular turnaround was. They once again worked as a team and unloaded the 50-gallon drums and put them inside the hangar with all the other drums they had already moved. By Peter's estimate, they still had over 1,000 gallons of diesel at their disposal.

"Back to the mess then, is it?" Glen suggested, once all the drums were stored.

"Sounds good to me. Nice cup of tea, see if we can find some fruit cake?" Peter agreed.

"Fruit cake? And where exactly are we going to find some of that then?" David asked.

"Come on, follow me, and I will introduce you to the delights of military-grade tinned fruit cake, gentlemen," Peter answered and once again they all jumped into their respective vehicles and headed back up the hill to the parking area by the main office, then walked to the accommodation block and entered the mess hall.

"Well, the beans have certainly survived the move and I have planted some potatoes to see if we can get a second crop this year. The tomato plants in that area at the side of the mess hall by the window are doing okay. Just have to remember that they need plenty of water, especially if this warm sunshine keeps up." Becky paused as she looked through her notes.

"I have some sweet peppers in that area too and I am trying to grow some cucumbers from seed. Just experimenting really. The soil is not as good up here, but we always knew that, I suppose, and I am hopeful of some more onions, leeks, carrots, parsnips and maybe broccoli if I can dig out some more of the ground where we re-planted all the stuff when we moved up here. That's pretty much everything. We have a reasonable store of the veg that we brought with us, but it needs looking at in the dry store; it won't last forever, and it would be criminal to let it go to waste. Margaret, maybe you and Minnie could make some large quantities of soup? That way, we use all the veg before it goes off and we can, of course, freeze the soup." Becky stopped to look up at Margaret and Minnie, who both nodded and smiled at her. "So that's pretty much it. Any questions?" Becky asked as she sat back down at the tables they had pulled together in the officers' mess dining room to create a large square for themselves.

"Thanks, Becky." A small round of applause stopped Peter as he spoke. "Do you have enough help from us all at the moment?" he continued.

"I do, while I'm planting and tending everything; it's when it comes to getting everything harvested, then I could do with a hand," Becky replied.

"Understood. Well, just say the word and we can all lend a hand, when that time comes," Peter offered. "Duncan, how are you getting on using the catamaran and the limited fishing gear that we found on board?"

"I won't lie, losing the trawler was a blow; we had all the nets and lines we needed, plus all the fish finding equipment, made the catching so much easier, but we are still getting fish and the storage freezers are much better here than back at the cottages, so we still have good supplies of fish to offset using the rations all the time. Coupled with the crops from Becky's field, I would say we are well set for the colder weather when it sets in at the end of next month." Duncan presented his facts clearly for the group around him.

"Margaret, Minnie? How are you getting on in the kitchens?" Peter asked the two new resident cooks, since they had moved to the base and embarked on cooking for the entire group.

"Well, dear, the ovens are okay, but one of them doesn't hold the temperature like my old Aga back in town. To be fair, we like to cook for a larger group, it's more economical and there is definitely less waste," Minnie offered. It was a rare thing for her to speak to the group, so everybody looked up as she described the kitchens.

"We both like the big walk-in fridges and freezers; we can store all the fish that Duncan and the boys bring back from their trips. Going forward, it would be lovely if we could get some hens; fresh eggs would be delightful and help me make some more cakes, other than that tinned stuff Peter found in the rations," Margaret added to the discussion.

"Let's make a note to see if we can get some hens from somewhere then," Peter smiled.

"Scotty, how are you liking the gym and exercise hangar?" Peter gently tried to include Scotty into the chat, having spent some hours coaxing him out of his room in the officers' mess to organise some fitness sessions for the rest of the group, as a way to try and take his mind off the loss of Sonia.

"It's not a bad gym; there is plenty of equipment, running machines and bikes, cross trainers and free weights. I've dusted and oiled all of the equipment and repaired some of the lights and found an old CD player, so you can have music while you exercise. Please come and join me when any of you get a chance." Scotty had clearly worked hard in the gym hangar to make the place a usable space for the rest of the group.

"Nice one, Scotty. I'll be down there to join you," Duncan said as he leant forward and patted his fishing buddy on the back.

The rest of the group all applauded as Scotty broke into a small grin. "Awright! Fuck off, will ya!" he quietly spoke, smiling back at them.

"Is everyone okay with the amount of space you each have in the mess? I mean, it's not as if you can't spread out some more if you wish!" Peter joked. Everyone looked up and nodded.

"I think we are all okay. No one was sure about this idea you had to transfer up here, Peter, but from my short time at the cottages to moving up here, I think you made the right suggestion, and we are going to be okay here for the time being," Glen spoke supportively.

"Okay, now the tricky bit; we have to talk about defence of the base and what we need to do," Peter said.

"Go on then; we are all here," Duncan answered.

"Right, I believe we need to have a 24-hour watch on duty, with the ability to see the land to the south, the channel and our jetty and bay area, the base itself and also the cliff area the other side of the base. This watch needs to be armed with a radio, one of the high-powered rifles, binoculars, a flare gun and a whistle, until I can find another louder warning system."

"That all makes sense, and where do you suggest we take up this watch, and who is going to have to do it?" Glen asked.

"The most obvious place is on the gantry around the light of the lighthouse. It's in an elevated position, with views of every part of the island and beyond. Now we can make it as comfortable as possible; put one of the mess chairs up in the light room and put blankets and maybe a small stove up there, and I have a couple of thermos flasks which can be filled with hot drinks, soup, whatever anyone wants in an effort to stay warm as winter sets in and the position up there becomes more exposed."

"You've thought about this then?" Duncan said.

"What do you think, Glen?" Peter sought the opinion of Glen, which he had started to do in most discussions since Glen had become part of the group.

"It's definitely a good spot for a lookout, going to be pretty cold at night, and once winter sets in up here, I think you will be in need of those blankets and hot soup alright," Glen added.

"Who is going to do the actual shifts on watch then?" Becky asked.

"Well, certainly myself. I thought Glen, Duncan, David and also Scotty." Peter looked up at Scotty to see if there was any reaction to being included in the group of lookouts, but he detected nothing. No one else reacted to Scotty being included either.

"When I was a copper, we used to do eight-hour shifts, but I am not proposing an eight-hour shift up there; I'm not sure it's possible to keep an attentive watch over eight hours. If the five of us are willing to, then I think we should pair up, with one spare, who will relieve someone in a cycle," Peter said.

"Hang on, that's not making sense," David spoke.

"Let him finish, David," Glen interrupted.

"My fault; I didn't explain it well enough. Basically, we do two hours on as lookout, with two hours off, between a pair of us. The member of the pair during their off two hours can go and eat, relieve themselves; we can set up a comfortable area in the buildings next to the lighthouse if necessary. After 12 hours of this, they are both relieved by another pair, who then do their 12 hours on and off. Does that make sense?" Peter asked.

"And the fifth member?" Duncan asked.

"The fifth member will relieve one of the other four and we all rotate at being the fifth member in a shift pattern. I will work that out as we get going," Peter answered.

"Could the rest of us lend a hand or get involved?" Helen asked.

"Of course. Everything I said was only a suggestion that we need a lookout posted and I didn't want you to think I expected you all to do it, but anyone who wants to be part of the shift pattern can be included," Peter answered, smiling at Helen, glad of her support.

"Right, when do we start with the lookout then?" Becky asked, keen to show that she was prepared to be part of the team included in the shifts to conduct the watch.

"If you don't mind, Minnie and I would rather not be included," Margaret interrupted, to peals of laughter from around the room.

"Margaret, timing, as ever, is everything. We shall do our utmost to find some hens so that you have fresh eggs with which to dazzle us with some freshly baked cakes," Peter answered, laughing along with the rest of the room.

Peter hooked the trip wire around the iron peg he had previously driven into the hard-packed soil between some rocks. The wire was at ankle height and stretched some four metres between the iron peg and the top of the lethal-looking Claymore M18 mine, which he had also driven into the ground, facing south, away from the lighthouse compound. Peter had thought it very generous of the designers of the mine to have the words, "FRONT TOWARD ENEMY" written on one side of the mine plastic cover to assist in their deployment.

Peter stood up and walked back to Glen, who was stood on a small rise, still about 20 metres from the gate in the lighthouse compound wall.

"Okay, that is the last of the trip-wired ones," Peter said.

"We have about 10 of the command-wired ones in the bag; how do you want to arrange them?" Glen asked.

"Let's create a kill zone in a crescent just in front of the wall and the track off to our right; put them close enough that we can unspool all the command wires and bring them through the gate so we have a line of the clackers within the compound," Peter replied.

"Do you think all this is necessary?" Glen asked.

"I don't know, and I really hope that it isn't, but we have all of this defensive stuff; we might as well make use of it. I am not sure everyone agreed with putting mines out and we will all have to keep our eye on Talisker and possibly Callum, but if an attack comes from the land in front of us, at least we can slow them down enough to get the group together and make for our shelter," Peter said.

"I still can't believe what's under this island," Glen spoke, shaking his head.

"Pretty well hidden, wasn't it, but it makes sense for them to have had a base like that so close to the yards where they were built and the channel where they were allegedly conducting sea trials and sound testing. Were you aware that the Chinese have similar underground bases, but that because their submarines were on the surface when they entered the base, they were visible to satellites?" Peter asked.

"So, ours are already submerged when they come in and depart from this base?" Glen queried.

"That's right and it must have been quite a job digging such a deep-sea trench to allow passage for a submerged nuclear submarine to sail under the cliffs into the base down there," Peter added.

"What do you think the group made of the discovery yesterday?" Glen continued with his questions.

"They all need a chance to have a look down there and see for themselves. Maybe we didn't explain it properly," Peter replied.

"Well, when we get back after this shift tonight, we can have another go at describing the layout of the place and maybe take them down there to check it out for themselves," Glen went on.

"That sounds fine with me. So, I'll get back up into the lighthouse if you are okay creating the crescent of mines and spooling out the command wires?" Peter asked Glen, and he walked back into the compound, up into the lighthouse and out onto the gantry. He lifted the binoculars to his eyes and scanned the area looking south down the channel between them and Skye. He then walked completely around the circle of the gantry and scanned as far as he could see in all directions. Nothing! He watched as Glen unravelled the command wires from the Claymore mines, brought them all inside the walled compound of the lighthouse and connected them to each "clacker" firing device.

Peter went back inside and sat down in the recently added comfortable chair. He poured himself a coffee from his flask, sat back and thought about the last 12 hours and the additional discovery that he and Glen had made that existed probably several hundred feet under where he sat now, looking out over the sound of water towards what was, he supposed, the mainland of Scotland.

He had, just yesterday, decided that he ought to show Glen the extent of the base, and to that end, he had taken him to the building marked PEN 1 and 2 at the back edge of the facility, which was built up against the rugged rock outcrop at the very northernmost point of the compound. Peter had explained how he had just unlocked and walked into the building and found it to be a shell, with the two large industrial-sized warehouse-style lifts at the far side of the room from the door. At the bottom of the lift shaft, as the doors opened, Peter had extended his hand to allow Glen to walk out into the vast expanse of openness beneath the rocks above them. His reaction had been the same as his; sheer awe and surprise at the extent of the facility, the scale and engineering mastery that had created it, coupled with the fact that it had been constructed without anyone's knowledge.

"I take it you had no knowledge that any of this existed?" Peter remembered asking Glen.

He replied he had not, and they had then taken a slow wander around the extensive dock area, taking more time to look at what the subterranean chasm contained. There was an array of large electrical sockets and switches on either wall by the side of each long jetty. A closer inspection helped both Glen and Peter conclude that by using the thick neatly coiled cables at their feet, the island base could be connected and presumably powered from the reactor of the submarine. Peter had recalled reading an article somewhere, possibly about Barrow-in-Furness and that the new class of submarines had sufficient power to be able to conduct continuous operations for up to 25 years, but that also the reactors within these new submarines were capable of powering a small town, provided there were the correct cable couplers and other electrical transformers and trickery.

Peter had imparted all of his knowledge to Glen, who had remarked that he couldn't see why there was a need to use the submarines to power the base when the base had its own power supply on the surface. Things began to make more sense upon Glen's discovery of a recess in one of the walls, which had not been visible from the extent of the investigation Peter had made on his last visit down to the underground docking space. Within the recess was a large sturdy-looking smooth concrete block, marked "BLAST DOOR". Sited to one side of this large sheer block was a control panel, which Glen studied, and then he pressed the large circular green button marked "OPEN".

For a split second, nothing happened. Then there was a warning alarm and a red light flashed above the blast door. The entire smooth concrete monolith in front of them started to move and swing out towards them slowly. They both took a step back as the block continued to swing out and reveal a brightly lit corridor that led down and away to the left. The concrete block of a door must have been about a metre thick. Peter recalled they had delayed entering this new section, fearful that the door might swing shut behind them, entombing them below the island. Glen walked forward after some hesitation and found some more controls on the inside of the blast door, similar to those outside. This set also included locking instructions to prevent the doors being opened from the outside once they were locked.

They both decided that it would be alright to proceed further and entered the corridor. After 10–15 seconds or so of walking, they came to a large circular area with another bank of large lift doors. This time there were four of them, arranged in the far half of the circle from the corridor, which they had just walked down.

Peter remembered Glen's remark yesterday, "Well, in for a penny, laddie?" as he had pushed the button next to one of the middle two of the lifts. The doors silently opened and again the lift cabin was filled with bright white artificial light. They had both entered and Glen pressed the down button. The doors closed smoothly, and the lift descended. They both felt the speed of the descent, and both felt their ears pop. The doors opened onto a clean smooth-walled, well-lit atrium. The area was well signposted, with instructions directing to the central control, mess halls, accommodation area, library, medical wing, cinema, games room, lounge, gymnasium and swimming pool. The signs pointed down the myriad of corridors that led away from the central atrium, where they stood. Both men stood and stared, unable to take in the extent of the new level they had discovered. Peter had decided they ought to go to the control room first and see what all this was for, although he was starting to have a pretty good idea.

The motion-activated lights suddenly bathed the vast bank of computer screens and other smart TV screens, including one wall entirely made up of monitors. Peter had remarked to Glen; "Did you ever see a film in the 1980s called *Wargames with Matthew Broderick*? They had a control room that was supposed to be NORAD. I tell you, it was just like this, with a tiered bank of monitors with chairs and a wall-sized screen that could pretty much project whatever you wanted onto it. This is just like that."

Glen had, unfortunately, not seen the film. Peter bemoaned that his nerdish movie knowledge had not reached the environs of Skye as of yet!

They both walked slowly around the room, taking it all in, then up an aisle to a central half-moon of desks that seemed to be at the centre and rear of the room, commanding a position where everywhere else in the room and all the screens could be seen easily.

Peter had sat down behind the middle console and marvelled at the array of buttons. One which caught his eye was marked, "Closed circuit TV base security cameras". Peter tentatively pushed a few buttons below this sign and the screens at the front of the room were suddenly filled with images of the base above them. Peter counted at least 50 camera views, each one numbered, timed and dated.

Glen had spotted Becky on one camera, tending to the crops she had planted. There were views of the bay, a view out above the rocky crags on the western side of the base. There were views to the south from a camera clearly on the very top of the lighthouse tower.

"You can watch the entire base and surrounding area from this room. You can even see inside the communal areas, like the mess hall, the gym, the kitchens, down at the jetty; it's an incredible system," Glen had remarked.

Peter and Glen had spent some time looking at the various controls in front of them, marvelling at the air purification system, the power supply coming from an internal automated reactor, the ability to switch between the base reactor and that of the submarines that used the base. Clearly this place and that on the surface had an inexhaustible supply of power to heat, light, purify and scrub the air down here. There were monitors and detectors to check for air quality on the surface, any radiation, and a range of other biological and chemical impurities. Peter had pulled a plastic binder out of one of the shelves in front of him as he sat in what he reckoned to be the command chair. Glen leaned over, and between them, they read of the base being capable of supporting up to 270 persons for an unbroken period of two years. There were instructions on how to operate the facility at this maximum capacity, how the food should be rationed, how to change out carbon filters and how to vent fresh air from above, through various other filters. Glen and Peter sat and read the binder for about half an hour.

Glen pointed to a section on how to communicate with a selection of other seemingly similar bases and to contact submarines and also certain surface vessels around the globe. Glen had remarked that there was clearly a part to be played by the controllers here, to facilitate the arrival of a submarine and make access to the underground base possible.

Peter and Glen had realised that staff were needed here to make it possible for a submarine to use this place. Peter and Glen decided that they would return to the surface, Peter taking the binder with him to show and explain the significance of this latest discovery to the others. They walked back down one of the corridors to the atrium. They spent some time deciding whether or not to explore other areas but ended up getting back into the lift and returning to the upper circle and from there back to the blast door. Once outside the orbit of the concrete block, Peter pressed the closed button and the door slowly swung back into position and they both heard a hiss of air seals around the door as it locked closed.

Once back on the surface, they had debated when to tell the group and had mutually agreed to inform the rest of their colleagues over dinner that evening, before Glen went to relieve Duncan and David from watch duties with Scotty, it being Peter's night off!

"So, that is what we found. Does anyone have anything they would like to say?" Peter sat down after having revealed and talked, along with Glen, about the day's discovery of a large self-contained full nuclear shelter built under the base which they were now using.

"So how far down is this place?" Becky asked.

"Rough guess, I would estimate about 300 feet below us," Peter replied.

"Do you think it's safe that far down?" Helen asked.

"Well, I know the rocks in this part of the world are all igneous; you know, old volcanic rock, so pretty hard, and it looks to me like a sizeable amount of concrete and steel has been used down there to make the bunker stronger and probably capable of withstanding a direct hit, but that's just a theory. The best defence this place has is that no one knows it's here," Peter added.

"Doesn't it feel a little claustrophobic down there?" Minnie quietly asked.

"It's a pretty big place. The ceilings look and feel quite high, and the air feels fresh, and the lighting makes it feel welcoming and spacious, so no, my initial thoughts are that it's not claustrophobic, Minnie," Glen answered.

"When can I go see it? It sounds brilliant. Come on, Mum, let's go see, please?" Callum sat forward, keen to impress on his mother how desperate he was to see the underground shelter for himself.

"Hang on, wee man," Duncan interrupted his son's pleading. "So, you twos have found this place and it sounds the perfect shelter for us, but when would you want to move us to this underground living?" Duncan continued, looking at Peter and Glen.

"Well, that's just it, Duncan; we don't need this place. While we are able to make do up here and feel safe, then we are much more comfortable in the fresh air, here on the surface. What I think Glen and I have found is our ultimate fall-back position, should our safety and security here on the island be compromised," Peter said.

"Peter's right, we make this base as safe as possible, we plant mines on the far side of the lighthouse and monitor the bay and surrounding areas from the lighthouse tower. We can continue to plant vegetables, Becky, and we can continue to fish, Duncan. We simply leave this underground bunker for a time when we have no alternative to survive," Glen entered the debate.

"Are you sure you have to put mines up on the headland beyond the lighthouse wall?" Mary asked.

"It makes sense, Mary. I know it puts that area out of bounds to all of us too, but it might give us the time in an emergency to run to the PEN building, get to the underground shelter and lock the doors behind us," Glen answered.

"Well, you take note, Callum; the area beyond the lighthouse wall is completely out of bounds!" Mary ordered Callum.

"We will all have to keep a closer eye on Talisker too," Peter said as he spotted the small Terrier rooting about under the table.

"Maybe we can build a fence across from the lighthouse wall, covering the track to the side, down to where the flat ground drops away," Duncan suggested.

"Well, I think there is some wire in the hangar where the torpedoes are, and I am sure we can find posts in one of those maintenance sheds near to the gym hangar. Can I ask you to have a look for us, please, Scotty?" Peter asked.

"Aye! I'll have a look in the morning if someone can cover my watch shift, please, just for a couple of hours?" Scotty asked.

"I'll cover for that," Becky volunteered.

"Thanks, Becky, and thank you too for that, Scotty." Peter acknowledged the cooperation between the group was becoming almost instinctive.

Peter returned to his present position in the lighthouse, put down his beaker of coffee, picked up the binoculars and once more walked out onto the outside gantry and surveyed the land and seascape around him. He waved as he watched Glen place the last of the mines, unspool the command wire, bring it inside the compound and connect this last wire to its clacker. Glen waved back and shouted, "They are all armed and ready. My back's killing me. I am going back to the mess to get some hot food and will see you in about an hour."

"Thanks, Glen, enjoy and see you in a while," Peter replied and watched as Glen walked down the track inside the compound, past the lighthouse buildings and out of sight, only to re-emerge as he continued down the track past the helipad and then around the corner of the landscape out of sight once more.

Peter had one more good scan of all that he could see before returning once more to the chair inside the light room. *Bloody hell, 25 years since I left the Diplomatic Protection Group and here I am doing two hours on and two hours off again*, Peter thought.

Although it would be an exaggeration to suggest that life returned to normal at the base, there was definitely a sense of routine and developing friendships and cooperation as the group of locals and Helen and Peter bonded to ensure their survival on the small island. Scotty had built an effective fence between the side of the walled compound of the lighthouse and where the flat ground dropped steeply away. It was designed primarily to keep people away from the Claymore mines but would also serve as an additional defensive barrier to slow down any potential threat as it presented itself.

Becky had planted a late crop of potatoes in her newly dug field in an attempt to provide fresh new potatoes on or around the Christmas period. There had been a good crop of tomatoes from the pots in the mess hall, starting to wane now, as the sun shone less in the sky, replaced by more frequent high winds and heavy rain. Becky, with much assistance, had pulled up a reasonable number of vegetables, which were then prepared into a meal by the now almost professional pair of resident chefs, Margaret and Minnie. Scotty had welcomed most of the group to what was now by common consent referred to as "Scotty's Gym" and enjoyed keeping busy, helping others keep themselves fit, more so now as the weather pretty much put paid to any outside activities.

Peter and Glen had walked around the footprint of the base to see what could be done to enhance the defensive measures they planned to put in place, in addition to those already done.

While digging out the supply of Claymore mines from the armoury storerooms, they had found some Browning .50 calibre heavy machine guns. Glen had wondered if they could deploy one up on the wall of the lighthouse compound and one overlooking the bay area, to protect the jetty and quayside. Peter had weighed this up but had an alternative suggestion.

"Maybe we could mount them on the roof of the Land Rovers so that we have a more flexible field of fire, and we can deploy them to wherever a threat appears to be coming from?" Peter suggested.

"On the roof or in the back?" Glen questioned, then continued. "Might you not be too exposed up on the roof, and the operator would be in quite a precarious position?" he countered.

"Shall we give it a try anyway? Then if it doesn't feel safe, we can revert to a static position, like you said?" Peter replied.

Between them, they hefted a machine gun out onto the tarmac in front of the armoury and went to work screwing the tripod to the roof rack. Once the tripod was secured, they lifted the M2 machine gun up onto the roof of the vehicle and attached it to the tripod. Peter had found a supply of belt-fed cartridges, about 300, he reckoned, per ammunition box. Not being conversant with the weapon, Peter returned to the armoury, found a binder about the M2 and brought it out to assist Glen in loading the gun and understanding the weapon and its effective range, any limitations and other facts, which were not readily apparent.

Peter recalled his wife's criticism that he always liked to refer to a manual or instruction guide, no matter what the item, utensil, machine or product. He acknowledged that it was part of his make-up to consistently refer to guides and advice manuals when about to operate or use anything that was new to him. Helen was much more likely to get the object out of the box and begin using said item before the user guide had been removed from the packaging. It just wasn't his way, and why, he thought, should it be any different when getting to grips with a Browning M2 .50 calibre belt-fed machine gun, with an effective range of 2,000 metres and capable of firing 600 rounds per minute. Plus, he thought, how do you load the thing? How do you feed the belt of cartridges into the gun? So, while Glen was up on the roof, checking the range of movement of the gun attached to the tripod, Peter sat in the driver's seat and flicked through the manual, noting sections on over-heating, muzzle velocities and then loading a belt of ammunition.

Now armed with the information he required, Peter climbed up onto the roof of the Land Rover and joined Glen. Peter explained how to feed the belt of cartridges into the gun, and after a little bit of experimentation between the two of them, the belt of ammunition was loaded. Peter had read that the weapon could fire a single shot if the bolt action was unlocked into the UP position. The bolt latch must then be released manually by the gunner to send the bolt forward. Before they embarked on a test firing, Peter suggested they move down to the quayside and fire out into the bay.

So, they both jumped down off the roof and into the front of the Land Rover, and Peter drove the short journey down to the jetty. Peter angled the vehicle so the majority of the moving axis of the gun was facing out into the sea. He put the hand brake on, and they both clambered back onto the roof.

"Right, Glen, your honour, sir. Just remember this is Rona, a small island off the coast of Scotland, not downtown Mogadishu!" Peter joked, laughing as Glen settled himself behind the blunt end of the heavy machine gun.

"So, it should be a single shot? Is there much recoil on one of these things?" Glen asked.

"Yeah, just one shot and I've never even seen one fired before, so as regards recoil, well, we shall see," Peter replied.

"I am aiming across the bay; what is the range of this thing?" Glen asked as he shifted his weight so he was more comfortable.

"The manual says effective range of 2,000 metres and a maximum range of about 7,500 metres, so aim at the rocky outcrop on the other side of the inlet; we should see a rock shatter. I'll try and watch through these old binoculars we found in the glove box," Peter replied.

"Right, ready!" Glen shouted.

"Go on then," Peter shouted back.

There was a loud report from the weapon as Glen fired.

A couple of seconds later, Peter, looking through the binoculars, saw a puff of smoke and shards of debris explode on a rockface on the other side of the inlet.

"Okay, let's put the bolt back and then lock the latch down and have a quick blast on automatic; what do you think?" Peter asked Glen.

"Aye!" Glen smiled, warming to the task and delighted that he was going to fire again.

Peter helped Glen unlock the bolt action and then stood back again.

Glen fired a short burst of 10–12 rounds, then stopped, the noise report echoing around the bay and no doubt beyond.

Peter jumped down and picked up a radio in the cab.

"Duncan, receiving? Over."

"Aye! I take it that was you and Glen firing that cannon you found," Duncan's voice came back over the radio.

"Yes, sorry, Duncan. We should have told you first that we were going to test fire it, sorry. Over," Peter apologised. "Where are you? Over," he continued.

"I'm up near the lighthouse, just checking the fence is secure. Bloody loud, that thing!" Duncan responded.

"Okay, we're done now. Just to say we now have a mobile heavy machine gun on the roof of one of the Land Rovers, which we can deploy to any location as the need might arise. Over," Peter added.

"Okay. David and I will see you later at changeover," Duncan finished.

"Understood, Duncan. Out," Peter said, putting the radio back on the dash as Glen joined him in the front of the vehicle.

"Well, they heard it up at the lighthouse. Let's park it up by the road near to the mess hall and then I reckon it's time for tea," Peter suggested.

"Yep, tea and a biscuit sounds good to me," Glen replied as Peter moved off and drove back up to the road junction near to the mess hall and went in search of some tea.

Peter leaned on the gantry rail of the lighthouse platform, binoculars lifted to his eyes. He scanned the horizon, out across the sea to the north and to the west, looking first towards the Hebrides and then back at the shoreline of mainland Scotland. The days were noticeably shorter now; the sun had already disappeared from view and darkness would quickly follow, and it wasn't even 5pm. Peter knew from previous visits to the north of the UK that at the height of winter, it would be dark by 3.30pm and then not fully light until 8.30 to 8.40am. A lot of hours of darkness, making life just slightly more difficult for them all on their island retreat. Peter moved back around the gantry to have another look out into the channel between where they were and the Isle of Skye, also scanning the southern section of the land mass of the island. Peter watched a familiar figure walking up the track from the base complex as she continued past the helipad and then disappeared from his view behind the lighthouse buildings. As she reappeared from within the compound, Peter saw the unmistakable stride of Helen, just as she looked up and waved to him while she walked up to the lighthouse and entered the building below him.

"Brought you some hot fresh tomato soup, Minnie's special recipe. She's made tons of it from Becky's tomato crop," Helen said as she handed a large, insulated flask to Peter just inside the light room.

"Thanks, love, just the ticket. Clear sky, going to be cold tonight," Peter said as he unscrewed the lid of the flask and poured some of the thick soup into a mug.

"When does Glen take over?" Helen asked as she casually picked up the binoculars from a small table and looked out into the approaching gloom.

"I said I would stay here until Duncan and David take over from us both at 7pm. Glen was looking tired, so he's got his feet up in the main building," Peter said, pointing to the main buildings within the lighthouse compound.

"Just thought I'd come and see how you are doing," Helen continued as she took a seat back inside the room.

"Today or generally?" Peter replied.

"Well, both, I suppose. Time passes so quickly, and we have been at this base for nearly three months now," Helen contemplated.

"Today I'm okay, feeling the strain a bit of these 12 hours on and off, but it's what I used to do, so I should be used to it," Peter said.

"That was over 20 years ago, don't forget! None of us are getting any younger," Helen came back.

"Generally, I think we are doing okay. I feel that as a group, we have the place working well. We have a good supply of food that hopefully will be sufficient to sustain us through the winter and a plan to get stuff in the ground as we get around to the spring next year." Peter folded his arms and continued. "We have a good defensive position, although yet to be and hopefully never to be tested. I feel we can keep people at bay, and if the numbers become too overwhelming, then my tactic would be to get to the underground bunker," Peter explained.

"I've had a brief look down there; are you sure that's where we should retreat?" Helen asked.

"I'm not 100% sure of anything. The alternatives would be to try and fight to stay on the surface or we get a chance to escape on the catamaran, but then we would be leaving our entire food supply, shelter and a magnificently secure secret defensive shelter," Peter explained.

"How long could we be down there?" Helen quizzed.

"Well, you know me, I read everything. There is a user guide and handbook in the control room down there that indicates that a larger group than ours, say 100 to 200 people, could comfortably remain down there for two years. There's 10 of us and a small dog; we could probably ration ourselves and be down there as long as would be required. If anybody infiltrated the surface base, they would have probably long run out of food and moved on before we felt any need to disturb them," Peter said.

"I know I should have been down there to have a look around. I know some of the others did after you and Glen discovered the place, but I just feel a bit unsettled by the constant preparation to move on again after we have continually moved around since we got here," Helen said.

"That's the thing; we have kept moving and reassessing our situation, so that is probably the reason we are still surviving. That's the nature of what we find ourselves in now; a constantly changing and evolving world which necessitates this level of upheaval to ensure our safety," Peter spoke quietly.

He went on; "Let's both have a look down there tomorrow. I'll show you the things I've discovered and there are still other areas to explore. I've not seen the cinema yet!" he exclaimed.

"Okay, I'd like that, a chance for us both to experience this subterranean world together. Now I'm off back to the mess because it's bloody freezing up here. See you after 7pm!" Helen leant forward and kissed Peter and disappeared down the stairs, leaving him thinking about life without fresh air in an artificially lit, heated and ventilated world.

It's the premise of a Jules Verne novel, he thought. Then he recalled, as a boy, reading *The Machine Stops* by E.M. Forster, which had always held a fascination with him. The construct of a society living away from the surface of the planet, being managed and controlled by an all-encompassing machine. *The things you remember from your childhood*. His mind wandered back to those formative years due to the time and space that his current situation afforded him, allowing him to reimagine images and events through his life.

The light of the day had disappeared, replaced by a complete blackness now that they had disabled the revolving light of the lighthouse. He found his gloves and his favourite black woollen hat. He put them on and once more walked out onto the gantry to check the surrounding scene for any sort of threat. The dark was so complete; there was not even a hint of anything but darkness away to the south and out across the channel. They had disabled the exterior lights for the entire base, a decision arrived at to try not to advertise their presence here. He could just make out one or two lights in the mess hall area, a couple of windows where the curtains had not yet been drawn. This low amber light partially lit the Land Rover parked outside and the recently accessorised M2 Browning heavy machine gun attached to its roof. This caused Peter to smile and wish for a Toyota Hilux as he leant back on the door frame and waited for his relief to turn up.

"I just think we should try and talk to them, that's all!" Becky insisted as they sat together in the mess dining room.

"What, like they talked to us before they blew Sonia away in your own house?" Scotty argued back, clearly still raw from the senseless slaughter of his wife.

"Yeah, but the alternative is we always have to be on our guard here. Peter has posted a 24-hour watch over us because we are living in fear of not knowing what these people want," Becky replied.

"Becky, they fired at us, without any questions. They stalked us back to where we live in town, and then without a word of warning, they shot poor Sonia in the doorway of your house, in front of David," Duncan entered the debate.

"Well, I'm just saying, can we sustain this defensive position forever? At some stage, we will need to venture out and it might help if we at least had an idea of who they are and what they want," Becky continued.

Peter had listened rather than interfere in the discussion. After all, despite everything, both he and Helen were still visitors, still tourists to the area. He could see Becky's point of view. *Perhaps it would be prudent to at least know our enemy*, he thought as he listened to the talking around the table.

Peter decided to offer his thoughts. "This may surprise some of you, but I actually think Becky has a point. I have spent the past few weeks improving our defensive position. I have investigated and worked out that we could fall back to the underground bunker as a place of safety, should we be attacked and overrun by anyone who comes. But, as Becky quite rightly points out, maybe we ought to have something other than a defensive strategy. Maybe we should be thinking of trying to engage with the people in your town, even just find out if they are still there?" Peter looked around as he spoke.

"Well, look at you! Never thought I would hear you offer a placatory idea. You've been all about the defensive line and creating a stronghold here. You have moved us from the distillery to more and more remote locations in an effort to isolate us from the illness and from the danger from other groups; now you want to entertain an idea of dialogue with other people. Peter, I have to say I'm flabbergasted!" Helen spoke to her husband in the company of the group around the table.

"I just think Becky has a point. I am not all about the defensive stronghold. Yes, I have spent time working out how best to defend ourselves here, but I am just floating the idea that we perhaps need an alternative to ultimately ending up living underground. Does anybody else have an opinion?" Peter asked.

"I have been heartened by the way we have come together as a group in this different environment, removing ourselves from our homes, but I am sitting here wondering about the bigger picture. We have no communication with the outside world; we don't know what's going on beyond this island. I would support a tentative foray across to Skye, have a look at what's happening, and from a purely selfish perspective, it might be nice to see how my cottage in the north is," Glen spoke for the first time.

"Scotty, I don't know how you must feel, but I'm guessing you are against the idea?" Peter tried to gently sound out Scotty's opinion on the idea of venturing out.

"You lot can go if you want to, but I'll not be leaving here. If I see one of them bastards from town, well, enough said, with the lad here." Scotty stopped, acknowledging Callum's presence at the table.

"Would you be happy to take charge here if a few of us decided to take a trip across the channel and check out what's there?" Duncan asked his mate.

"Aye, I can understand what you are saying, Becky, and it kind of makes sense, but I just don't feel ready to confront anyone just yet, okay?"

"Come here, you big sook." Becky crossed to Scotty and gave him a hug as he sat in his chair.

"Okay, who's going and where to?" Peter posed the question to the group as the mood in the room became calmer and a decision had been arrived at.

20

"Come over to this side; you'll get a grandstand view of the waterfalls as they flow over the cliffs here at Staffin," Glen offered to Helen as the catamaran motored north from the channel, into the more open expanse of sea as they closed in on the larger land mass of Skye.

Helen moved to the left side of the open deck, wrapped up against the cold now that autumn was giving way to winter.

"Do you think Margaret and Minnie would have liked to come, Peter?" Helen asked as they both looked out at the sheer cliffs as they came closer.

"They probably would have enjoyed a change of scenery, but until we know how risky it is when we explore Skye, then we can't really take them. Perhaps the next trip," Peter replied.

Becky joined them, staring at the impressively tall cliffs. "It's nice just to get some fresh air and a chance to explore," she said as they watched the water cascade over the top of the cliffs from their vantage point some 150 metres offshore.

"How long have you had this cottage then, Glen?" Peter asked the stocky policeman as they carried on north along the east coast of Skye.

"I knew a farmer that used to come down to Portree for feed supplies and to sell his stock; we have known each other for years. When his son took over the farm, we got chatting about retirement and he offered me one of the old farm cottages that was empty. It was in need of some fairly major repairs, but that's what I've been doing since I acquired it, which was about five years ago now," Glen explained.

"How far have you got?" Peter continued.

"All the structural work has been done and I've replastered, put in a new kitchen and bathroom. It just needs a bit of decorating, and the windows will need looking at soon," Glen said.

"So how are we going to get to it?" Peter asked.

"I've never got to it by sea, so it's a bit of a gamble, but there is a small inlet right at the top of the island that is pretty much the view I have from the front room of the cottage. The bay is sheltered and shallow and we should be able to get in relatively close to shore. We will probably have to get our feet wet, but the boat should be able to get in close enough for us to pull a mooring line up the beach and secure it while we have a look around," Glen said.

"Okay, let's see what David thinks. He is the seafarer among us, after all," Peter said as he and Glen walked back inside the cabin, where David was controlling the boat's route north towards the most northerly tip of Skye.

"The inlet is just coming up ahead of us," David said as he pointed out through the window and steered the boat slightly to the left, following the line of the coast.

Peter and Glen silently watched as David slowed the engine as they drew level with the inlet to the small bay.

"It's funny, I've sailed past this inlet virtually every day of my working life but never had a close look until now," David commented as he slowed the revs further and turned the boat into the inlet.

"What can we do?" Peter asked.

"Okay, someone on the front to give me an actual idea of the depth, beyond what the gauge tells me, and then someone else ready with the anchor. We'll put out the front anchor, maybe throw out a rear anchor too and also pull a mooring line with us as we walk up the beach. Tell the others to hold on," David instructed.

Peter and Glen left the cabin and Glen walked forward to the front of the boat while Peter pulled a small anchor out of a locker on the deck.

"Girls, can you be ready to drop this anchor when David shouts. Glen and I will do the same at the front, is that okay?" Glen asked.

"Yeah, we've got it," Becky answered.

David inched the boat forward as much as he dared, small movements dictated by the signals from Glen on the bow, until Glen put his hand across his throat to indicate that they should go no further. Glen dropped the anchor at the front and David reversed the boat to snag it. He then shouted, "Okay, Becky! Let the other anchor go."

Becky and Helen lifted the anchor over the gunwale and dropped it.

"Okay, everyone get their Glocks ready. Glen, David and I have the MP5s with spare ammo. Everyone put on their armoured vests. Just need to be careful," Peter instructed.

Glen and David pulled the small inflatable around from the rear, which they had been towing across the channel from their base. "Peter, can you grab the mooring line and that metal pole," David asked, pointing to a four-foot-long metal stake.

Glen and Becky got into the inflatable craft, followed by Helen, then David and finally Peter, who passed the pole down to Glen and then, with mooring line in hand, he lowered himself into the small rubber boat and between them they pushed away from the catamaran and Glen and David rowed the 10 to 15 metres to the shingle shore. Peter jumped out and Glen handed him the metal stake. Peter walked up the beach and rammed the pole into the surface of the beach, found a large rock and bashed the pole in until he felt it was secure, then tied the mooring line to it.

While he did that, the others got out of the small inflatable, pulled it up the beach and joined Peter by the pole.

"Right, Glen, which way?" Peter asked.

"Okay, stay together. It's up this track to the right, not far. In fact, the cottage should come into view once we get off the beach," Glen replied.

Just as Glen had described, the lone cottage came into view the moment they crested the slight rise at the top of the beach. It was a whitewashed building, sitting within its own land, with one or two other isolated properties visible further up the slopes of a rocky peak, known as Ben Volovaig. It took them less than five minutes to reach the property. The small group crouched down and waited while Glen moved forward, and after an inspection right around the boundary of the building, he stood back, turned and called the others to join him.

"It still appears secure; the locks look as they were when I was here about nine months ago. Let's have a look inside," Glen said as he pulled a set of keys from his pocket and slowly opened the door.

"Lovely spot, Glen. I can see why you would have chosen to retire here," Peter said.

"Aye, it's not bad, I suppose. Once I get the decorating sorted, I'll be quite comfortable here," Glen added.

"I love it, Glen, so much light and fresh air up here, even compared to back in town. Let's hope you can enjoy it if things ever return to normality," Becky said as she looked out of the large lounge window towards the sea and the view of Rona.

"Everything looks to be in order. You really have to know these houses are here and where the road is just to get to them. It doesn't lead anywhere else; part of the reason I bought it," Glen went on.

"If you want to wander on up the track to the farm, there may be some hens about, or even sheep. The farmer's name is Daniel. I'm just going to pack some fresh clothes and see if there is anything else useful I can take back to the island."

"We're happy to wait, Glen," Peter suggested.

"Okay, well, I won't be long," and with that Glen disappeared upstairs and some banging was heard as wardrobe doors were flung open and draws were slammed shut.

"Put the four panels together on their side, then we can float them out to the boat," Glen suggested as they lay the fence panels down on the beach. The expedition had been a success in so far as they now had five hens and had spotted some sheep and cattle further up the slopes of Ben Volovaig for a future mission. David and Peter somehow got the fence panels onto the deck of the catamaran, then Peter returned in the small inflatable to pick up the others and the flapping hens, who seemed nonplussed about an excursion over water. By the time they climbed aboard, David had loosely nailed the panels into a square on the rear deck of the boat and the hens were gently placed within its confines. Peter made another return to shore to collect the pole and mooring line, and once he was back on board, the two anchors were lifted and the boat retreated out of the inlet, then David put the engine into forward and they motored back out into the channel, with Skye now on their right-hand side.

"Daniel should have come with us," Peter said to Glen.

"Aye, well, maybe we can persuade him on another trip here. At least we know that the place has not been invaded by any of them maniacs from Portree," Glen said.

"They seem to be doing okay with supplies and have some more agricultural weaponry at their disposal should the need arise," Peter observed.

"His son, Alex, is a cracking shot too, so they will certainly do everything they can to defend themselves," Glen said.

"Well, I hope they felt our offer to join us on Rona was a genuine one," Peter said.

Becky, who had been listening, said, "It might be good to have another place on the main island where we are made to feel welcome and can perhaps trade or swap stuff with them. I mean, they gave us these hens, they have a store of summer produce and livestock which need tending, but they will be essential as we try and rebuild anything in the future."

"That is an excellent idea and probably how we are going to manage as we move forward." Helen applauded Becky's suggestion.

"Do you want to head back to the base or head down for a closer look at your town?" Peter asked the group.

"It might not hurt just to have a closer look. I'm not saying we need to go too close or go ashore or anything, but just to have a look," Becky asked.

"Okay, then!" Peter pulled a white square of cotton material from the drawer under one of the shelves in the cabin. "I thought this pillowcase could serve as a white flag in case we see anyone and feel confident enough to try and engage with them," he went on, mortified at using the term "engage", but unfortunately, in the circumstances, that was probably what would be needed to understand the intent of the people they had run into on their last visit to the town.

"We are then at least prepared for whatever we may come across," Glen added as David steered the boat due south down the middle of the channel, passing the inlet for their base on the left, and they watched as the east coast of Skye drifted past.

Peter could see some broken windows of the houses that fronted onto the bay from his binoculars as they approached the inner part of the inlet, still some 200 metres or so from the quayside of the town of Portree.

"Ease back on the engine and hold steady here, David," Peter instructed as they all had a clearer picture of their town. "Has that radio above the control panel got a PA system?" he asked.

"Aye, I think it can be set to PA mode," David replied.

"Are you sure it's wise to announce our presence here?" Becky looked from David, then back to Peter.

"Peter, rig that white cloth to the mooring pole and one of us can raise it on the fore deck," Glen suggested.

"If I wave the white flag, maybe one of you locals should use the PA. Might be better if they hear a Scottish accent," Peter commented.

"I'll do it!" Glen said.

Peter tied the pillowcase to the metal pole and made his way outside to the area in front of the cabin, raised his makeshift flag above his head and waved it.

Glen then addressed the town through the PA system.

"This is Glen Ritchie; I'm a local of Portree. Is there anyone in town that can hear me? We are here to talk to anyone who is here in the town of Portree. We just want to talk to anyone in Portree." The sound of the PA was quite tinny, but it echoed around the bay of the town as the catamaran bobbed in the water, holding station about 200 metres away from the quayside.

No response. Peter looked around the town and then back at Glen in the cabin. "Try again, Glen!" he shouted through the window to the town's local police sergeant.

Once more, Glen stated who he was and asked if there were any people that could hear him. Still nothing stirred in the town.

"David, do you want to move in a little closer and then try the PA again, Glen?" Peter shouted. David revved the engine and the boat slowly moved forward towards the quay. "Okay, that will do, David," Peter said, now reckoning they were about 70 or so metres offshore.

For a third time, Glen announced them over the PA to try and see if there was still anyone present in his own hometown.

Suddenly, the glass on the left-hand side of the cabin shattered, followed by one of the front panes, and shards of wood and fibre glass flew everywhere around Peter as the catamaran began to receive multiple hits from various firearms. Peter dived for cover onto the front deck, screaming, "Get us out of here!"

David reversed the boat at speed, turned it and engaged forward and the boat sped out of range while receiving still further small arms fire and birdshot rounds. Peter scrambled around to the rear deck and into the cabin, where all he could see was a river of blood running across the wooden interior deck.

Becky was hunched over a figure on the floor, clearly desperately tending to them. Peter could see Glen had a cut head, but he was still stood up, instinctively firing through the broken window of the cabin, back at the shore. David had similar cuts to his head and arms but was driving the boat back out.

"They were in the boats, hidden under all the nets and other stuff on the trawlers," Glen said as he changed magazines on his MP5.

"Peter, it's Helen; she's got a piece of glass in her neck, and I can't stop the bleeding." Becky looked up at Peter as he stood motionless, looking down at his wife.

Helen looked white and was on the verge of dropping into unconsciousness. Peter was used to blood, but not his wife's and not this quantity. He knew that it was bad.

"Keep as much direct pressure on it as you can," he shouted at Becky as he knelt down and stroked his wife's cheek.

"It's alright, love, I'm here now. You are going to be okay."

Helen tried to smile up at him, but she was too weak to form the smile. Peter leaned forward as Helen's lips moved. "Love you, love," she whispered. It was the last thing she said as the light quickly faded from her eyes. Helen was dead. Peter slumped back on the deck, staring at the body of his wife as Becky tearfully tried to mop the blood from her face.

"Becky, it's okay. I've got her now." Peter leant forward, putting his hand on Becky's arm, stopping her endeavours. Becky stood and went to David, where she buried herself in his arms and wept. Peter took the lifeless body of his wife in his arms and hugged her as they lay there on the bloodied glass-strewn cabin floor. He stayed in that position all the way back to the base.

When they had got within range, Glen had radioed Duncan, and when they arrived at the jetty on Rona, both Duncan and Mary were there to meet them. After some time just moored at the quayside, Glen spoke to Peter. "Let us take her for you. We'll carry her up to the mess hall for you and put her in one of the rooms."

Peter looked up at Glen, tears streaming down his face. Very slowly, he loosened his grip on the body of his wife and Glen and Duncan very gently lifted Helen between them and carried her out of the cabin and up onto the quayside, where Mary had opened the rear door of a Land Rover. Becky came back into the boat cabin and knelt down to Peter.

"You come with David and me. Let's get back to the mess, get ourselves cleaned up." She then very carefully, with David, lifted Peter to his feet and led him slowly back up to the jetty and towards the vehicle.

"Do you mind, I think I'll walk, Becky, thank you, give me some time and space to think. Thank you all. I'll see you all back at the dining room soon." They looked at Peter, then Glen quietly ushered them all into the Land Rover and Mary drove them away. Peter stared blankly out to sea, at the channel between the islands. He stayed staring at the view for a good 20 minutes before slowly turning and walking off the jetty and around the crescent of the bay, back towards the accommodation block.

The chill of the shorter days had now given way to the freezing, driving rain of true winter. Short grey days with long wind-swept nights. The sea around the island crashed unerringly against the cliffs and crags. The waves had angry, white-topped peaks as they broke through the channel between the islands. The first isolated squalls of snow showers were followed by more prolonged blizzards that covered the entire island in a blanket of white, and the ground became frozen and hidden beneath this white cloak. This adverse weather was perhaps the greatest defence against potential assault from elsewhere. Any passage across the channel between the islands was going to be a treacherous undertaking. Despite this, the hardy group of island dwellers kept up a 24-hour watch from the lighthouse tower. Even when visibility was down to nothing, there was someone in the tower. More often than not, that someone was Peter.

Since the loss of Helen, Peter had taken over the watch duties virtually single-handedly. After a few weeks of despondency, Peter had raised his head one day and looked hard at himself in the mirror. He felt it was an important moment. Either he lost himself to the pit of the despair he felt with the loss of his wife, or he buried these feelings and kept himself busy, working for the others in this makeshift group of displaced locals. The rest of the people around him had been fantastic, both giving him the space to grieve but also supportive in readmitting him into the daily running of their communal home. There had been some initial awkwardness around him, but as time passed, he had found their sensitivity around him to be a burden, and after telling them so, things became easier. The easiest time for him was in the gym sessions with Scotty. His undoubted empathy meant that the two of them found themselves bonding more closely than with the rest of the team.

Duncan had been rarely able to venture out to fish because of the poor weather conditions. They were lucky that he had preserved his previous catches so well and the freezers in the kitchens were well stocked. Likewise, Margaret and Minnie had used the excess tomatoes from the crop to create a thick broth, mixed with some pearl barley and other pulses, which they had chilled, then stored in the freezers too. The store of flour, though depleted, was still plentiful enough for Minnie to bring forth fresh bread and rolls and onion-flavoured bagels. The hens had been given a space and a shelter to call their own and now they had fresh eggs most mornings, which had broadened the scope of recipes available to the redoubtable chefs. Fresh meat was still missing from the menu, but it was not inconceivable that this could be obtained from Glen's farming neighbour on a future trip to Skye if safe and when the weather allowed.

Callum had persuaded them all to make paper streamers to decorate the communal dining room and attached lounge, and they had built a tree out of bits of wood and coat hangers, upon which Callum placed more of the paper decorations he had been manufacturing. It was not as they had ever known it before, but it was Christmas. Duncan made the hard decision to sacrifice one of the hens for their Christmas lunch. Becky had pleaded the case for the hen's survival, but in a democratic vote, the hen wound up on the Christmas dinner table. It might have been a time for both Peter and Scotty to dwell on their respective losses, and perhaps to an extent, Peter found it incredibly hard on his own. But in the company of his island comrades, he put on a cheery demeanour and joined in with as much game playing and Christmas drinking to allay the fears in the others that they were being insensitive to both his and Scotty's loss.

Several days after the Christmas Day delights, Peter had wandered outside, as the weather had calmed itself and allowed for a day of clear skies and bright winter sunshine. Peter walked up to the lighthouse. He did the daily check on the detonation controls, now hidden inside a makeshift canvas tent by the gate in the whitewashed wall. Peter ventured no further. The winter's snow covering had made the positions of the Claymores all but invisible and to walk anywhere beyond the wall compound of the lighthouse would be suicide. So, he checked the firing mechanisms of the mines they had laid. He waved up at David, who was taking a turn in the lighthouse to keep watch. Peter walked back the way he had come. He ambled past the helipad and the accommodation blocks. Peter pulled the tarpaulin off the roof of the Land Rover parked there and checked the mechanism of the Browning .50 machine gun on the roof. Happy it was in good order, he replaced the tarpaulin. He carried on past the main office and down to the small crescent bay. He walked slowly round and onto the concrete jetty. The sea was calm today and there was a faint warmth coming from the winter sun, which was pleasant with no wind chill. Peter sat down on the dock edge and looked out across the inlet towards the sea channel. He glanced around him, then secure in the knowledge that he was on his own, he let himself think of the monumental loss Helen had been to him. He fought back the tears for a while, but eventually, he let them come. He forced himself to sniff and wiped his eyes. He reached inside his jacket and pulled out his hip flask.

"I miss you, love. I miss you more than I can put into words." He took a long deep swig from the flask and closed his eyes as he thought of his wife.

Peter conducted himself, outwardly, like he was coming to terms with his loss. He threw himself into the daily tasks that living on the island necessitated. He spent time cleaning and preparing firearms and kept them ready for use in a storage room, near to where the store of rations was held. He dragged boxes of ammunition and other equipment out of the armoury and brought it up to the accommodation block and still more up to the lighthouse compound. Everyone watched him working, hoping that this was a sign that he was slowly recovering from the devastating loss he had endured. Glen and Duncan spent time during the day helping secure loose fence posts and strengthening the barbed wire barrier that existed between the lighthouse compound and the cliff edge. Margaret and Minnie continued to create culinary masterpieces that kept everyone's spirits up during the long winter.

There had been no sign of any activity from the area of the town of Portree, but as Peter continually pointed out, it was probably a lull caused by the extremely poor winter weather, and that at no stage should they drop their heightened alert state. It was the constant fear of the unknown that led to Peter's strategy to take the fight to the mob responsible for the death of his wife. He had initially thought that it was something he should share with the group. It should have been discussed and voted on, as all the major decisions had been. But Peter was not thinking as he had before the terrible events of his last trip to the town. The rest of the group genuinely thought that Peter was getting over the worst of his loss and time was healing the morbid feelings around him, but Peter hid his emotions well. He knew he had once been known as a deep, secretive person. But with Helen, he had been able to find a sunnier disposition and more affectionate side to his character. With her gone, these traits had deserted him, replaced by a seething feeling of anger and resentment for the loss of his wife.

A brooding, menacing temper had overtaken him. He was able to act positively around the others, but the darkness in his soul was being brought back into the light, not by a recovery, but by a determination to reap his revenge upon those that had taken so much from him.

Working subtly around the armoury at the times of his ammunition resupply, Peter had secured another Browning .50 heavy machine gun and been able to hide it aboard the catamaran in the small harbour. On another trip, he had taken the firing tripod, and at the pretence of refuelling the boat, he had brought boxes and boxes of the belt-fed ammunition for the gun onto the boat. He found some heavy-duty packing straps, the ones with the ratchets, used to secure things on the backs of lorries for transportation. In an effort to conceal his activities, Peter decided he would rig his weapons system on the boat once he had left the harbour and was away from the compound. Once he was far enough away from calls for him to rethink his plans and generally be talked out of his endeavour. He added still more arms to the boat's inventory with the addition of grenades, smoke cannisters, his sniper rifle, the M16 shotgun replica, and he would, of course, have a Glock and MP5 anyway.

The weeks passed and nothing much changed around the base. Margaret and Minnie had been taken down to the subterranean base by Glen to have a look around. They marvelled at the size and scale of the complex and brought some industrial-sized tins of baked beans and some similarly gargantuan tins of processed meat to the surface in an effort to vary the rather limited winter diet. Becky was becoming restless and frustrated by the still frozen soil and her inability to sow any crops yet. Finally, the weather relented and there was an increase in the average temperature and the days started to become longer. Duncan began to plan a fishing trip to stock up on their dwindling freezer supply of fresh fish. Peter knew he would have to implement his plan soon; Duncan would quickly spot the weaponry concealed under a tarpaulin on the boat.

Peter decided he would go on the next suitable day. He woke early, around 3am, and quickly dressed in warm winter clothing and heavy walking boots. He had his faithful black beanie hat on, a decent pair of gloves and a small torch in his pocket. He struggled into the body armour and decided that he would take a helmet today. He strapped the gun belt around his waist, loaded a fresh magazine into the Glock, racked it and slid it into its holster. He picked up his MP5 again, loaded a 30-round magazine, cocked the weapon and put the safety catch on, then put the carry strap over his head and slung the gun to one side. He knew that there were binoculars on the boat. David and Duncan had boarded up the shattered glass windows of the boat's cabin, but it was still going to be bitterly cold, especially this time of the morning. Peter silently let himself out of his room and into the early morning darkness, walked deftly to the jetty and climbed down onto the rear of the boat. Peter started the engine, then loosened the mooring lines, eased the catamaran away from the jetty wall and moved slowly forward out into the bay. Once Peter was a little way across the bay, he steered towards the far side of the inlet and then threw out the rear anchor. He then went forward and let the front anchor go. Once he felt the boat was secured to the bed of the inlet, he began assembling the tripod, and using the packing straps, he was able to fix the tripod firmly in position. He then lifted the heavy Browning machine gun onto the tripod so that it was facing out over the stern of the boat. *Like a Toyota Hilux on water!* Peter thought.

Peter eased the boat out of the inlet using the ambient light from the moon and the stars on this clear night. It was cold enough to put a slight sparkle and sheen onto all the exposed surfaces of the catamaran. Peter kept the engine revs low; after all, he was in no hurry. He suspected that his departure could have been noted by David, who would have been in the lighthouse tower lookout during this night. He knew David was as diligent as the next person, but he suspected that during the quiet cold hours of winter darkness, he was probably sat in the comfortable chair just inside the light tower and his eyes might be closed. The lack of calls on the short-wave radio on the control panel of the boat indicated that Peter had been correct, and his departure had gone seemingly unnoticed.

The boat drifted into the bay of Portree. Peter eased back still further on the throttle of the boat and gently allowed it to drift in towards the quayside. When he was some 200–300 metres from the line of moored trawlers and the quay itself, he cut the engine and went to the front of the boat. He knew the anchor chain would clatter to the seabed, but at this time of the morning, he was hoping this would not be heard by anyone in the town. Once the front anchor was down, Peter went to the rear of the catamaran and dropped the smaller rear anchor over the back of the boat to doubly ensure he was well secured in his position just out in the bay.

Then he loaded the first belt of ammunition for the Browning machine gun and prepared the other similar boxes so it would be a simple job to reach over and load the next box. Peter then took the sniper rifle from its case and opened the folding stock, loaded a clip of five rounds and laid it carefully on the deck beside the Browning. Peter went back inside the cabin and down to the lower forward area and brought out an old collapsible deck chair. He returned to the rear deck, opened the chair and placed it in the middle of the deck behind the machine gun and sat down. He checked his watch; 4.45am. He rose again and went back inside the cabin. Once again he returned, this time with his trusty dented old Stanley thermos flask. He poured himself a coffee from the flask, sat back down in the chair and looked out at the shadowy town in front of him. He tried not to think of the others in the group from the island, knowing that they would have objected to his actions this morning and done everything they could to stop him. Hence the reason for the secret and underhand way he had slipped away from the island in the dead of night, and now he waited for those resident in the town to wake and show themselves to him. He wasn't tired. Since losing Helen, he didn't sleep much anyway. His outward signs of recovery could be shed like a camouflage, and he could be his true self this morning. A brooding, seething rage of anger welled up in him as he waited to take his vengeance.

While he waited, he wondered how many there were in the town; 20, 30, 100, 200? Did they use the trawlers to fish? They had the benefit of the two massive storage tanks of fuel, painted a dull matt green, situated just behind the harbour buildings at the end of Quay Street. Peter picked up the sniper rifle for the fifth or sixth time and sighted the weapon on the trawler moored in the middle of the fleet. Focused as he was, he was still nervous about the events to come, but he knew that nothing would deviate him from his actions. He spotted seagulls in the air now, indicating that the darkness was giving way to the brightness of a new winter's day. Not quite a year since he had travelled with his wife Helen to this beautiful remote spot. A year of cataclysmic change that was now ending with Peter ready to reap his vengeance on the people directly responsible for the death of his beloved wife.

He felt that by mooring the catamaran as he had, it would be easy to hide in plain sight among the other boats in the bay, and it would allow him to see people emerge onto the streets and afford him the element of surprise he felt he needed. The grey sky was brightening with every minute now; Peter could sense that he didn't have long to wait. He had lined up a dozen or so smoke cannisters and had a canvas bag full of a variety of lethal anti-personnel grenades should he need to venture closer to the shore. Finally, he stood and picked up the sniper rifle. He had laid a blanket down on the deck, and he lay down now, and using the two forward legs of the rifle resting on the edge of the boat, he steadied himself behind the sights of the rifle, flipped open the telescopic sight covers and scanned the street along the bay front of the town through the cross hairs of the gun sight. Still no movement visible to him in Portree. He assumed the power might have been out, but one or two faint yellow lights could be seen in a couple of windows, indicating lit candles or torches perhaps.

A bang from the town caused Peter to lift his head in time to see a darkly clad figure emerge from the hotel where both he and Helen had first encountered Margaret many months before. The figure placed a black woollen hat on his head, very similar to the one that Peter was sporting that morning. He then slammed the door and began to walk up the side of the street towards the town, away from Peter's position. *Not long now*, Peter thought as he watched the figure walk slowly out of sight. Three more doors opened in the buildings lined up along Quay Street and one that faced out into the bay. Shadowy figures all made their way up the street and out of sight into the town.

Another half an hour to 45 minutes passed and Peter grew cold and stiff in the morning air. He stood up and walked around the deck, doing that thing where you flap your arms around your body in an effort to get warm. He walked into the cabin and returned to the deck with a pair of binoculars and scanned the town now that the light was sufficient to see the streets along the sea front and detect movement. Suddenly, a group appeared, walking casually down the hill and out along Quay Street. Peter counted about 20 men, all dressed in dark or camouflaged bulky coats, with heavy-looking boots and various colours of head gear. Peter scanned closely, trying to spot the leader. Maybe the chap at the front with the peaked tweed cap, smoking a cigarette. He began pointing at the other men, and even from this range, it was clear he was giving instructions or orders as they all walked along the street. Peter slowly put down the binoculars and reached for the sniper rifle. He lay down on the long seat along the edge of the deck and rested the legs of the rifle on the rear of the boat. He once again fixed the telescopic sight on the chest of the person he perceived to be the leader. It was almost too close range for this weapon. Peter breathed more slowly as he prepared to fire. Then as the man momentarily stopped, Peter gently squeezed the trigger.

The man flew backwards with the force of the impact, dead before he landed. There was a moment of incredulity from the people around the victim. This gave Peter the opportunity to jump to his feet and take up position behind the .50 Browning heavy machine gun and commence firing. He fought the weapon to keep his aim low, firing through the masts and rigging of the moored boats and into the rapidly dwindling group of people. Peter paused for a split second to check his aim, then recommenced with a sweeping ferocity, directing the arc of the gun side to side. Great chunks of flesh and bone could be seen tearing from the many victims as they dove for cover. Peter paused again, this time throwing several smoke cannisters towards the quay. He reloaded another belt, cocked the weapon and began firing again. This time he deliberately fired at the boats, watching the wooden cabins disintegrate and glass and fibreglass explode everywhere. As people moved from cover, he found them with a short burst. One man was running down the street; Peter caught him in the back with several rounds, and he literally came apart as he fell. Peter continued to rain fire down upon the moored boats in the harbour, finding a fuel tank and exploding one small pleasure cruiser. This fire began to spread to other boats moored next to it. Peter reloaded another belt and surveyed the carnage. He had spotted several men cowering near to the large olive-green fuel tanks. A quick adjustment of the angle of the tripod and he once again fired. The wood and glass of the quayside office came apart in front of him, several seconds before the first fuel tank exploded, sending a great orange ball of flame into the early winter morning sky, followed by a huge billowing cloud of thick black smoke. A few seconds later, another enormous explosion indicated that the second tank of fuel had also exploded. Peter watched to see if any of the people he had seen sheltering near there had survived.

Peter stood, brought up the rear anchor and then went to the front of the boat and raised the main anchor. Starting the engine, he moved slowly further away from the town, then arced the boat around and moved back into the bay, close to the other boats that had been moored, like the catamaran, out in the bay on fixed buoys. Peter once again slowed the engines to idle and stepped out and surveyed the result of his assault. The whole quayside was concealed beneath a thick pall of smoke and flame. The fires from the fuel tanks had set light to the buildings in Quay Street and it was spreading along the line of terraces. Peter caught sight of some movement up above the quay and returned to the Browning. Several reports indicated that small arms fire was being aimed in his direction, but the range would be extreme, in his opinion. He reloaded yet another belt of ammunition for the Browning, angled the weapon as high as he dared and fired a quick burst across the front of the buildings along the bay. Glass and brickwork were shattered in equal measure as he rained fire at the town. Any firing that had been previously heard was now silent. Peter slumped down in the deck chair and stared out at the devastation around him. He felt a wetness on his cheeks. He had been crying tears of anger during the entirety of the attack. After a minute or so he roused himself and returned to the cabin. Increasing the revs of the engine, he moved the catamaran back through the moored boats and out into the wider bay towards the channel. Once safely into the main channel, he slowed the engine again and walked back out onto the rear deck of the catamaran. He stared back at the appalling sight of the town of Portree, hidden beneath a blanket of thick smoke, with great eruptions of flame still billowing from the fuel tanks and the buildings close to them. He suspected that the group he had left behind on the island would have seen the explosions from their position. *Oh, well, this might take some explaining*, he thought.

He took a final look at his handy work and said, "That was for you, Helen, and for you, Sonia."

He returned to the cabin, gunned the engine and headed north out into the channel, back to Rona.

They at least waited for him to safely moor the vessel to the jetty on the island and clamber up onto the quayside wall before they started on him.

"What the fuck, Peter!" Becky opened up.

"Morning, all, um... err... there were some things that needed doing. I apologise, but I was never going to rest until I had retaliated in some way." Peter vainly tried to justify his actions to the group gathered on the jetty.

"Aye! Well, good on you, Peter. Just wish I could have come too." Scotty walked forward and patted Peter on the back. One person, at least, that Peter knew would always support him.

"Well, without discussing it with us, I suspect you knew that we would have disagreed with your actions," Glen said.

"Peter, I thought you were recovering from the loss of Helen?" Duncan said.

"I don't think I will ever recover from losing Helen, but today will go a long way to starting that process," Peter replied.

"We could have talked about your feelings. We could have tried to understand," Mary spoke for the first time.

"At the end of the day, you would have all been fantastic, as indeed you have been, but it would have ended up with you inevitably trying to talk me out of taking this action today."

"So, what exactly did you do, apart from seemingly blowing the hell out of everything?" Glen asked.

"I waited until I saw a group of people approach the trawlers, presumed they were about to do some fishing. I identified someone who looked to be in charge and shot him. Then before the rest could react, I opened up with the machine gun, causing the fuel tanks on the jetty to explode and start some fires to neighbouring buildings. I suspect I killed quite a few of them," Peter said. As he did so, he nodded to the .50 Browning machine gun sitting proudly on the rear deck of the catamaran.

Duncan looked down at the deck of the boat and raised his eyebrows at the mountain of spent brass cartridges littering the deck. "Fired a few rounds then? We'll be shovelling those brass cases out of there for weeks!"

"Look, what's done is done. I can't change that. I was never going to seek or get approval from you all. I hope in time you can understand and forgive me, but if it's all the same to you, I am tired and I am going to my bed." Peter indicated he was finished talking and walked stiffly past the group and headed around the bay, back to the accommodation.

The others stared sadly at Peter's hunched figure as he walked slowly away from them.

"What do we do now?" Duncan asked the rest of the group.

"He may have ended the problem of the people from the mainland. He may have killed their leader and decimated their numbers to remove them as a threat to us as we move forward. But part of me worries that he may have just poked a stick in the hornet's nest, and we may not have heard the last of the people who now inhabit our town," Glen surmised.

"Aye! So, what do we do now?" Duncan looked around at the others as he asked the question.

"In the immediacy of Peter's action, we must maintain our 24-hour watch and be prepared to defend ourselves at all times," Glen replied.

"But Peter may have killed the majority of the occupants of our town," Mary said, trying to make sense of what had occurred.

"Mary, we don't know. We have never had a chance to see the true picture of the number of people that came onto Skye all those months ago. We could have a situation as Glen described, where Peter has perhaps killed 15 to 20 of them and they still have over 200 people living in our town." Becky almost shouted her reply at Mary in frustration at Peter's actions and the very real danger he could have possibly placed them all in.

"Look, the man was clearly devastated by the loss of his wife, and unlike me, he actually did something about it. I don't understand why you lot cannae understand that the man felt he needed to take a more direct approach. My only regret is I never got to join him in what he just did. Now I am going to go and pour Peter a large drink and toast the wives we have both lost." Scotty turned away from the group and he too walked off around the bay, back to the base.

Glen watched Scotty go and then looked back at the rest of the group. "Peter saved you lot when he brought you here. I suspect the people who took over our town may not have been so generous. He was part of the group that pulled me out of the town and brought me here too. He discovered this place, as a tourist. We, who have lived here all our lives, never even knew of the existence of such a facility on our doorstep. While I am not happy with the actions Peter took this morning, I do understand where he was coming from. I am also prepared to give him a break and hope we can all move on from this." Glen set out his position.

"Oh, bloody hell. I wish he hadn't done it, but we do owe him, so I agree, we must give him some slack and pray that he hasn't caused more harm than good." Mary endorsed Glen's stance too.

"Well, I think he's a fucking idiot, but that's my opinion and I will keep the ideals of the group together and hope I can learn to understand his actions. It may just take me a little longer than the rest of you," Becky exclaimed, clearly still very angry, then she walked back to the Land Rover and opened one of the rear doors. "Come on, let's get back to the warmth of the dining room and have some tea before we all freeze."

Glen, Duncan, Mary, Callum and David all turned as one, walked over to the Land Rover, jumped in and headed back to the base.

Life on the island began to return to a more outdoor experience as the weather started to improve and the days became longer. Becky was still frosty around Peter, and he learned that he needed to try and spend a little less time with her than the others. The ladies in the kitchens continued to provide excellent meals at the end of each day. Scotty brought some of the gym equipment outside into the early spring sunshine so people could exercise in the fresh Scottish air. Glen and Peter once again found a bond through their past lives as police officers and maintained the shift pattern of 24-hour watches over the island. They also checked the Claymores and fences up by the lighthouse on a daily basis. Some of the wire on the fence needed tightening after the long winter.

Becky was once again busy planting seeds and digging larger areas of land near to the base to try and increase the quantity of fresh vegetables they might have available as they embarked on another season of survival on the island. Duncan was as good as his word and literally shovelled the spent brass cartridge cases from the .50 Browning machine gun off the deck of the catamaran. He took the boat out with David, headed due north and put over his first lines for quite some time. The catch was not one he would have been proud of as a commercial trawlerman out of Portree, but for a single day's fishing, he was able to fill one entire chest freezer, and while out near the north coastline, he threw over some makeshift lobster pots he had constructed from old bits of wood and some camouflage netting he had found in one of the armoury stores.

Callum was growing up fast and it was actually Peter who suggested to Mary that he would be happy to provide some rudimentary school classes for him, as both a way to help Callum, but also as a way for Peter to have something tangible to do. Callum was a little dubious at first, but when Mary sneaked a look through a crack in the door of one of the empty rooms where Peter was teaching Callum, she found them laughing and talking about the books of Charles Dickens. Not wishing to interrupt, she quietly left them to it. Later over the dinner table, she chanced upon her moment.

"So, tell me, Callum, what was so amusing today about Charles Dickens?"

Callum looked up at his mother and then across to Peter, who just subtly nodded.

"Well, err! Peter was talking about the character of Miss Havisham and her sitting in her wedding dress for all those years. Peter was telling me about one of the times when he was a policeman in London, and he had been called to deal with a complaint about a bad smell coming from a house. Peter couldn't get into the house, and no one was replying, so after a while, he broke a small window by the front door and entered." Callum drew breath and looked over to Peter.

"So, I walked into this old mansion-like house, with rubbish and filth everywhere." Peter took over telling the story. "It was just like I had always imagined the house of Miss Havisham from *Great Expectations* would have been like. We were laughing because as I tried to walk through all the rubbish and filth on the floor, I placed my boot squarely on a full carton of milk that literally exploded all over me. Now, this milk must have been weeks old, and I was covered in this foul-smelling cream-cheese-like substance. If the smell had been bad before my arrival, I had simply made it 10 times worse. We called the council, who cleared the empty house, and I returned to the nick, where my colleagues decided that I had to remove my stained and foul-smelling uniform in the yard and walk down to the locker room in my underwear, much to the amusement of all of them, and of Callum today, when I told him the story."

The table all laughed at Peter's retelling of his story.

"Thanks, Peter. It's kind of you to take such time with Callum and it's so nice to hear you laugh again," Mary spoke quietly as they enjoyed their dinner.

Peter was doing what he had always done. When things got too tough while he was a serving officer, he compartmentalised his situation. He had placed the trauma associated with the loss of his dear wife Helen into a recess in his brain. He knew it was there, but he was able to function and shut out the ache and agony he felt over her loss. Outwardly he was the same thoughtful though rather deep individual. He was able to operate and interact with the others in the group, not necessarily as if nothing had happened, but he was more positive with them and provided a sunnier disposition when working, speaking and socialising with the group. Inwardly he was able to cope the majority of the time, to keep himself busy in order not to dwell on his pain. But the times on his own, when on watch duty in the lighthouse or alone in his room, the demons came and unlocked the compartment in his brain and made him relive the death of his wife over and over again. Sometimes in bed, he would wake up in a cold sweat, thinking he was cradling the bloodied corpse of his wife in his arms. When with the group and especially with Callum, he did his utmost to bury these thoughts and try and move forward with the demands placed upon them all by the challenging life they had made for themselves on the island.

There was no sight or sound of anything in the vicinity of Portree. Duncan had steered the catamaran south in the channel a couple of times on his fishing trips in order to see if there was anything going on in his town, but apart from the odd wisp of smoke from the burned-out Quay Street properties, there was nothing to be seen. To be fair to Duncan, he hadn't ventured all that close to the bay and had not had any vision on what might have been happening on the opposite shore of Raasay, especially around the jetty where the ferry had last been moored. Between the men of the group, they kept up the 24-hour watch from the tower of the island lighthouse. This onerous task was becoming easier as the daylight grew longer, and the weather began to improve. Peter and Glen conducted a daily routine of inspecting their defences, ensuring that all the Claymores were still connected, and the command wires and clackers were protected from the elements and ready for immediate use.

During one evening around the dinner table, Peter had suggested that they ought to have a drill in place for what action should be taken in case of attack and perhaps some sort of practice, including the withdrawal from the base to the subterranean facility, to give them an idea of how long it would take them to secure themselves underground from when an attacking force was first seen. Becky had been a little critical at first, wondering if such action was still necessary when nothing had been seen or heard from Portree or anywhere for so long. But Peter, perhaps with his customary sixth sense and naturally cautious nature, had insisted that such a drill might pay dividends if an attack became a reality.

As was now usual with the group, they debated the idea over the meal, and after everyone had voiced their point of view, they cast a vote. By a majority, it was decided that such a plan to practise a move to the underground shelter in the event of attack was a legitimately good idea.

For the purpose of the test, David was the lookout in the tower of the lighthouse. Becky was where Becky would most likely be, tending the ever-growing field of crops. Margaret and Minnie would be in the kitchens. Glen would be down by the jetty area, or in the Land Rover on the bay road, prepared with the roof-mounted .50 Browning machine gun, should it be required to slow any assault from the jetty. Callum and Mary would be somewhere within the base complex. Scotty would be down by the gym area, closest to the entrance to the underground shelter. Duncan would be in the lighthouse building, technically resting between watch duties he shared with David. Peter decided he would be on a roving patrol, based more up towards the lighthouse, where he could have a view of any potential assault from the sea towards the jetty and also any land-based attack from the south. The signal for an attack in the drill, and in reality, would be given as three blasts from a gas cannister klaxon Peter had found in the armoury. Everyone knew that the drill would happen, but only Peter knew at what time he planned to sound the klaxon.

Peter walked over to the edge of the cliff, near to where the makeshift wire fence had been erected. He looked back up at the lighthouse tower and waved at David, who was surveying the island from his vantage point. Peter could also see Glen sat casually behind the blunt end of the machine gun on the roof of the Land Rover. He had sited the vehicle on the rise of the approach road, just outside the gate of the complex, with a broad field of fire out over the bay towards the jetty and the sea channel beyond. Peter looked back south, down the length of the island and could make out one of the odd stark olive-green Claymore mines half-buried in the undergrowth. *I need to camouflage those better*, he thought.

Peter checked his watch; it was a little after 4pm in the afternoon. He suspected that people had been on tenterhooks all day, waiting for the three blasts from the klaxon.

He prised the aerosol cannister from his pocket, pulled out the red plastic trumpet from another and affixed this to the top of the can. A quick shake and he depressed the button on top three times...

"Armageddon, Armageddon!" David shouted over the radio; their agreed signal that an attack was happening, and they should make for the shelter. Peter ran to the command tent and the Claymore controls. David descended from the lighthouse tower and joined him and Duncan, who had emerged from the main lighthouse building. Glen took up a firing position on the Land Rover. Margaret, Minnie, Callum and Mary all made their way swiftly to the gym, where Scotty was waiting to escort them all to the entrance building to the underground centre. Becky had been in the crop field, and she made her way to Scotty and the others. Scotty was tasked with getting this group in the shelter and taking up control duties underground and, with Mary and Becky's help, was to monitor the surveillance cameras and spot the rest of the group as they retreated to the shelter. Once Scotty was sure that all were accounted for, he would close, seal and lock the bunker's main door.

Glen stayed in position for the agreed 10 minutes. Peter, Duncan and David did likewise. Glen then drove the Land Rover back to the gym area and made his way underground. Peter, Duncan and David waited the allotted time and then all jumped in the tactically positioned Land Rover, and they too drove down the hill to the gym, parking next to Glen's vehicle. The three then all made their way underground. Scotty, monitoring all this, watched on camera as the three appeared and joined Glen in the underground dock and walked through the bunker door. Peter then contacted Scotty on the intercom. Scotty confirmed that all were within the safety of the shelter and Peter closed and locked the blast door. Once the door was securely locked, he checked his watch. *Twelve minutes*, he thought. *Would that be long enough in reality?*

That evening over supper, they all discussed the emergency drill. Glen decided that he would take charge of the discussion; not to usurp Peter, but more to be a supportive comrade in arms and to take some of the burden from him.

"It was a bit unrealistic if you ask me," Becky snapped at the group. "I think it unlikely that any attack will actually come, and if it does, then we are almost certainly not going to be in the spread-out strategic positions that you put us in, Peter."

"I agree, Becky, but it was a case of just seeing what might happen and, more importantly, how long it would take us to get underground once an attack was detected," Peter answered.

"Becky, it was just a drill and that was always going to make it a little bit unrealistic, but we made a good fist of getting ourselves to safety." Glen put in his opinion.

"What about if it was at night, or similar to your tactic when you attacked Portree, Peter, very early in the morning before the sun rises?" David asked.

"Well, maybe we should conduct a drill with us all in bed in our rooms, with just the two watchmen up at the lighthouse," Peter offered.

"Enough with the drills, Peter. We are obviously going to be able to cope now we know what to do in the very unlikely event that any attack actually happens." Becky was now getting crosser with each sentence.

Sensing the hostility, David stood. "Anyone fancy some whisky? Let's not get bogged down in arguing about this. We did a drill; it seemed to work, and we got underground pretty quickly. I feel that we could do so from any position at any time, should it become necessary."

"Okay then, enough of the drills; you on board with that, Peter?" Glen asked.

"I'm fine, I have always only been trying the best I can to find ways to ensure our safety. I concede that it was not the brightest thing in the world to have ransacked the town like I did, but it's done now and all I can do is my best to protect us all," Peter stated.

"I'm sorry I got upset. I know you are trying to protect us. It just sometimes feels a bit overprotective," Becky said quietly as she looked at Peter.

"Point taken. Thank you all for your unwavering support these past months," Peter replied.

"Right, where's this whisky, David?" Glen said, sensing that the meeting was over and that, as a group, they each knew of their respective responsibilities.

23

The first shot woke Peter from his fitful sleep. He was slumped in an armchair in the main building of the lighthouse. He and Glen were on the night duty shift and Glen was in the tower while Peter had his break. The radio by his arm crackled into life.

"Shots from the south. I repeat, shots fired from the land to the south. Over," Glen shouted over the radio.

"Sound the alarm and warn everyone, Glen. Over," Peter replied.

"ARMAGEDDON, ARMAGEDDON," Glen shouted the alarm call over the radio, and almost immediately after this, Peter heard the three blasts on the klaxon.

By now, Peter was running up to the tower and the primitive tent structure that protected the command wires for the Claymore mines.

Glen was still in the tower as two more birdshot rounds struck the masonry of the tower several feet below Glen's position on the metal balcony.

"Glen, get down from there. You are too exposed," Peter shouted up to Glen.

"There's a ship coming into the inlet, heading for the jetty," Glen shouted.

"Duncan, are you receiving? Over," Peter called on the radio.

"Go ahead. Over," Duncan replied.

"There is a boat heading to the jetty; can you and David use the machine gun to defend that area? Scotty, get everyone else into the shelter, please. Over," Peter instructed.

"Received. Everyone is awake and on the move. Where is the shooting coming from? Over," Duncan asked.

"There is an assault from the land to the south; we'll try to slow them down. No sign of numbers, it's still too dark, but the light will be up soon. Over," Peter replied. "Can you see anything?" Peter shouted up to Glen, who was now sheltering inside the balcony door of the lighthouse tower.

"Use the radio. Over," Glen replied over the radio.

"Can you see how many? Over," Peter repeated quietly, using his radio.

"Numerous dark shadows. Could be upwards of 20 to 30. Over," Glen replied.

Peter took up his position behind the trigger of another .50 Browning heavy machine gun he had sited in a gap in the wall of the lighthouse compound. He had built a protective wall of flat stones and odd bricks he had found lying around. His position was now well protected, and he had an excellent field of fire, facing towards the expanse of land to the south. Several birdshot pellets struck the wall of the lighthouse compound as he seated himself behind the machine gun.

Duncan and Scotty were in the Land Rover and reversing into position at the fenced entrance to the base, with a view overlooking the bay. They could hear the low hum of a large diesel engine out in the channel and the sound was definitely getting louder. The light was just beginning to break through the darkness of the early morning and Duncan was looking intently at the channel through the binoculars from the roof of the Land Rover.

"Peter, receiving. Over," Peter heard Duncan say on the radio.

"Go on, Duncan. Over," Peter replied.

"It's the bloody ferry from Raasay, the MV *Hallaig*, and it's heading this way. Over," Duncan shouted over the radio.

"Duncan, do your best to hold them back as long as you can then get to the shelter. Over," Peter ordered.

"Understood, we will. Out."

"Scotty, receiving. Over." Peter tried to make contact with Scotty.

"Aye! Go on. Over," came the unmistakable Scottish burr of Scotty.

"What is your situation? Over."

"I have Margaret, Minnie, Callum, Becky, Talisker and Mary all with me at the underground entrance. Over," Scotty replied.

"Understood. Get underground; we will be with you as soon as we can. Over," Peter replied.

"Aye, get a move on. Over," came Scotty's reply.

Peter once more turned his attention to the manoeuvring dark shadowy figures in front of him.

"Glen, can you see anything from up there? Over."

"They are going for position and using the contours of the ground as cover. I reckon they are still a good few hundred yards away from the start of the Claymores. Over," Glen answered.

Several more birdshot rounds struck the wall either side of Peter's position and then he heard a more conventional round strike the wall somewhere off to his left.

"Glen, I think they must have some rifles, probably hunting rifles. Keep your head down. Over," he shouted into the radio.

"Yeah, quite a few rounds are now hitting the tower all around me. Over," Glen replied.

"Do you want to move down here? Over," Peter asked.

"Not yet. I've got a better view and can spot for you in the first instance before we make a retreat. Over," Glen answered.

In the next instant, the glass of the lighthouse tower began to shatter as a hail of shots hit their target and shards of glass were ricocheting everywhere. Glen felt a sliver of glass strike his cheek and embed itself there as he ducked down below the parapet of the glass.

"Glen, time to move down here. I can see more clearly now, and they are almost at the Claymores. Over."

"Understood. I am on my way. Over." Glen crawled over to the stairs, then followed the staircase down to ground level and was almost immediately alongside Peter at the small redoubt Peter had constructed.

"Glen, you okay? Your face is covered in blood," Peter observed as he stared at the blood pouring down Glen's left cheek onto his jacket.

"It's just a piece of glass; I'll leave it where it is for the moment," Glen replied.

They both turned and surveyed the enemy arranged in front of them.

"Glen, over to the left." Peter pointed at five or six figures moving closer.

Glen picked up a Claymore mine clacker from the ground and squeezed the mechanism.

Instantly, a deafening explosion blasted three people back the way they had come, the deadly array of small steel ball bearings within the explosive of the Claymore mine lacerating and tearing into the flesh and bone of the group Peter had spotted. No one in that area got up.

Duncan heard the explosion from his position at the jetty side entrance to the facility as he was stood behind David, who was hunched over the trigger of the Browning machine gun on the roof of the Land Rover. The MV *Hallaig* was now almost upon the bay, maybe 100 yards from the jetty, and looked to be increasing speed as it entered shallower waters.

"They're going to run the thing up the beach of the bay and get off the boat there," Duncan said as he watched with horrified awe at the progress of the ferry.

Several reports of discharged guns were heard, followed by various strikes to the Land Rover and the surrounding rocks.

"It's the Raasay ferry they are using to assault the beach in the bay. Over," Duncan informed the rest of the radio users.

"Received, Duncan. Hold them back as long as you can, then get to the shelter. Over," Peter answered as he too now opened up with the machine gun.

David aimed at the superstructure of the ferry and squeezed the trigger. A thunderous roar of firing now deafened the two fishermen on the roof of the vehicle.

David deliberately swept the machine gun from the top of the control booth of the ferry to the deck area. Great pieces of wood and glass shattered and splintered, and Duncan and David both watched in horrified fascination as the men on the deck, at the front, simply came apart as the torrent of ordinance tore into them.

As Duncan reloaded another belt of ammunition for the machine gun, up by the lighthouse compound, Peter and Glen were now engaged in a full-on fire fight. Glen was firing his MP5 at the more distinct figures approaching both his and Peter's location. Peter had reloaded another belt of ammunition and began a sweeping arc of firing into the melee of people as they tried to move forward from their cover positions. Glen suddenly knelt down, picked up two of the Claymore detonators and clicked them both at the same time. Immediately there was an explosion just left of centre of the ground in front of them and there was an audible shriek of pain as several figures went down under the withering volley of ball bearings buried in the Claymore mines explosive. Peter paused to assess the carnage they were causing.

"Peter, receiving? Over." Duncan's voice was quite high-pitched over the radio.

Peter depressed his radio talk button as he looked at the land in front of him during a brief lull as the attackers presumably regrouped.

"Go ahead. Over," Peter responded.

"There's loads of them on the ferry; we are getting quite a few, but some are making it to cover and moving away to our right. They may be trying to flank us. Over." Duncan sounded quite desperate.

"Move back to the gym area and make for the shelter. We will be right behind you. Over." Peter ordered Duncan and David to bug out of their position and get to the underground refuge.

"Glen, let's get ready to move. You drive the truck and I'll fire as we retreat," Peter instructed his colleague. "Duncan and David are outnumbered, and then some."

Glen stood, and as he did so, several shots ricocheted off the stone wall close to him. He ducked and depressed several more Claymore command wires. Three more explosions halted a stealthy group of attackers over on the right-hand side and caused a cessation in the firing. Glen was up and running to the truck; he got in and reversed up to Peter's position. Peter picked up the last two boxes containing the belts of ammunition for the machine gun and carried them to the Land Rover. All he had left behind was the still smoking machine gun. Peter returned to the redoubt and scanned the ground in front of him. The attackers were regrouping and beginning to move within the range of the last line of the Claymores. Peter watched closely until the force massed against him was into the kill zone he and Glen had created all those months ago. He picked up each command wire in turn and clicked the detonators one after the other. Two people were thrown backwards as the first mine exploded, then two more were literally blown apart by the second. The third took the arm off one and the leg off another attacker. The final three explosions ripped into a group trying to outflank Peter's position on the left, cutting them to pieces and thwarting their progress.

Peter jumped up and ran for the Land Rover, launching himself into the open rear door, and swivelled round to be able to bring his MP5 to bear. Glen gunned the engine. Several shots whistled over the top of the Land Rover, and one struck the rear left-hand light reflector, smashing it. Peter emptied his magazine of thirty 9mm rounds at the gap between the walled compound and the cliff edge as Glen drove down the hill past the helipad. As they rounded the right-hand bend, they could see the MV *Hallaig* Raasay ferry beached in the bay and a swarm of figures, too numerous to count, sweeping along the road. There was no sign of Duncan or David.

"Take the path, go to the right of the accommodation block. This is going to be tight, mate," Peter observed to Glen.

They bumped over some rocks to the right of the road and then they were on the grass and paved footpath, slewing around the low accommodation to the far side of the complex, where the ferry had landed. Glen fought to keep the Land Rover on the footpath to get better traction and make better progress. They came around the back of the block and continued down the hill, bumping hard over a series of small rocky outcrops but still moving in the right general direction.

"Scotty, control, receiving. Over." Peter tried to raise the underground control centre.

"Yes, Peter, what is it?" Mary's voice came over the radio. Peter smiled in the heat of all this as he picked up on the absence of any radio procedure.

"We are just getting to you. Have you got Duncan and David? Over."

"Peter, we have seen David enter the building and the lift is descending, but not Duncan. Over." Scotty's voice was now on the command centre radio.

"Glen, we have to find Duncan," Peter shouted as Glen brought the vehicle to a halt by the entrance to the subterranean shelter.

"Understood," Glen replied.

Peter jumped out and saw the other Land Rover lying on its driver's side about 100 yards away, near to Scotty's gym. Without hesitating or waiting for Glen, Peter raced to the vehicle and immediately saw Duncan inside the stricken off-roader. Glen came up, as Peter was now stood on the passenger door, in the air, trying to force it open. Several shots rang out as they began to hit the back of the vehicle and strike the road.

Glen took cover and began to return fire, trying to give cover to Peter as he wrestled to open the door and get to Duncan, who appeared to be stuck behind the steering wheel.

A glass bottle sailed out from behind a rock in a large arc, almost in slow motion. It shattered loudly on the road just behind the Land Rover, engulfing the whole of the road in a great burst of orange flame.

"Petrol bombs! Hurry, Peter," Glen shouted as he saw Peter finally wrench the door open and literally bend it back further than its design, using gravity to assist his size 10s.

Peter crawled into the vehicle and immediately saw that the seat belt mechanism was jammed. Duncan was also bleeding from his head and right arm, just above the elbow, but he was conscious.

"Come on, Duncan, stop pissing about," Peter called, and he cut the seat belt with his Leatherman, freeing

Duncan. Between them, they managed to clamber out of the Land Rover as two more Molotov cocktails landed. One found the rear of the vehicle and ignited the interior, setting Peter's trousers alight as he fought to clamber out. Peter had become disorientated by the flames and smoke, and it was another 10 seconds before he emerged and jumped clear, his legs completely on fire. Glen quickly tried to smother the fire on Peter's legs with the well-known technique of a rugby tackle and pat-down. Peter got up, still smouldering, grabbed the stunned Duncan and half-carried half-dragged him back up to the refuge entrance building. The petrol bombs were working in their favour now, as they shielded them all from view of the attackers. Glen fired off a magazine full of MP5 rounds for good measure and they all made it to the door of the PEN building.

"Reckon we have held them off for as long as we can. Let's get underground and secure the shelter," Glen ordered.

Peter picked up Duncan and walked him into the building and into the lift. Glen turned to survey the carnage behind him, the burning Land Rover and roadway. His eye was drawn to an object in the sky that appeared to be hovering about 200 to 300 feet in the air, just above the likely position of the ferry down in the bay.

As he turned and closed the building door behind him, he tried to work out what he had seen.

He joined Peter and Duncan in the lift and pressed the descend button.

He looked at the other two men, Duncan's bloody head and arm and Peter's still smouldering trousers and spoke. "I reckon I have just seen a drone outside…"

They laid Duncan down on one of the beds in the medical wing of the underground complex. He was still conscious, but only just. He was bleeding heavily from a large laceration to the left side of his head. His upper arm was broken with a compound fracture, the bone visible through his torn, bloody clothing.

"Glen, try and stop that bleeding on his head while I check for any other wounds," Peter shouted as he began a top-to-toe fingertip search of Duncan's body for any other wounds or injuries.

"It looks worse than it is; all head wounds bleed a lot," Glen answered as he applied direct pressure with a field dressing to the left side of Duncan's head.

"Okay, his sweater is saturated in blood," Peter shouted. "There is another wound here somewhere," he added as he lifted Duncan's jumper and shirt to get to skin.

Duncan began to cough up blood. To Peter's alarm, it was bright red and frothy around his mouth.

"Found it. It's a gunshot to his chest. Reckon it's hit his lung," Peter exclaimed as he found a comparatively small hole just below Duncan's left nipple.

Mary burst into the room as Glen and Peter tried to lever Duncan onto his side.

"Oh God! Duncan, no," she cried as she saw her stricken husband on the gurney.

"Glen," Peter quietly attracted Glen's attention. "He's got another gunshot to his stomach and one just above his groin and I haven't checked his back yet," Peter whispered as they continued to treat Duncan.

"He's slipping out of consciousness," Glen replied.

"Mary, come and hold his hand, talk to him, keep him awake," Peter shouted at Mary.

Mary ran over and grabbed her husband's right hand. "Duncan, it's Mary. Stay awake, love. I am here now. You'll be alright," Mary spoke, holding back her tears as she watched her husband's eyes glaze over.

There was a flicker of recognition in Duncan's eyes and an attempt at a smile before his body went limp in Peter's arms.

Mary shrieked, "Oh God, no," as she realised that Duncan was dead.

"Peter, you are bleeding," Glen observed as he looked across at Peter. Peter followed the line of Glen's eyes and saw that the lower half of his left arm was covered in blood and had run down to his hand and was dripping on the floor from his fingers. He shrugged off his jacket and lightweight shirt.

"That's a gunshot, looks like it might have gone through," Glen said as he looked around at the rear of Peter's arm.

Becky was now in the medical room, and she moved forward towards Peter.

"Let me dress that and try and stop the bleeding. Minnie, can you have a look at Glen's cheek." Becky now took charge as Minnie and Margaret entered the treatment room.

"Peter, get those trousers off too," Becky ordered.

"Umm! I think they might be stuck to my legs," Peter commented as he looked at the burned and charred remnants of his walking trousers that had indeed adhered to his skin as they had burned.

"Margaret, can you look for some painkillers or morphine in that cabinet on the wall." Becky now took over the treatment of the injured.

"David, are you shot or injured?" Becky shouted across to her dazed partner, who was sitting quietly in a chair by the side of another bed, staring vacantly straight ahead. "Minnie, can you check on David, see if he has any injuries, if he's bleeding from anywhere," Becky asked as Minnie stood next to Margaret.

Minnie went across to David and managed to get him to take his jacket off and then his shirt. She slowly checked his upper body for any wounds or injuries beyond the bruises and superficial cuts she could see pretty much all over him.

"David, David, it's Minnie, how are you feeling?" Minnie asked as she looked at David.

David stared back at her for a second, then seemed to snap out of his stupor, turned his head and looked up at Minnie. "Zoned out there for a second; possibly the most terrifying experience of my life," he said and chuckled!

"Mary, we need you, Hen. Peter is going to go into shock. We need to get some painkillers or morphine into him. His legs look really bad, and that gunshot wound is still bleeding," Becky shouted across at Mary, still laid across the prostrate body of her husband, Duncan, clutching his lifeless hand. Mary looked up when she heard her name.

"Mary, I need you to help me with Peter or we may lose him too. Come on, please, Mary; we need you now," Becky shouted hard at Mary.

"Here's some morphine," Margaret announced as she offered a box to Becky.

"Take one out of the box and just stab him in the leg and squeeze the container, then pull it out. Find something to write with and put a big letter M on Peter's forehead."

Margaret took out a small syrette; basically, a small flexible metal tube (like toothpaste) with a covered needle at one end. Margaret removed the needle cover and jabbed the needle straight into the muscle of Peter's left leg and squeezed the tube full of morphine, then immediately withdrew it and threw it in a yellow sharps bin in the corner of the room.

Mary rose and walked over to Peter, who was now lying on another bed. "I'm so sorry, Mary. He was such a great bloke," Peter whispered to Mary as she stood above him, tears streaming down her face. Margaret reappeared in Peter's eyeline, brandishing what looked like a hideous shade of pink lipstick.

"Just what do you think you are going to do with that?" Peter inquired of Margaret as she leaned over him, and he drifted into unconsciousness.

The four sleek ribs spread out once they moved off. The engine mufflers made the boats virtually silent as they sped across the still water in the pitch black of night. Two headed for the inlet towards the natural entrance to the base, one continued down the coast, heading for the Island manager's cottage and holiday lets. The fourth headed around the north headland towards the high cliffs of the east coast of the island. Each boat contained 12 heavily armed black-clad figures, all wearing armoured vests, respirators and carrying huge quantities of spare ammunition. At precisely the same time, the four craft disgorged their occupants onto the island, and in a sweeping professional way, they began to capture or kill any opposition they met. The inlet group tasked with securing the base landed next to the beached, abandoned ferry in the bay and fanned out across the headland, searching for any persons. Two lookouts sat smoking were swiftly and silently despatched with knives. The team moved on, coordinating their movement with each other as they proceeded past the main office and towards the accommodation block, where lights could be seen. Slowly and deliberately, they split into smaller teams and took up station at each of the various entrances of the block. The team leader whispered, "Units one to six, sit rep. Over." Each of the four-man units responded in turn; "Unit one in position. Unit two in position. Unit three ready. Unit four in position. Unit five set. Unit six in position."

There was a pause followed by a clear, "Go! Go! Go!" from the leader.

A deafening cacophony of noise burst the island stillness as 24 heavily armed marines and SBS troops stormed the accommodation block, hurling thunder flashes and smoke cannisters in through each entrance before following inside and capturing the majority of those there. There were some small pockets of resistance, but these were snuffed out in an instant and the entire block was quickly subdued and those still alive were rounded up and made to sit on the floor of the dining room with their hands on their heads.

At precisely the same time, the group to the east were scaling the cliffs near to the lighthouse compound. Once all the squad had reached the summit, they moved slowly out and surrounded the walled compound of the lighthouse buildings. The team leader could see one or two faint yellow lights within the main building. "All units, move in and secure the compound," he whispered the order into his radio and moved off himself with his partner. The squad moved inside the compound and quickly cleared the lighthouse tower, killing two sleepy guards up by the remains of the redoubt Peter had built.

The squad moved down to the main building and quickly and silently surrounded the structure, covering all the entrances. Once more the team leader instructed, "Go! Go! Go!" A split second after the first explosion was heard from the accommodation block, four thunder flashes were hurled through the windows and doors of the building. The deafening explosions were followed by a full incursion by the team and the building was swiftly secured. There had only been three people inside; all three had been asleep and were cuffed and face down on the floor before they knew what had happened. The compound was made safe, and the leader left four of his men at the lighthouse and marched the prisoners down to the accommodation block with the rest of his squad.

The boat heading south cut their engine as they neared the rocky entrance to the small natural harbour. The squad of heavily armed troops went ashore by the headland and walked the short distance around the rocky coast until they came across the track and then fanned out as they moved down towards what had been identified to them as the Island manager's cottage. They moved stealthily down the slope of the path, keeping to the folds of the ground as they approached the long thin cottage. Two of the team had spotted some fine wires that appeared to be trip wires for active mines. In an instant, they halted the team and dealt with the wires, marking them with a tab of fluorescent tape.

The team moved forward, more slowly now, mindful of other mines and potential booby traps. The leader crouched down, and with some vigorous arm waving and finger pointing, the team moved slowly around the cottage, surrounding it. A distant blast away to the north was the signal for the team to assault the cottage. Several thunder flashes and smoke cannisters were smashed through the windows. After the blasts from the devices thrown, the men burst into the building. Two men were shot at the kitchen table as they dived for their weapons. Three others, asleep upstairs, were quickly subdued and cuffed and marched unceremoniously out into the morning air.

"Are there any others?" the leader asked quietly to one of the kneeling prisoners.

"Fuckin' nearly broke my arm there, Chief," one of the three responded.

"Are there any other people in those buildings?" The leader of the assault team repeated his question, pointing towards the outbuildings and a cottage closer to the shore.

"Aye! There's a family; John and Silvia and their boy Darren." The same man weighed up the situation and gave up these facts.

"Come with me! Des, bring him." The leader ordered one of his men to bring the prisoner as he and two others headed to the other buildings. "Secure these two and gather the squad together. Hopefully, we'll be back shortly," the leader said to his other team member as he pushed the talkative prisoner in front of him.

True to his word, the leader returned within 20 minutes, now accompanied by a very sleepy and confused couple and a young boy of about five. The youngster was busy chewing his way through a Mars bar, a big chocolaty grin on his face.

"These good people are joining us for an early morning stroll north," the leader exclaimed as he joined the rest of his troop, who were quietly sat outside the cottage. The leader smiled as he spotted that his team had got a brew on while he had been away.

"Tea before a walk and medals, boss?" one member of the group offered.

"Splendid idea. John, Silvia, sorry, I don't know the rest of your names, but would you care for a cup of tea before we head north up the road?" The leader politely offered some refreshment to his prisoners.

"But, what, um! Who are you?" the man identified as John asked as he was sat down next to the other captured men.

"We, sir, are representatives of Her Majesty's armed forces and you are now our prisoners." The leader identified his team.

"What is going to happen to us?" the female, Silvia, asked.

"You are going to be taken to the northern end of this island now, and from there, we will arrange for you to be transferred to the new northern Scottish holding facility, near Inverness, where you will be processed, required to quarantine for 14 days, before eventual return to your homes." The leader of the assault team briefly summarised their impending journey.

"Are we in trouble?" John asked.

"Not my remit, sir. There will be an inquiry, no doubt, and witnesses will be questioned, and decisions will be made," the leader hypothesised.

"Oh! I see," John replied quietly.

"Now, Des, where's this tea? And see if you can find some fizzy pop or something for the young gentleman to wash his chocolate bar down with." The leader sat down with the group, waiting for his tea...

25

There was a piercingly bright light above him that appeared somewhat blurred. Slowly the light became more distinct as his vision cleared and he recognised the cold stark artificial ceiling lights of the medical wing of the underground bunker. Peter sat up from the bed he was lying on. He took in his bandaged legs, swathed from ankle to groin. His left arm was similarly covered in bandages. It was all coming back to him, as was the pain of his injured arm and burned legs. Peter looked to his left and saw the recumbent figure of Glen lying in the bed next to his, his face and neck wrapped in clean white dressings.

"Glen, you okay?" Peter whispered across to his colleague.

No response!

"He's asleep, leave him. He wouldn't let us treat him until you were taken care of, stubborn old bugger!" Becky moved into Peter's field of vision and stood at the end of his bed.

"Hello there, you had us worried for a while. How are you feeling?" Becky asked in a strangely compassionate way.

"My mouth's dry; have you got any water, please," Peter croaked a whisper.

Becky brought a small container with a pipe fitted and helped Peter draw some water into his mouth.

"Thanks, how long have I been out? How is Glen? Are we secure? Is David okay? What about Mary, poor Mary, oh! And Callum, does he know?" A stream of questions tumbled from Peter as the memory of the previous events returned to him.

"Whoa, easy there, Peter, one thing at a time. Just lie back and I'll tell you." Becky gently but firmly eased Peter's head back onto the pillow and did a cursory inspection of his dressings before returning to her station at the end of his bed.

"You were unconscious for roughly 12 hours, I think. We have dressed the gunshot wound to your arm. It has missed the bone and gone right through, so we cleaned and stopped the bleeding, then dressed and bandaged it." Becky imparted this information in a matter-of-fact way. She continued; "Your legs are pretty badly burned, and the fabric of your trousers had melted onto the skin. We have removed most of it, but we have not got all of it. You lost a lot of blood and fluids, hence the intravenous drip in your arm." Becky pointed to the catheter in Peter's right arm. "Glen has a nasty cut on his face, but we managed to remove the glass embedded there and he will have a suitably heroic scar in time. David is back up in the control room, watching the footage of you behaving like Captain America, racing back to the Land Rover to drag Duncan out and get him back here. It's difficult to know how he is. He seems fine physically, but he was really quiet and withdrawn when he first got back here, so I just don't know." Becky paused, obviously bothered by the condition of her partner.

"The marauders have either gone, been taken prisoner or are dead. Mostly dead by what we can see from the monitors in the control room," Becky went on.

"Now! Peter, let me introduce you to, well, what I suppose are the owners of this establishment." Becky shuffled to the left and was replaced by an average height, stocky man wearing the uniform of a naval officer. Peter noticed the beard and rather oily, damp smell that seemed to emanate from this person. The man smiled down at Peter.

"Sir, I have the privilege to introduce myself to you. I am Captain Damian Havelock, officer commanding Her Majesty's Astute Class Submarine HMS *Ambush*." Captain Havelock saluted the now wide-eyed Peter. "You appear to have stumbled across our base here during the pandemic and have maintained and ensured the security and viability of the facility, for which I thank you."

Peter just stared. He had no immediate words with which to answer the captain.

"My men have retaken the surface base and secured several prisoners, both here and further south on this island. Our orders are to defend this base while also liberating and recovering the local area, including Raasay and the Isle of Skye," the naval man continued.

"It's very nice to meet you," Peter croaked a quiet reply, still not fully awake.

The captain was about to continue when a small Terrier barked his presence in the room and jumped up onto Peter's bed.

"Talisker, Talisker, get down." Callum ran up and picked the small Border Terrier up and placed him firmly on the floor.

"Hello, Callum. I am so sorry about your father; he was a brave man and had become a good friend." Peter could see that Callum had been crying and that tears were once again forming with mention of Duncan.

"I'll take my leave, sir." Captain Havelock again saluted Peter and walked back out of the treatment room.

"Mum said you were injured trying to save my dad and that you and Glen had given the rest of us enough time to get safely underground." Callum spoke slowly and quietly to Peter.

"He would have done the same for me; we were a real team, like an extended family, mate," Peter replied to the young lad.

"What happens to us now?" Callum asked.

"I don't know; it looks like the military are in charge now. We will have to see what has happened to the world this last 18 months," Peter answered.

"Mum is being strong, but I know she has been crying," Callum mentioned his mother Mary. At that moment, Mary came into the room and walked across to Peter's bedside.

"They told me you were awake. Just thought I'd pop in and see how you are." Mary's voice was trembling, but she managed a smile as she spoke to Peter.

"Callum, go and see Becky," Mary shooed Callum away across the aisle to go and talk to Becky, who was sat on the side of Glen's bed, checking the dressing on his cheek.

Callum smiled at Peter, grabbed the small dog and walked over to the other bed.

Mary looked across at Becky, and she looked up and caught the expression on Mary's face.

"Come on, Callum. Those navy boys have a host of chocolate bars and some fresh milk with them; let's go and find some," Becky instructed Callum as she led him out of the treatment room.

Peter and Mary were suddenly alone, apart from the sleeping Glen. Mary looked down at the injured man who had tried to save her husband, the man who had saved them all from the perils of Portree and kept them safe through the recent incursion by his dogged determination to be prepared for just such a threat. They looked at each other, suddenly searching for the right words. "I have asked the captain if we can bury Duncan at sea; it's what he would have wanted. He loved the sea; it was his life and where he spent so much of it," Mary said, her voice breaking as she spoke of Duncan.

"Of course, Mary. It's the right decision," Peter responded.

"They are going to take us out into the sea beyond the islands on the submarine and lay him to rest there," Mary continued, tears now streaming down her face.

"Would you come with us, please?" Mary quietly asked.

"Mary, it would be my honour," Peter replied. He took Mary's hand in his, lay his head back on the pillow and drifted off to sleep.

About the author

Guy Robin

Guy grew up on the South coast of England, near Bournemouth. He lost his father when he was five and was brought up by his mother, who then secured his education at Reeds School in Surrey. At 21 he joined the Metropolitan Police Service, serving for 30 years in a variety of roles and departments, but regards his time at Battersea Police Station to have been his most enjoyable time in the Job!

Since retirement Guy has worked as a document collection and statement taking agent. He has been a driver for several driving agencies and private clients. Guy is married to Paula and they live in a quiet town in Sussex. The time and solitude afforded to him by the recent lockdown restrictions led to a fulfilment to write a piece of fiction.

Guy's interests are many and varied. He played hockey for many years for the Police and then for Crowborough Hockey Club, where he met his wife. Guy enjoys the outdoors, particularly walking great distances across the South Downs and beyond. He collects stamps and Scottish Malt whisky. He is a keen motorcyclist, awaiting the time when it is easy to once again tear around the highways and byways of Europe. Guy has more work in the pipeline and he continues with his writing as a pleasurable and cathartic hobby.

Lightning Source UK Ltd.
Milton Keynes UK
UKHW041533250222
399235UK00002B/34